SHIELD OF FAITH

Danney Clark

To Darlene with warm wishes—

Dan Clark

DanScribe Publishing

DEDICATION

Dedicated to all who follow Jesus even when it is difficult
and those who work tirelessly to achieve and advance
God's kingdom here on earth.

ACKNOWLEDGEMENTS

God, our Creator and provider; Dale Erickson and Larry Patrick for their encouragement; Robert Williams for his advice and computer expertise; Kelly Roberts for her editing and attention to detail; and Scott Buffaloe for his creative graphics design.

INTRODUCTION

Who is Cady Miller? What is his story about? Is this just another book about the struggle between good and evil, or something more? Something more, I certainly hope. About a man's search for himself and his discovery of God in the process. About what legacy a man might leave behind him and how we are all interwoven into the fabric of God's creation. So let's jump in and let the story tell itself...

– ONE –

It was a mixed bag, to choose the shortest route, or the least difficult one. The winter snows in Idaho had left the mountains blanketed in white, with the northern slopes heavily laden long into the spring. The southern exposures were still covered, but with heavy, wet, melting snow, with bare spots beginning to show mud.

There was an obvious lack of wildlife, most of the larger animals had moved down to their winter ranges earlier in the winter, with predators following behind. In the high country, only birds and smaller animals forged on to stay alive during the bitter cold. Bears remained in hibernation, while coyotes, wolves, cougars and the smaller cats were predators of opportunity, making their homes near their natural food supply.

Cady was a miner and sometimes trapper, living north and east of Idaho City, Idaho Territory. The town had grown up around a discovery of gold, the miners spread out over the mountains like locusts, staking both placer and hard rock claims from the Tetons south to the southern deserts. Many Confederate soldiers migrated west in an effort to find gold to help finance their fight against the north.

When silver was also discovered in the southern reaches, the wilderness spawned towns at every water hole. The Oregon Trail cut across the state only 40 miles to the south, bringing with it those eager to sell goods and supplies necessary to support the rugged life.

He found some relief from the heavy snow when he was able to use ridges running parallel to his course. Wind had often cleared them of snow or at least pushed the drifts off the crest. Sometimes he could follow a frozen creek bottom, but just as often, as in life, found himself fighting waist deep snow in an effort to keep to his course. The fact that he was dressed for the weather prevented him from frostbite or worse, but made busting through the drifts no easier.

Cady had hoped to make it until spring before returning to Idaho City for supplies, but had not been able to make his provisions stretch. He lived with the economy of necessity, eating well but not with variety, relying mostly on wild game for his meat, also using salt pork to supplement and stretch his rations.

Cady lived and worked his claim alone since his partner had taken sick and died of a burst appendix the previous year. There had been no way to get him to town and no doctor would come out from the camp in mid-winter. Their first hole had run to nothing, but rather than closing it up, they had fashioned a door across its opening, making it secure from animals. While staying cool year around, it kept fruit and vegetables fresh and meat from spoiling in the summer's heat.

They had found 'color' in the small creek bed while panning, then followed it upstream to a spring coming right out of the hillside. When the placer ran out, they began digging out the source of the stream only to find a small vein which grew as they got deeper into the mountain. By the end of the second season they had thirty ounces of dust with another twenty in nuggets before the vein played out. By then they had built a shack and had established themselves in the area, with hopes of finding another and larger vein.

That summer they found a natural hot springs with a strong sulfur smell to it which often indicated the presence of gold. They began the second hole within sight of the first and close enough to the shack to make life easy. The gold they found here was ore, meaning that the gold was dispersed throughout the rock and required milling and smelting. This changed their operation considerably, making it necessary to own animals and equipment to transport the heavy ore to the 'basin', as the valley surrounding Idaho City was called.

Early in the gold rush, the ore was freighted by heavy wagons to Boise to be processed, later on the basin had developed its own mill and light rail to take it to town. The train ran twice a week, taking logs and ore to the flatland and bringing back milled lumber and staples in return.

Cady had elected to leave the mules behind, preferring rather to travel light and not risk injury to one of them. When the melt came he'd take the ore to town and lay in a stock of the supplies which civilization offered. 'Store bought' meant poor quality to some, but to him some of the store bought stuff gave him more time to mine and less time to sew and fuss with stuff. A man could waste a day per pair skinning, curing, cutting and sewing up gloves which lasted little longer than the store bought kind, or he could dig and maybe find enough gold to buy ten pairs.

Cady lost track of time when he was working, enjoying the labor and the sense of accomplishment it gave him. Now, more than one hundred feet underground, it would have been a pleasant 55º except for the hot water which ran constantly from the mine.

At first they had used a skid to ferry the ore from the hole into the open. Then, as they got deeper, they'd had to add wheels so the mule could pull it up and out. Finally, a second mule was rigged up in front of the first to make the trip with the heavy ore. Cady knew if the vein held up that it was time to buy some rail and an ore cart.

He had held off, not because of finances, but because word of his purchases would indicate that his hole held promise. He knew many in town would rather steal than work and would kill without compunction. Not that he feared any man, but he was wise enough to know this type would shoot a man in the back rather than fight fair.

Cady had spent a fair amount of time thinking over the situation, not wanting to cut in a new partner, but needing another hand. His sister, Kate, and her son lived in St Louis and were his only living relatives. She had been widowed nearly five years and her son, Ben, should be nearing twenty by now. Since he was single, and appeared to remain so, gold had held little value for him. It was the search for it which drew him on and not the riches. Cady had expected to leave what he had to his sister someday anyhow, so he had decided to invite her and the boy out to Idaho.

The south and east facing slopes were clear of snow but still muddy when Cady received a letter from his sister. The north and western ones still claimed winter's fury, evidenced in their drifts. By rail he expected the trip to take more than ten days, which would make their arrival about the first of May. He planned to improve the cabin's accommodations to make them more for fitting for guests should they decide to live with him, but remained unclear of his sister's intentions.

She may want to live in Boise, or even Idaho City, where life was less severe. Ben, however, had written of his eagerness to join his uncle in the mine and learn the trade, just as Cady had hoped. It was nearly ten years since he had last seen them, Ben being just a boy and Kate still a young mother. Her husband Bill worked at the railroad in St. Louis, making a good living, before being struck with consumption. He had found it increasingly difficult to breathe, causing him finally to become frail and home bound. After his death, there was a small monthly railroad pension which allowed Kate to live, as well as working part time doing housekeeping and ironing.

Cady would be forty 40 the coming summer, with his sister only two years his junior. Their only sibling had died at birth with their mother. Cady's father had been killed in a logging accident, leaving him to raise his younger sister, who had just turned 15. Although forced to drop out of school, he had completed the eighth grade and knew how to read, write, and cipher, having been told he had a quick mind.

Like his father, Cady was a big man in that day, a shade over six feet with broad shoulders and heavy chest, muscled as a result of hard labor. First taking his father's place in logging, then learning how to wrangle cattle in the big stock yards in St. Louis, he became well suited to the outdoor life, which he now enjoyed.

A short time after his sister had married, he had met Tom Clark and they had become friends. Tom, several years older, had experience in mining and had persuaded Cady to move west with him when the news of the gold rush reached him. Together they had settled and done well in Idaho until Tom's unfortunate death.

The shack had been originally been built only as a place for he and Tom to get in out of the weather, with little thought of comfort. Some 20 feet square, built of lodge pole pine, it still had a dirt floor and only one window, which faced their claim. The window was not glass, but of an animal hide with hair removed, that had hardened to a translucent bronze color, letting in light but not winter's cold wind. In summer the frame around the hide was removed from the shack to allow for air movement.

He and Tom had first covered the roof with bows from trees, cooking over an open pit in the floor, but found it to be a poor plan after the first snowfall. They'd been forced to reinforce the rafters and cover them with slab wood and bark the first winter, replacing them again in spring with tin, purchased in town. Having an adequate roof, they were forced to build a fireplace into one wall, venting it through the roof. It provided both heat and light, in addition to a location for cooking indoors.

America was a contradiction of progress, with the eastern states already thinking in terms of electricity, indoor plumbing and water pumped from wells. While the west lived much the same as it had 100 years previously, the exception being the 'iron horse' which connected the two. The railroad had moved civilization westward at an alarming pace, causing the cultures to be at odds to one another. The 'old west' tried vainly to hold onto its traditions, while eastern culture steadily threatened them.

The year, 1862, found Idaho City the largest town in the territory. While the north and south were fighting over slavery, men with high expectations and low morals shot each other in its streets. History records the gold taken from the area surpassed both the California and Alaska gold rushes.

Cady enjoyed the solitude and the absence of neighbors nearby, going to town only when necessary. Twice, hard men had attempted to encroach on his claim, Southerners by the look of them, dressed in Confederate gray, panning gold in the stream near the cabin. The first time they had moved on after Cady had taken up a rifle, making plain his willingness to protect his claim. The second required a warning shot before they left the little valley.

Most were here for the quick and easy money, expecting to get rich overnight, few like him were willing to dig it out of the hillside. The first and easiest gold long gone, he'd heard of a dredge being assembled in the basin to eat its way down stream, processing gold as it went, leaving only worthless rock behind. But Cady was like a farmer, he who was content to take his living from the land but wanting to leave the land intact when he was done.

He had named his little stream "Meadow Creek" simply because it flowed through his meadow, providing water for the natural grasses, yellow buttercups, purple lupines and wildlife that lived along its banks. Several beaver dams stored the water in sufficient quantity to bathe as weather allowed, and providing a marsh that often brought elk and moose.

Hanging now in his #1 tunnel was still more than a quarter of moose meat which had made him work just to get it on the mule for transport. Its hide, more than nine feet long, had been tanned and covered his cot, giving protection on the coldest of nights. Cady took care not to disturb the natural balance of nature, often passing up easy game to allow it to reproduce itself.

As he stepped out of the tree line into the meadow, his hand went to his rifle, taking immediate notice of the door to #1 tunnel being open. On the far side of the shack were two horses, packed high with furs and gear, tied to a tree with no sign of their owners. They lifted their heads and cocked their ears forward but made no sound as he stepped back into the trees.

Cady set down his pack, removed his snowshoes, and checked the breach of his new Henry 44, making sure of its load. It was better than two hundred yards across the open with only a light breeze blowing down the valley. Cady was confident of himself and his weapon at nearly twice this range if it became necessary to use it. He waited.

Then the wind carried the sound of voices to him from the tunnel, excited voices. They had apparently uncovered his stash of gold which had been buried under the carrots and potatoes. A head appeared in the doorway sporting a fur cap, looking around, then quickly disappeared again.

A decision had to be made, and quickly. If they left, even without the gold, the word would spread and others would come when Cady was not prepared to defend himself. If they appeared with just food he'd not challenge them, but if they were carrying the gold they'd have to die.

Using a small tree to steady his aim and partially hide himself, he centered the sights in the open doorway and waited. Several minutes passed before the fur hat appeared again, peering cautiously left and right, before slowly exiting. He was followed by a second, also dressed in furs, who struggled to carry the heavy bags of gold from the tunnel.

They talked quietly, moving toward the horses and stopping to rest frequently. Cady waited until they were walking abreast of each other before bringing the iron sight to rest on the neck of the nearer man, then squeezed the trigger. The men fell as one while their horses reared and jerked at their tethers. A third man peered out of the opening just as Cady chambered another round, but retreated before Cady could fire.

Secure that he had not been seen, Cady waited. The horses quieted and nothing stirred in the little valley. Still he waited. Then a voice cut across the clearing, "don't shoot, I put the gold back, I won't tell no one nuthin'." Cady did not reply, the last sentence told him what he needed to know, the man would tell everyone everything.

The man finally filled the opening, holding up his hands, but still gripping a long rifle in them as he walked out. The echo of the shot still filled the air as the lifeless body fell forward. Cady waited. Several minutes passed as he kept watch. Finally he picked up his gear, confident that no others were present, and crossed the meadow.

Trappers they were, and thieves of opportunity. They had apparently been following the creek and came upon his vacant claim. Greedy eyes had seen the color in the ore piled at the mouth of #2 tunnel and they began to look around. After ransacking his cabin, they moved to the #1 tunnel, finally finding his cache hidden with the vegetables.

A hard lesson he had learned, he'd take more care in finding a secure hiding place. Cady knew that although he was in the right, that the law could not be depended upon to keep his secret any more than the trappers would have. Word would get out. It took him all day to move the food to the cabin and store it, he thanked God for the season which kept the meat from spoiling as he hung it high in the trees on long ropes.

The three bodies were moved into the tunnel just as they had fallen, Cady made no effort to search them or identify them. Their furs and provisions were removed from the horses and stored for his future use, but their personal effects were left on them untouched, as the horses were led into the tunnel, one at a time. Cady deeply regretted having to kill an animal who had no part in the event, but it could not be helped. Finally, using a significant amount of dynamite, he closed the tunnel, burying the intruders inside.

As he lay on his cot beside the dying fire, he felt grateful that God had allowed this to happen as it had, before Ben and Kate had joined him. He also wondered what would have happened if they had been there alone when the men had come. It was a bad but necessary thing that he'd been forced to do. He was unsure of how they would have felt, had they been a part of it, but he prayed that he'd be forgiven by God, before drifting off to sleep.

– TWO –

Indians still co-inhabited the west, but for the most part, had lost their ability to wage war against the white men. As they had for generations, they lived simple lives hunting, fishing, and living off the bounty of the land, while being systematically displaced.

There were several tribes, Nez Perce, Blackfeet, and Shoshoni, with which Cady had dealings in the past, never hostile, always honorable. The gold rush had brought a quarter of a million hopeful souls west seeking their fortunes, all of whom displaced the original Native Americans to some degree. They also brought disease and decadence which were foreign to the tribes. Alcohol, tobacco, and social disease soon decimated the vulnerable Indians, taking away pride and independence, which conquering soldiers could not.

Cady took a few minutes from his labor in the mineshaft to breathe the fresh air of the coming spring and sat while eating his lunch. He heard the sound of horse's hoofs as they made their way up the rocky stream bottom. Since the approach was obvious, he was not alarmed, though it could be a ruse to disarm him mentally, while quiet feet crept up behind him. He only took precaution to grab his long gun and stand while surveying the meadow.

Moments later two braves, and a squaw leading three mustangs, came into view. The horses were heavily laden with furs, gear, and a small whitetail buck tied securely across their backs. Cady raised one hand in universal gesture of welcome, which was returned by the leader. He then made a gesture toward his small fire with its remains of elk roast and coffee dangling over it. They hesitated, then smiled, moving forward, while leaving the squaw holding the horses at the edge of the stream.

They, more than he, could communicate, having picked up enough English to understand much of what he said. Gestures, grunts, nods and smiles affirmed when understanding became clear to the group. They ate the offered elk with relish, using their knives to cut portions for themselves. The woman remained at a distance, with the men taking no notice of her, until Cady pointed toward her and gestured toward the waiting meat. They seemed to ignore him until he cut a large piece himself and again pointed her way. They nodded their approval but did not rise from their crouch.

Cady rose slowly, walking carefully toward her, while holding the meat at arms length. Her eyes darted from him to her companions for reassurance, but said nothing. He smiled, moving forward before stopping only a few feet from her, continuing to offer the meat. He waited, said nothing, but continued to smile. With a lightening-quick gesture, she grabbed the elk meat and began eating, all the while holding his gaze.

Cady dropped his hand and slowly turned away, returning to the fire. The Indians had no interest in his mine or gold. They were hunters, just passing through the area, heading south to the great Snake River, where they expected to join their tribe to harvest salmon coming up river from the ocean.

In both spring and fall, several tribes camped along the riverbanks in the sagebrush and desert lands, near the river. There were shallows nearby which had allowed the wagon trains to cross on the Oregon Trail, headed toward the Pacific. Further up the river in a small canyon, large amounts of water came out of the rocks from underground streams, dumping into the river.

Cady reverently opened his tobacco pouch, taking a pinch and offering some to his guests. A pipe appeared from nowhere and was quickly filled and lit, bringing smiles of satisfaction to the Indians as they grunted and passed it between themselves. Cady rolled his own and enjoyed his smoke while taking pleasure in watching them.

The squaw had tied the horses to a willow and sat nearby, quietly watching the men. She busied herself with a knife and some skins, scraping the meat from the hide in preparation for tanning. Cady remembered the furs which he had removed from his uninvited guests' horses. He had intended to take them to town when he next went, but wondered if opportunity existed here to trade.

He returned from the shack with the skins, dropping them before the men, signaling a desire to trade. He could see the eager glances between them as they looked the furs over carefully one at a time, discarding only two. They motioned the woman to join them in the inspection while speaking among themselves, nodding and smiling. When they had finished, their smiles disappeared as they got down to the haggle. Cady, having nothing invested in the furs, was feeling generous as the negotiations continued.

They had little that he really needed but one of the horses had caught his eye. A mare, large for a mustang, with paint markings of chestnut-brown and white would be more versatile than his mules for transportation. Their first offer had been for the woman, then the deer and the woman, finally they offered the older and smaller of the horses. Cady was having fun with it, shook his head and countered with the mare and the deer. The deal was closed with smiles all around when Cady offered a pouch of tobacco and the furs, all parties feeling they had bested the other.

After they tethered his new mare, they began loading the furs on the two remaining horses. Cady returned to the shack, coming back with a small metal cooking pot and a hand mirror which he had brought with him from St Louis. Walking over to the woman, he handed them to her, while watching her dark eyes dance as she inspected them. She caught his arm as he turned to leave, asking with her eyes what he expected in return. Cady smiled and shook his head. Nothing, nothing at all. was his message.

It saddened him to know that much of the world considered these people savages. The few he had known had been honest, simple people with better values than most of the 'civilized' whites he knew. Cady took the remaining slab of elk off the fire, offering it to his new friends as they prepared to leave.

The woman accepted it quickly, then held out a soft buckskin shirt to him, with a smile. The shirt represented many hours of her labor and should last several years if treated well. He knew it was worth a week's pay but knew also that to reject the gift was to reject the giver. He nodded, smiled and took it from her saying simply "thank you."

The shadows were long as they disappeared from view, with little of the day remaining. Cady had enjoyed the afternoon and had no desire to return to the hole, promising himself he'd get an early start in the morning. Inside the shack he suddenly felt lonesome, not something he had often felt. It would be good to have his family with him, he thought, as he banked the fire for the night.

It seemed that he had just fallen asleep when the report of a rifle brought him to his feet. He pulled on his boots, grabbed his rifle and jacket, as and went out the door into the darkness. A second explosion gave him direction as he broke into a trot, heading downstream away from the claim. He moved quietly, keeping to the marsh grass where it bordered the tree line, making him almost invisible in the waning moonlight.

His was mind racing, looking for an explanation, he knew of only two possibilities for the cause of the shots. Either someone defending himself against a predator or a human predator was looking for prey. Suddenly the Henry felt heavy in his hand, not from its considerable weight, but from the weight of responsibility it gave him.

As he reached the toe of a ridge he could hear voices, then screams. The moonlight showed two figures standing over two others lying motionless near a small fire, while a third was fleeing toward him. One of those standing raised his rifle, pointing it in Cady's direction while laughing hoarsely. Cady drew down on the man instinctively, watching as he was pitched backward over the fire when the round reached him.

As he levered in a second round, the other man dropped to the ground with his own rifle, looking vainly into the darkness for an assassin. Cady could hear heavy breathing and footsteps before he could see her in the darkness. The young Indian woman was running blindly away from her attackers, not aware that he was there. He stepped out from behind a tree as she passed, wrapping a large hand over her mouth and drawing her to him. Her eyes were those of a frightened animal as she fought to get free of his grasp.

Suddenly Cady felt a hot burning pain across his stomach as the blade of her knife cut through his coat. He knocked her roughly to the ground, pinning her arm under his as he lowered his considerable weight on her. Taking the knife he got to his feet, feeling the warmth of his life's blood soaking into his coat. She must have caught a view of him in the approaching dawn for he could see a flicker of recognition in her eyes as she regained her feet also.

Cady motioned her to follow him as he climbed the ridge away from the meadow, gaining elevation as he went. Finally he stopped, able to see the camp clearly with its inhabitants. The gunman had snuffed out the fire, making himself a harder target as he crawled away from the carnage. As he raised his gun, Cady noticed that the woman had followed him and was staring blankly at the horror below.

The heavy caliber bucked against his shoulder once more leaving the final assassin lifeless in the meadow below. Cady could make out, in the early morning light, three horses tied on the far side of the clearing, straining at their lead ropes. Their backs were piled high with furs and supplies.

A short distance from them, the mustangs, which he recognized from earlier in the day, stood with heads down also bearing their loads of furs. Cady speculated that the three men had spotted the mustangs first, noting their valuable cargo, then had shot the two male Indians from ambush with intention to use and probably then also kill the squaw. He was nauseated by the ruthlessness and greed of the men he'd been forced to kill within the last few days.

Suddenly he felt weak and tired, he lowered the rifle and turned toward the woman, then staggered sidewise and sat down on the hillside. With the adrenaline working it's way out of his system, the loss of blood from his stomach wound overcame him and he blacked out. Eighteen hours later, when he finally opened his eyes, he had trouble focusing on his surroundings.

He could hear the pop and crackle of a fire and feel it's warmth, its light dancing across the timbers overhead. After a few moments he attempted to sit up but fell back, sweat running down his face. Pain, white hot like a branding iron, seared his stomach in the attempt, causing him to gasp. She moved toward him as if in a dream, gliding without a sound. He felt the cold wetness of a compress against his skull as she attempted to soothe and cool him. Even in his fever, memory began to return and he began to recognize his surroundings. In the flickering firelight he could see just the outline of her face as he went back to sleep.

Morning of the second day came, its light flooding through the doorway as he opened his eyes. There was no sign of the woman but Cady could smell food and felt a compelling hunger and raging thirst well up inside of him. I will live, he thought, I cannot be this hungry and still be dying. He was still unable to sit up, but did manage to turn his head and move his legs sidewise off the cot.

Cady must have groaned with the effort because she came through the door in an instant, motioning him to remain lying down. Before he could object, she had lifted his feet and put them back on the cot, then raised a tin cup to his lips. A hot bitter mixture burned its way down his throat, spilling across his bearded chin and onto his shirt. She did not stop pouring until he had swallowed the last few drops.

He could not completely identify the ingredients but felt better already with something in his stomach. He surmised that it was an Indian remedy brewed from nature's own pharmacy. His hands fell to his stomach and found it covered with a heavy moist poultice of moss and herbs, covered with clay.

With her back toward him, he watched her as she filled a tin bowl with a thick, savory smelling stew. She was slight built, weighing a hundred pounds at best, and maybe a little over five feet tall. Cady marveled at how she could have brought him here from where he had fallen more than a mile downstream.

As she spooned the stew into his mouth, he could see the hint of pride in her eyes as he chewed and swallowed with great relish. He gestured for a drink, croaking out the word 'water'. She understood and repeated the word "water" as she lifted the dipper from the pail to his lips. Cold and sweet, it soothed his raw throat and raised his spirits considerably.

After a second bowl of stew he felt bloated but satisfied, drifting back to sleep. This time he dreamed of pleasant times in his childhood, running and laughing as he and Kate played in the forest among the flowers and trees. when his father was still alive. Cady opened his eyes and began to stretch, big mistake, as the pain shot across his wound. She came toward him, a smile obvious in her childlike face asking, "water?" He nodded and said "yes." She repeated his words, "yes, water." Once again, the water thrilled him with its pure clean refreshment. "Thank you," he replied at last. And again she repeated, "thank you."

It was obvious to him that she was eager to communicate so he pointed to himself and said "Cady." She looked puzzled for a moment then pointed to herself and said "Cady." Although it pained him to laugh he could not resist it. Shaking his head sidewise, he again pointed to himself saying his name, then pointed to her in a questioning tone asking, "you?" Several minutes passed without a sound as Cady watched her trying to make sense of his question. Finally she looked at him and repeated his name, motioned to the water and identified it correctly, then pointed to herself once again and said "Shau-nna." Cady grinned and repeated after her "Shawna," watching as she nodded affirmation.

Her hands were like whispers of wind as she cleaned and redressed his wound. The poultice removed, he could see the eight inch scab which represented the healing wound to his abdomen. He counted it fortunate that he had worn a heavy coat as he considered how much worse it could have been. Any deeper and it would have opened his insides to infection and he would have died slowly and painfully.

Soon after, with her help, he was able to stand and walk short distances outside the cabin, where he observed two fresh dirt mounds, covered with rocks to discourage predators. Cady did not know how to bring up the subject so he did not try. He observed that their two horses had been staked out in the meadow with his mare and two mules. Curiously he saw no sign of the dry gulcher's horses, bodies, or gear. In reflection he supposed they had been left where they had fallen, she being unwilling or unable to deal with them, while their horses would have eventually gotten free or been taken down by predators.

Shawna had been sleeping on furs in one corner of the shack while he convalesced until one morning when Cady pulled the covering off of Tom's cot and placed hers on it. She watched silently, then moved to the cot and straightened the furs. Cady smiled and pointed saying, "Shawna's cot," expecting a positive response. He got none. Worse yet she grew quiet and sullen.

When Cady attempted to return to the mine, he had neither the heart nor the stamina for it yet, so he busied himself using the horses to drag in more lodge poles. He had no idea of what to expect from his guest long term and did not know how to raise the subject. He supposed she'd want to join her people at some point but was unclear on how he might help her do that. Perhaps others might pass through and offer to take her with them, or maybe Kate would have some insight when she arrived in a few weeks. While she was eager to help in the chores, the closeness they had shared in the beginning had faded, making her seem more like a hired hand.

From the meadow came the calls of crows, finches, and mourning doves, lending a joyful feel to the outdoors. Cady had peeled and notched the poles, having previously cut them to length. Leveling a piece of ground using rock from mine tailings, he then began to assemble them on a piece of ground south of #2 tunnel, where there was good drainage.

After he had laid the fourth course, he improvised a swing boom to help lift and place the poles. The boom was attached to one of several nearby trees, lifting the poles easily while Shawna guided them into place. It was late in the afternoon when the boom over-swung, causing the balance to fail and letting the butt of the log smash into her upper leg. Reaching her in a few quick strides, Cady lifted her up and headed to the shack at a half run.

Her leg was starting to swell and dark blood pooled under the copper skin, turning it black. There was no break in the skin indicating the severity of the wound and no way to easily know if the bone had been broken. She made no sound but the tears in the corner of her almond eyes showed the pain. As he laid her on his cot, a half smile passed across her quivering lips, unnoticed by Cady.

He at first was unsure of what to do since there was no wound to dress, but then remembered how soothing the mudpack had felt on his stomach. Taking a pail, he hurried to the stream, scooping large amounts of the sandy clay from its bank. Then, at the shack, he placed the clay carefully around the injured upper thigh area where the swelling was most evident.

She watched him silently as he gentled his touch, fearful of causing her pain. When he looked up, their eyes met and she smiled. In that moment he knew love for the first time. Embarrassed, he quickly looked away, then returned his gaze to her. At once he understood why she had turned cold and distant. She had taken his offer of the second cot as rejection rather than simply an offer of comfort.

With their roles now reversed, he offered the dipper of water to her. then wiped a cool cloth across her forehead. Half his age, she was beautiful and delicate lying there looking up at him quizzically, questioningly. He wanted to hold her, to make her pain go away, to let her know his deep feelings for her, yet he did nothing. He felt clumsy and awkward, unsure of himself as he continued to gently wipe her brow. Then, as if answering his unasked question, she took his large rough hand in both of hers, pressing it lovingly against her cheek.

Though it was several days before she could walk without pain, it was obvious that no bones had been broken. Cady had pulled the second cot up beside his own and had tended and cared for her from it. Holding her hand, but never being intimate, they shared closeness brought on by circumstance. During the convalescence they spoke often, not always fully understanding, but always enjoying the conversations. She was Shoshoni, had seen the seasons change nineteen times, and had been traveling with her brother and cousin, they had been her only living relatives. Cady told her of his sister and nephew, but was not certain that she fully understood him when told of their impending arrival.

It was the third week of March when they set out for Idaho City with the ore wagon. It was loaded with ore trailing two horses piled high with furs behind it. The first year Cady and Tom had scouted out a trail down the valley and into the basin. It was still muddy and wet in places, but maintained a southern exposure to avoid snowdrifts that lingered on the northern slopes until mid summer. Twice they had to mount the mustangs, tying them to the mules to pull through a particularly muddy sink hole. They were blessed to be going down hill with their burdens, but even so it took two long, grueling days.

The town was a sprawling tangle of shacks, buildings and tents. It boasted brothels, saloons, a sawmill, livery, assay office, general store, and a blacksmith. There was a periphery of assorted businesses that provided additional and necessary services like the bank, laundry, restaurant, doctor, Sheriff, tailor, barber, and feed store. The mill, located east of the railroad tracks, crushed and separated the ore from the waste before being shipped south to the smelter. That was their first stop.

The mules were unhitched and led to the livery to be fed, the wagon was chained down to the platform that was rotated, then elevated, causing it to dump its load onto the waiting conveyor. The conveyor moved the ore to the mill to be crushed and sorted before being weighed and assayed, then loaded into an ore car attached to the train.

Cady and Shawna stopped by the assay office and checked in. They would later return to receive an assay slip verifying the quality and quantity of their ore, after they had sold their furs. The fur buyer tried to play it cool when he unloaded the furs but the glint in his eyes betrayed his interest. They were prime quality, taken in the heart of winter, and preserved by experienced trappers. The load consisted of some of Cady's own hides, those traded to the Indians that had previously belonged to the three thieves, and those Shawna and her family had taken themselves.

While Cady left the inspection and sorting to the furrier, Shawna kept an eagle eye on him, arguing when he tried to devalue a pelt. She proved to be a shrewd trader. In the end, he gave them a voucher for well over a thousand dollars to deposit in the bank. Vouchers were something new and were the subject of some distrust among the miners. Cady found them both a convenient and a more easily protected way of carrying large amounts of money. The bank would either deposit it or convert it to gold, at it's owners request.

Next, the couple went to the train station where they found that the passenger train from St. Louis stopped in Salt Lake before coming to Idaho. A spur line went north to Idaho City from the Les Bois valley line that continued west toward Portland and the coast. Coming from St. Louis, the train master guaranteed Kate's arrival date within one day of the promised ticket date, seeming proud at their efficiency. That left Cady and Shawna less than a week to spend in town before heading home with Kate and Ben.

Idaho City sported bathhouses, with the natural hot springs all along the basin full of medicinal minerals, making them a destination for visitors. Cady nearly lost his temper when the proprietor of the establishment at first refused to allow Shawna inside. He finally acquiesced when, with firm determination, Cady added a gold nugget to the price of admission. She was hesitant to enter, preferring to wait outside and bathe in a stream. But Cady assured her, insisting that she was his guest and welcome where ever he went.

Finally they entered, men going to the right and women to the left. They were given a towel and a place to leave their clothes, then were pointed to an area where steam rose off the clear water. The pool was divided only by a curtain down the center to separate men from women, with water entering the pool continuously from a natural spring.

Cady immediately soaped his body, running his fingers over the raised scar across his flat stomach. He washed thoroughly several times before settling back, relaxing and closing his eyes. He was awakened to the sound of coarse laughter and women's voices. Two men had lifted the curtain and were staring and making gestures at the women on the other side.

When he heard the word "squaw" from a pair of leering lips, he came up out of the water and moved quickly toward them. They barely had time to turn their heads as his fist found the side of the first man's face. The second's nose splattered blood onto the curtain before he went down into the water. Cady grabbed both men by the hair, dragging them to the side, then throwing them out onto the rocks. The first man, still out cold, made no sound, the other blustered and cursed Cady through the blood. Cady cuffed him along side of the head with an open hand, silencing his foul mouth, then raised himself from the pool.

As he dressed hurriedly he wondered why it mattered so much to men what their race or color was. Why men always seemed to take offense at anyone different from themselves. When he met Shawna outside, he felt guilt for forcing her to endure the men's taunts and ridicule. She, better than he, had known better than to enter the 'white man's world' and expect to be accepted.

Together they returned to town, stopping at the barber shop along the way. Inside, the chair was filled by it's owner who was reading the paper, with no one else in sight.

"Got time for a shave and cut?" Cady questioned, stepping through the door as Shawna followed.

"No Indians," came the quick reply as he saw her enter.

"She's with me," thundered Cady. "You want to cut it or not?"

The barber sized him up for a moment, then changing his tone said, "Have a seat."

Cady showed Shawna to a seat by the door where she perched nervously like a small bird ready to fly, then took the offered chair.

A few minutes later, as they left the shop, Cady felt ten pounds lighter and looked ten years younger. Shawna looked up at him like a child, eyes full of wonder, then softly touched his smooth cheek, smiling. Cady laughed as he realized she had never seen him without a beard and had never seen the other men in her life with one.

Their next stop was the bank where he tendered his voucher, depositing much of it into his account, while keeping some 'hard money' in his pocket. With several days to kill there was no reason to buy provisions, so they walked the long boardwalk to the Boise Basin Mercantile and went inside. The few patrons were a diverse lot, hard men with guns on their hips, women with children at their sides, two Chinese from the laundry, and the local parson. They entered together without raising an eyebrow, walking across the rough plank floor. A portly woman, looking very much in charge, greeted them as she filled orders and collected her due.

Once again Shawna took on the look of an amazed child as she stared at the wares displayed around the room. A large, round, pot bellied stove dominated the room, giving off its warmth to the visitors. A step down in a side room was the millinery and soft goods that had attracted the women visitors. There were bolts of cloth, batting, and assortments of thread and needles, as well as 'store bought' dresses, hats, shoes, and women's apparel. There, too, were the catalogs from which a person could order nearly anything they desired.

Taking Shawna by the hand, he guided her there and opened the book for her. She went through the entire book one picture, one page at a time, her mouth open. Looking up at him from time to time, she said nothing but pointed and gestured as if maybe he had missed something. He was filled with love for her, badly wanting to tell her but not knowing how.

Cady was somehow wise beyond his years, knowing it would be

wrong to try and change her and make her 'white' by dressing her white. So he waited, let her look, let her decide what she may want without interfering. Suddenly her fingers stopped, her eyes lighted up, she stared down at a cameo displayed in the pages of the catalog. She looked up at Cady, eyes filled with the excitement of a child.

The woman finished handing a few items to the parson, then turned to them and asked, "and how can I help you?" in a most pleasant and jovial voice. Cady first handed her his list of supplies, asking if they could pick them up later in the week, then handed over the catalog pointing to the cameo. The woman smiled and turned, retrieving a wooden display from the sideboard behind her.

It was filled with jewelry and trinkets including the very cameo they had wanted. Cady asked to look at it, then handed it to Shawna who literally squealed with delight. He paid for the cameo and signed for the supplies with a promise to return when they were ready.

As they exited onto the boardwalk, they encountered the parson who appeared to have waited for them. Pleasantly he asked, nodding toward Shawna, "your wife?"

Cady, finding himself caught off guard, answered, "not yet, someday though if she will have me."

The parson smiled, then gestured up the hill, "the new church is just up there a block, when you get the details discussed, come see me." Then he turned and started to walk away.

Cady, for the first time, considered the possibility of having a home and family. "Parson," he said, "some are not open to whites and Indians marrying, what are your thoughts on that?"

"My thoughts?" he replied, "my thoughts are not important, but I can say that God made all of us and He made us perfect in His sight. I respect both the creation and the Creator's work."

"Thank you," said Cady, taking Shawna's hand and crossing the street.

Back at the hotel, the saloon was busy, filled with rowdies, fancy ladies, loud music and gambling. It was not a place where Cady could take Shawna without expecting trouble. They opted instead for the boarding house a few doors away that catered to a longer term and quieter clientele. Cady purchased two adjacent rooms, paying for the week in advance, without needing to explain himself or his intentions.

Each room was only ten feet square, furnished with a bed and cotton mattress, chair and table, oil lamp, and crude wardrobe. On the table beside the lamp was a pitcher and bowl for washing. Behind the building were two privies. It was his intention that he and Ben would eventually bunk on the floor while the women would have the beds, before they returned to the mine. Meanwhile, they each had a private room.

Once in their rooms, they changed from their travel clothes into clean ones, Shawna pinning the cameo to her buckskin dress at the neckline. They then met and returned to the sitting room while waiting for dinner, which came with the price of the rooms. Room and board meant breakfast and supper, served family style to the guests, in the large dining room. Another couple joined them, while two nondescript men, who eyed Shawna openly, talked quietly in one corner. Just as the proprietor announced dinner they were joined by a loud and very obese man and woman with pink complexions.

The eight found chairs at the long table and sat while the owner and his wife brought the steaming food to the table, then joined their guests. Several bowed their heads, privately blessing their food, while others jumped right in. Shawna looked ill at ease sitting beside Cady but said nothing, mimicking the movements of others unobtrusively.

Hot black coffee stood in a massive pot while guests helped themselves to it. A thick, rich stew with vegetables and large pieces of meat in brown gravy dominated the table, while a large serving bowl filled with mashed potatoes made the rounds. A dozen fresh rolls disappeared in an instant and were replaced by another. Homemade butter and fresh huckleberry preserves made the rolls almost a dessert. After the first plate, the group settled down a bit, taking time to look around and speak to one another, as they helped themselves to seconds.

Cady took time to compliment their hosts while others nodded in agreement. One of the men motioned to Shawna asking rudely, "what's the story on the Indian?"

Cady composed himself before speaking, giving the man a hard look, "She'll be my wife, if she'll have me," he answered, "not that it's any of your business."

The table was hushed for several seconds before the man responded, "I mean no offense, just curious. Most of them have already gone south to the Snake to fish."

Cady relaxed a little before he answered, "no offense taken, her family was dry gulched and she was left alone."

No one offered comment and the moment passed with the fat man making small talk to his wife. As they settled back in their chairs with a collective sigh, the hostess proudly announced, "I hope you saved room for pie, I worked all day on them." She sat a peach and two apple pies on the table and began cutting them into generous pieces. No further invitation was necessary as every plate found a home and coffee cups were refilled.

After dinner, the men retired to the sitting room while the women cleared the table. Cady watched as Shawna quietly imitated the other three women before he joined the men. He talked little, but listened as they discussed the war in the east, the prices of gold and furs, and the latest news of new inventions from the east coast. They talked of the new hydraulic mining, using high pressure water to erode the soil and its effect on the land.

As the women joined them, Cady saw the smile on Shawna's face and an odd look in her eyes as she looked at him. The atmosphere was pleasant and subdued as the meal did its magic. One by one they began to excuse themselves and head for their rooms at a little after seven, leaving just Cady and Shawna alone with the owner and his wife.

Catherine, as she introduced herself with a broad smile, and Harless, her husband, had owned the boarding house just a little less than two years. They had moved west from Ohio after their only child had been killed in the war between the states. Both loved the open country and enjoyed the life in the boom town, with the exception of the violence that came with it.

Apparently the women had been able to communicate with Shawna while in the kitchen and she had become aware of Cady's comment about his intentions for her. Catherine apologized for letting "the cat out of the bag," assuming that they had already discussed marriage. Cady actually felt relief, he was able to tell that Shawna felt the same as he, as he hadn't any idea how to approach the subject.

Finally, Catherine winked at Harless and made excuse that the dishes needed cleaned up as they returned to the kitchen. Cady took Shawna's hand in his and looked into her eyes for a long moment before telling her what was on his heart. He was unsure if she fully understood until she nodded and threw her arms around his neck, holding him tightly. Cady left her at her room, returning to his own with a light heart and high hopes for the future.

Morning came, announcing itself with a blustery cold wind and sprinkles of snow against the small window. Cady dressed in the leather shirt that Shawna had given him, taking time to shave and wash up before knocking on her door. She answered with a smile, wearing a dress that he had never seen, with the cameo at the throat. Apparently Catherine had been up to the room earlier and had offered her a dress to wear.

Cady had wanted to wait for his sister and her son to arrive to stand up with them, but saw this as an opportunity not to be passed up. They would see the parson today if he was available.

Breakfast was as plentiful and delicious as dinner had been, with sourdough flap jacks, real maple syrup, eggs, and slabs of cured smoked ham waiting when they arrived. Some were seated and already eating while others came in behind them and joined in the feast. Catherine nodded her approval at Shawna as she sat, smiling at Cady, Harless, and the other guests.

She lifted her glass of apple cider in a toast to the 'bride and groom', as Cady and Shawna gave embarrassed smiles to the table. The others laughed, winked, and gave their encouragement to the couple as they ate.

As they stepped through the door into the street, the wind bit into their warm coats, forcing them to put on their gloves and hats. Although the snow had stopped, overhead the clouds were heavy with moisture that threatened to return later with a vengeance. The mud had frozen hard during the night, supporting their weight easily as they walked the rutted street toward the church.

When they entered the church they could see no one, but could hear a cheery whistle from farther inside. The sanctuary was a single room, possibly 16 feet wide and twice as long, with three tall narrow stained glass windows on the sides. Several rows of crude benches were positioned on each side, leaving a walkway between them that lead to the pulpit at the far end. A small door on the side lead to an anteroom where the parson was working on a piece of furniture. As they neared, Cady called out and was rewarded by the smiling face he had met yesterday at the Merc.

"Welcome, welcome to God's house," was the pleasant greeting. "Hoped to see you again," he added.

"I... er, we would like you to marry us, if you will," Cady blurted.

The parson smiled again then said, "will you join me in the parsonage for coffee and fresh cookies while we discuss this union?"

Cady nodded, then followed him out the door and into a homey little bungalow that was attached to the rear of the church. When they were seated around the small table, the parson stood, then introduced himself and his wife who had entered the room. "I am Orville Ricks, this is my wife Sarah."

Cady rose also and spoke, "Cady Miller and Shawna, pleased to meet you."

They shook hands awkwardly while Sarah placed steaming cups of coffee and warm cookies on the table before them. Pastor Ricks blessed the food quickly before passing the plate of cookies around the table, then asked, "Mr. Miller, would you tell us a little about yourself and why you feel ready to make a lifetime commitment to this woman?"

Cady was caught off guard but began slowly, telling the story of his childhood, the loss of his parents, of his sister and his trip west to Idaho. He hesitated, wondering if it were necessary to tell the story of the three thieves, so he elected not to. Then, seeing no way around it, he told of meeting the Indians, trading, then the treachery which placed Shawna in his life. His audience listened quietly without comment, then the pastor asked, "do you understand what the word covenant means?"

Cady, unsure of himself, shook his head.

"It means a promise, a sacred binding promise made before God. Do you believe in God?"

Cady had never really considered the matter seriously until then. He remembered when he was small, his mother and then his father, reading from the Bible. He remembered attending the small church with his sister after their deaths and hearing the stories from it. He even remembered at times in his life, when things seemed hopeless, praying to God in his own way.

"Yes," he answered after consideration, "I do, although I do not know much about Him."

"And Shawna, does she understand to Whom she'll be making a promise?" the pastor asked.

Cady shook his head, "no, I suppose she doesn't, we can barely communicate in words."

Sarah Ricks moved her chair closer to Shawna and, covering her hand with her own, spoke gently, "do you understand what marriage means?" Without waiting for an answer she lifted her hand displaying her gold band, then pointed to her husband.

Shawna hesitated, pointed to Cady, then nodded smiling. "Marriage," she repeated, fingering her cameo as if it were a ring.

There were smiles all around the table as Pastor Ricks spoke again, "How long do you expect to be in town, Mr. Miller?"

"Three, maybe four days," he answered, then continued, "my sister and her son are coming in on the train from St. Louis."

"I have an idea," the parson offered, "if you are willing. I have a friend who was a trapper who speaks several Indian dialects, I'd like to ask him to meet with you. He may know a few tricks which may make your communication problem easier to handle."

Cady was excited. "When?" was his answer.

"Soon, if I can arrange it. I'll speak with him today" said Pastor Ricks. "Where are you staying?"

"We have two rooms at the boarding house," Cady offered.

"Two?" queried Sarah Ricks.

"Yes ma'am, one for her and one for me."

The pastor and his wife smiled at each other. "I'll speak with my friend and meet you here this evening for supper at 5:00, if you are available," said Ricks, standing.

They left the parsonage holding hands and smiling as they walked down the hill toward town. Stopping at the Mercantile on their way home, they went inside, gathering close to the stove and enjoyed its warmth. The same stout, pleasant woman was behind the counter when Cady approached and asked if she might have a wedding band.

Her smile brightened the room as she laid the tray, that previously had also held the cameo, on the counter. Shawna, standing discreetly behind him, could see them but said nothing until Cady beckoned her forward. He chose first a solid gold band, holding it up for her to see, then pointed to the others remaining before them. She touched each one gently, then picked up one with colored stones inset into it.

Although it was not a traditional looking wedding ring, with plain gold or diamonds, it was indeed beautiful and sized to fit her small fingers. His eyes asked her the question, she nodded, and the deal was made with little further conversation. The woman behind the counter put it in a nice box and collected payment from Cady.

Things seemed to be moving quickly, almost too quickly, thought Cady to himself, wondering at how easily things seemed to be coming together for them. They had gotten busy the previous day and had forgotten to return to the assay office to pick up their assay slip. They were entering the office just as the two men from the bathhouse exited, giving them hard looks and mumbling something to the effect that "this is not over yet," as they passed by. Both men sported bruises, one had both eyes blackened and his nose askew in his broad face.

Cady let the matter drop but looked over his shoulder, making sure they were not going to pursue the matter with his back turned. He knew well they had been humiliated by their appearance and would want revenge at some point in time. He watched as they entered the saloon, then turned his attention back to the business at hand.

"Miller," Cady said to the man behind the counter, "left my ore by the mill yesterday."

"Yes, Mr. Miller, I have your numbers right here," answered the assayer, handing the slip to Cady. "That was a nice load you brought, with good numbers. Must have found a good vein."

"Hope it holds out," Cady answered, "last one petered out on me."

"They do that more oft' than not," the man said, returning to his work, "the bank will honor that slip when you present it."

"Thank you," said Cady as they turned to leave. They went to the bank right away, the slip could have been negotiated by anyone if lost or stolen. Cady wanted to make sure neither happened, he had invested six months of hard work. Placer miners did not have that problem. What they found, whether dust or nuggets, was negotiable as it came directly from nature. However, they still had the problem of protecting it from thieves.

Most passing by them showed little interest, but occasionally someone would smile or nod, and now and again a rowdy would leer at Shawna, in spite of her escort. Cady made note of the two men in Confederate dress who had paid special attention to them when they had left the assay office. It was nearing 4:00 and Cady was tempted to stop by the lumber yard, but opted to wait another day. He did not want to be late returning to the parson's house.

Instead, they stopped by the millinery which was on the way. Only two other customers had braved the blustery wind to come shopping. They stood at the counter while the woman behind it expertly cut cloth, folding it neatly, while complimenting them on their selections. She looked up and nodded to Cady and Shawna, then returned to her work. As they walked about, Shawna seemed to want to touch everything, feeling its texture and admiring the colors. Cady felt quite out of place but did enjoy watching her, nodding and smiling each time she offered something for his approval. In the end, they purchased nothing, but planned to return once Kate arrived.

It was nearing 5:00 when they knocked on the parsonage door and were welcomed inside. Already seated at the table was a jovial looking dark skinned man and his portly Indian wife. Both had missed few meals and both wore smiles across their pleasant faces that said they enjoyed life. As Pastor Ricks introduced them, Sarah came over to Shawna and embraced her with a hug.

Alphonso, or Al as everyone knew him, had come west as a boy with his family. They were Basques who tended sheep for their livelihood, enjoying the outdoor life and the rough countryside. Al had begun trapping while tending the flocks. Then, finding it more exciting for a young man desiring adventure, he pursued trapping all over the northwest.

He lived among and traded with many tribes, making it necessary to learn their languages and customs. He finally had fallen in love with and married a young Nez Perce woman, and they had grown old together. Later he had become a farrier and together they ran the blacksmith shop at the edge of town. Sadly, they had never had children.

Cady could see they were as comfortable with one another as old moccasins. He envied them, hoping to find that same happiness with Shawna. The three women gathered in the living room talking, while the men remained in the kitchen having coffee.

Al finally spoke up, "heard you had a little run-in at the bathhouse. You know that goes with the territory don't you?" Cady didn't answer for a moment so Al continued, "some can never put their prejudices behind them, always looking for a reason to cause trouble."

Cady answered, "yes, I know that. Have you ever wished you'd made another choice?"

Al answered immediately, as if he'd anticipated the question, "never! Not one time in thirty years. But I have wished I could have sheltered her more from the hurt she has had to endure. We were never blessed with children. I think God chose not to give them to us because of the problems they would have had, half-breeds never quite fit in anywhere, they'd have it worse than we did."

Cady could hear the women visiting in the next room, both in English and their native tongues. Neither tribe shared the same language but they were close enough to communicate well. He heard Shawna laugh out loud for the first time, unknowing of why.

Pastor Ricks was direct when he spoke, "do you know Jesus?"

Cady was surprised and unclear of the question.

He continued, "do you know what will happen to you after you die?"

Still Cady hesitated, not wanting to say the wrong thing.

Al jumped in, "he's asking you if you know that there is life after death. If you can believe that Jesus is God's Son and our Redeemer, then you will be born again in heaven."

Cady recovered enough to answer, "I remember when I was young hearing about that but I did not understand it. I haven't thought about it in years."

Al continued, "Linda and I do believe, we know that when we die that we will be together again with Jesus in heaven, forever. It makes it easier to live without worrying about her if something were to happen to me."

The pastor spoke, "we believe in a promise made to all men, that we all may live in happiness forever, even though we have died here on earth, because one man, Jesus, died in our place. God cannot abide sin and even the best of us cannot help but to sin. So, by dying once for all of us who believe, we can become sinless as Jesus is. Does that make any sense to you?"

Cady shook his head, "clear as mud, but I find the idea interesting."

Pastor Ricks persisted, "can you read?"

Cady answered, "yes, graduated eighth grade."

Ricks asked, "Would you read something for me?"

"Now?" questioned Cady.

"No, not now, take it back to your room with you and read it when you have time," the parson said as he slid a Bible across the tabletop.

"I've marked a chapter in John that may give you both answers and questions." With that, he called to Sarah, "got any food for some hungry souls?"

The six of them ate nearly two full fried chickens and cleaned up their plates of baked squash, pickled beets and fresh bread, before settling back in their chairs. Cady was comfortable, enjoying their company and marveling at how life had changed for him in a few short months.

Al turned to him and said, "if you have time to come by tomorrow I can try to teach you a little Shoshoni while the wife works with Shawna on her English."

"We'd be grateful," Cady answered, "it's hard trying to guess what is on another person's mind."

All three men laughed, then Pastor Ricks spoke, "don't think speaking the same language means that you'll understand each other any better." They all laughed together while finishing up their dessert.

Shaking hands at the door with the Bible under one arm, Cady thanked them, then turned in surprise when he heard Shawna say, "good night" in English. The four walked together to the foot of the hill where Al and Linda turned left and headed home. Cady and Shawna turned right onto the main street and walked to the boarding house. It was almost 7:00 when they entered, with only the proprietor in sight. She said simply, "didn't hold dinner for you."

Cady responded, "I'm sorry, I should have told you that we were having dinner with Pastor Ricks. I hope that none went to waste."

Softening her voice she answered him, "Nope, nuthin' ever goes to waste here. Hope you enjoyed your supper, Sarah's a good cook."

As they settled into their respective rooms for the night, Cady lit the oil lamp and opened the book where it had been marked for him. "In the beginning was the Word..." he read until he had drifted off to sleep.

He awoke with more questions than answers, but with a desire to know more. It felt as though he had always known these truths but had never understood them. He had known that he had a moral compass, knew right from wrong, but had not known where it came from.

Since he had awakened before daylight, he relit the lamp and continued to read, giving Shawna a chance to sleep. Sometime later there was a knock on the door and a soft voice asked, "eat?" Opening the door he found her dressed and ready to begin the day, starting with breakfast, which announced itself to him with the aroma of frying bacon.

The guests, like himself, were just gathering, with the promise of another fine meal in their nostrils. Fresh baking powder biscuits by the plate, bowls full of country gravy, and thick sliced bacon with eggs were brought to the table. The food was quickly blessed before the feast was passed around. Little conversation ensued for several minutes until the first round had settled into the hungry stomachs.

As they began to refill their plates and coffee cups again, the hostess broke the silence, "Mr. Miller, may we ask you if congratulations are in order?" All eating stopped and all faces turned toward Cady and Shawna for an answer.

"Yes, I think so, by the end of the week," he answered blushing. When he looked, Shawna was nodding her head in agreement.

Nods, grunts, smiles, and congratulations circled the table as they resumed eating. Only the two single men failed to give affirmation as they continued eating. Pouring a final cup of coffee, the women joined Catherine in collecting the plates and silver to the kitchen.

Harless rose and slapped Cady on the back with a grin, "good for you son, we are happy for you," he said before wandering into the parlor.

Cady had not expected that they would be participants in his joy. It surprised and pleased him that others, who were almost strangers, would so openly endorse their plan to marry.

With the plans having changed, Cady spoke to Catherine about securing an additional room. Kate and Ben could arrive as early as tomorrow or as late as two more days, if the train master were to be believed. She was pleased to accommodate and agreed to add a bed to one of the rooms without charge.

When the women left the kitchen they were acting like school girls who had known each other forever, all talking at once. Shawna, who seemed to enjoy her new celebrity status, also seemed overwhelmed with the attention. Cady returned to his room, leaving Shawna to visit and plan, with intention to complete the book of John before meeting again with the parson.

He read slowly, trying hard to make sense of what he read as he moved along, making notes now and again on a piece of paper that Catherine had given him. He had not read anything for several years and many of the words were also unfamiliar to him. By late morning he closed the book, feeling puzzled and yet encouraged.

He knocked on Shawna's door without response, then, going downstairs, saw her sitting in a high backed chair while the women fussed with her hair. Apparently the men had tired of watching for there were none in sight.

They had removed the traditional braids and had combed and brushed her long black hair until it shone. Now they seemed to be practicing interlacing small flower blossoms in it. Cady guessed they were preparing in advance for when they would ready her for the actual wedding ceremony.

Now it was his turn to be nervous, he had expected it to be a short and private ceremony with just the preacher and his wife. He could see now that it may could easily turn into an 'event' once Kate arrived and became involved. Outside of the saloon and bar fights, he guessed that the town had little going on in the winter months. With spring here, folks with cabin fever would welcome any reason to get out and socialize.

It was after noon before he and Shawna stepped from the front porch and felt the crisp air biting into their nostrils. The sun was high and the sky was without a cloud, only a light breeze gave the air a chill. As they walked, even that disappeared. The walk to the blacksmith shop took only a few minutes and they were warmly greeted when they arrived. Cady and Al walked to the barn which contained the tools of his trade and was home to a menagerie of animals, while Shawna and Linda remained in the house.

Al began simply, as Cady supposed Linda was also doing, by saying a common word which they understood, then repeating its counterpart in the other language several times. Then Cady would repeat what he had heard in the same way. Cady remembered how Shawna had done similarly in her attempt to learn English early in their relationship, while he had made little progress in understanding her language.

Al moved about the barn doing chores, talking all the while, throwing hay to the horses, cows, then milk to the kittens who moved underfoot. An old brown dog lay near the door chewing on a remnant of last night's supper, the whiskers on his muzzle gray with age.

A call came from the house asking them to join the women. When they entered, the table had been set, with a steaming kettle of thin broth at its center and large hot chunks of fresh bread on a platter. Lunch was not a common practice for many, they took only time for breakfast and supper, but preferred to labor through the day. However, here it was a welcome break, offered simply and sincerely by new friends.

Purposely, Cady figured, Al directed his speech to Shawna in English, waiting for her reply, while Linda would speak in Shoshoni to Cady, as he struggled to remember what he had learned earlier. It worked effectively to draw them together, causing laughter to lighten the mood, while making them forget that they were learning.

It felt odd calling pastor Ricks and his wife, Orville and Sarah, but they had insisted as they had welcomed them once more to their home, following their time with the blacksmith.

Orville broke the ice. "How did it go with Al and Linda?" he asked.

Cady hesitated and Shawna jumped in, "good," she said. He was amazed at how much progress she had made understanding her new language. Speaking it would take more time.

Turning to Cady he asked, "and how did it go with John?" He was referring to the book of John.

"Pastor, I mean Orville, I am afraid I had a lot of trouble understanding it," was the response.

Orville smiled, "you read it all?"

"Yes sir, I did and took some notes too. I have so many questions to ask you," Cady blurted.

Pleased, the parson smiled saying, "we all struggle to understand the Word of God, we all have many questions. Sometimes it is easier to concentrate on what we do know rather than on what we do not, much the same as learning a new language."

Cady nodded, understanding the relationship.

The pastor had an awesome task before him as he moved forward, attempting to condense the Bible and theology into a few words in limited time. He prayed quietly that the Holy Spirit would guide both he and his charge as he plunged forward.

"We do know that God exists, we are told in His Word that He has always existed, that He created everything we see around us, including ourselves. He is perfect and will not allow sin in His presence and we live in sin. Sins are mistakes which we make that go against what God has told us to do. No matter who we are or how hard we try, we break the rules because we cannot keep them by ourselves. We need His help to do things right.

Have you ever done anything which you felt was wrong? We all have. We did it because we are not perfect as God is perfect. Later, after we have done it, we are sorry and wished we had not done it. If we pray to God and ask Him to forgive us for doing it, He will. Asking is called repentance. When we make mistakes and are forgiven, we begin to change and grow better. As we get better, God allows us to move in closer to Him. When we do, He helps us to make still fewer mistakes. Years ago God knew that men would never live long enough to be perfect. So they could never live in heaven with Him unless He changed things.

So, He sent His Son, named Jesus, to live on earth with us. He made it so that Jesus died and took responsibility for all of our mistakes upon Himself. When He did that, it made it so we could move close to God, then if we believed in this man Jesus, we could live with Him in heaven. Jesus is alive again with God, living in heaven with Him, waiting for us to join them."

Cady, Sarah, and Shawna had all listened carefully without interrupting.

Orville continued, "if we die before we make our commitment to God, we will never have the chance to change and go to heaven. Does this make some sense to you?"

Cady was quiet for a time thinking, before he spoke. "Yes, some. I usually know when I am doing something that I shouldn't. Sometimes I stop and sometimes I continue and regret it later. I'm not sure how I would ask to be forgiven."

Orville spoke quietly, "you speak to God just like you are speaking to me, from your heart. You can ask with words or you can ask with your heart, He hears both."

Cady was visibly moved when he said asked, "how do we know what His rules are? When we are breaking them?"

Orville answered, "many times we just know, we call it our conscience, it is God's Spirit who tells us. But the Bible also has the rules written in it to remind us when we loose track."

"Cady asked softly, "is killing wrong? Is it against His rules? I have killed men."

The pastor showed no emotion when he said, "murder is wrong, it is a sin because He loves all men who He created, even the bad ones. But, not all killing is murder. Your heart will tell you when it's murder. If you are not sure, just ask Him to forgive you, if you are sincere He will. He will know if you are not telling the truth because He can see into your heart."

As the evening wore on they continued to talk, with the conversation finally turning to the wedding.

"I wanted you to know God before you made a promise to Him so that you would keep that promise. I wanted you to also know God so that you and Shawna can live in happiness with Him in your hearts. And so your children would also know Him," said the pastor. "I asked Linda to tell Shawna this same thing when you were there so she would understand also."

Cady turned to her. "God," he said.

"God," she repeated, nodding.

Finally, darkness haven fallen long before, they said goodnight to Orville and Sarah and headed back to the boarding house. Cady was beginning to feel something working inside him, something changing. His mind was far away when two forms moved toward them in the darkness. The meager streetlamps did a poor job of illumination. With most of the shops closed, there were few on the street and except at the saloon, the town was quiet.

"Hey, squaw man, time to finish up what you started," came the harsh words from the darkness.

"We're going cut you up a little before we do the squaw."

Cady could make out the men moving toward them from between

two buildings where they had been waiting. They must have followed them earlier to the church, then waited for cover of darkness to play their hand.

"Shawna," Cady said, "go to the church." There was urgency in his voice, as he moved to place himself between them and her. She hesitated but a second, then took off up the hill.

The two from the bathhouse circled him, keeping their distance while brandishing knives. Cady held his skinning knife in one hand and a substantial leather pouch of gold nuggets in the other. Suddenly, the smaller man lunged toward him, feigning an attack, as Cady moved forward, rather than away, quickly closing the distance between them. Before he could withdraw, Cady hit him with the nuggets along the jawline, dropping him instantly. With a roar the other charged in, his blade slicing the air at Cady's back. Cady made no move to engage him, instead he sidestepped as the larger man passed by, nearly tripping over his fallen comrade.

"You think your nose hurts now," Cady taunted, "wait until I finish the job."

Cady could feel the hatred radiate out into the darkness as the man bore down on him wildly. He had accomplished what he had wanted, the other man in his anger had lost control and moved without caution. Again Cady easily sidestepped him, but not before feeling the blade cut through his leather shirt at the shoulder. Cady swung hard with the leather pouch, breaking the grip on the knife and causing it to fall free of the man's grasp. Cady then brought the butt of his big knife down like an ax, striking him high on the chest, breaking his collarbone.

The big man moaned, no longer able to raise his arm, just as Orville, Shawna, and Sarah arrived. Orville sent the two women down the street to the Sheriff's office while he and Cady prevented the man from recovering his knife.

As the Sheriff returned with the two women, the smaller man on the ground began to stir.

"What is going on here?" he demanded, turning toward Cady who had sheathed his knife.

"Had a run in with them at the bathhouse a couple of days ago, but it appears they wanted more," Cady responded. "They were waiting for us in the dark when we left the church."

The Sheriff laughed, "looks like they were over-matched, they should have brought some friends. I heard they took quite a ribbin' the other day at the saloon when they said they got whipped. They'll have a couple of weeks to think it over before the circuit judge comes through. I'm charging them with attempted murder. If they don't go to the state prison in Boise, you'll need to keep your eyes open. They won't forgive or forget."

Orville spoke, "we need to tend to your shoulder, before the blood ruins that new shirt."

Until now Cady had not noticed the shoulder wound and the blood soaking into the leather. They quickly returned to the parsonage where they washed and tended his wound. It wasn't deep and would heal without further medical attention. His prized shirt however was another matter. It was soft buckskin and would need the careful attention that only Shawna could give it, first removing the dark stain, then sewing up the cut made by the knife blade.

When they left the Ricks' a second time, it was nearly ten o'clock, with the full moon high in the sky overhead. Cady wore a borrowed shirt under his coat while Shawna carried the damaged one over her arm. They arrived at the boarding house with only a single lamp burning in the sitting room, with no one visible. But, as they started up the stairs, Catherine appeared from her quarters to see who had entered. They apologized for waking her and explained their delay in as few words as possible, hoping to get to bed. She would have none of it, she turned the lamp up and examined the shirt and had to hear the full story in every detail. Shaking her head frequently in disgust, she wondered aloud, "what this world was coming to".

– THREE –

Cady sat straight up in bed, every muscle taught, every nerve ending at high alert. A second knock on the door dispelled his alarm. Shawna spoke softly but insistently, wanting to make sure he was well, not willing to leave before he opened the door. He could not remember when he had slept this late, the adventure of the night before must have taken its toll on him. Together they descended the stairs just as the other guests were finishing up their meal with a last cup of coffee.

Apparently Catherine had given the other guests her version of the night's events, for all were eager to talk with them about it. In his modest manner, Cady downplayed it as much as possible, almost embarrassed to have been the victor. For the first time, the two single men showed interest and became involved in the conversation at the table. They had been in the saloon when the two had come in after the first encounter and had heard the ridicule they had endured. They also had heard stories of their intentions to "even the score" next time they met Cady.

Catherine returned from the kitchen with a plate of steaming hot flap jacks and several fresh eggs. Boysenberry syrup with fresh churned butter made them slide down like a dessert. Finally the guests began leaving, some to their rooms, others out the door to begin their day in town. Cady and Shawna went first to the Chinese laundry where they deposited Orville's shirt, then to the train station where they found that the train was on schedule and should arrive sometime after two o'clock. A passenger manifest was not available, so they pledged to return to see if it brought Kate and Ben with it.

They checked at the livery about the condition of their horses and paid the board current before walking to the blacksmith shop to enjoy another language lesson with Al and Linda. They were welcomed warmly once more, with the women talking excitedly in the kitchen while he and Al walked outside. Cady asked if Al would give the ore wagon a once-over before they left town. The mustangs wore no shoes but needed their hooves shortened while the mules needed shod. Al seemed happy to get the work, suggesting that they may as well go get them now. He could teach Cady while he worked.

"Heard you had another run-in last night, you all right?" Al asked.

"Fine," Cady answered, preferring not to go into detail.

"Word's all over town that they were lucky to have jumped you rather than some gunhand. They'd be heading for the cemetery instead of coolin' off in the jail." Al pressed.

Cady felt obliged to respond, "it wasn't that big of deal really, they just don't know when to give up."

Al replied, "worries me that now that they know they can't whip you, they may try and dry gulch you when you let down your guard."

"Sheriff is thinkin' that they may do some time in prison, have time to cool off and forget about revenge," answered Cady.

"Not likely, by my opinion," said the smith. "More likely they would get more bitter and more anxious for revenge when they got out."

They dropped the subject as they rode together in the wagon, returning to the language lessons.

At the barn Al carefully looked the wagon over, making verbal statements and mental notes as he went. The wagon was sound and well made, needed a few boards replaced, hubs greased, and one brake lining replaced. The metal bands on the rims still showed little wear and remained tight. On the harnesses, a couple of rivets had worked loose and the leathers needed re-oiled to prevent cracking. Cady himself had noted most of this before leaving the mine but preferred to let Al make his own assessment.

"The stock wintered well," Al noted as he checked over both mules and the horses, "they all look sound."

Cady nodded.

It was late afternoon by the time Al hammered the last nail into the hoof of the second mule and leaned back appraising his own work. "Should do," was all he said, feeling satisfied.

Cady elaborated, "a fine job, I do appreciate it. You've become a good hand at it, for a trapper."

As they both laughed they felt a kinship much stronger than just friendship. They knew that either would risk life or limb for the other.

"Got time for milk and cookies?" came the inquiry from the house.

"Youbetcha!" came the answer from both men simultaneously as they arose to their feet laughing.

"Is that English or Shoshoni?" Cady asked his new friend.

"Both," laughed Al.

Inside, they washed up and sat at the table, the aroma of the cookies wafting into their nostrils. Al quickly blessed the food and all of them dug in hungrily. As he washed down a second and then a third cookie with the cool milk, Cady wondered if a milk cow might be a nice addition to the menagerie of animals he seemed to be accumulating.

Up to now, he had just let the two mules graze in the meadow while laying away some grass hay in the lean-to each fall for when the snow became too deep. It would mean a corral and a barn as well as time to haul forage before snowfall. 'I'll probably need them anyway with the three ponies', he thought.

"Tell me about the cow," Cady asked suddenly, turning to Al. "I've never had no truck with them. But the milk and butter make me want to know more."

"Milkin' shorthorn," Al answered, "tough little thing she is, and a good keeper. She's raisin' her second calf and givin' us about a gallon a day for the kitchen to boot. I might be persuaded to part with her heifer when she's weaned if you are still lookin'."

Cady nodded. They played the word game for a while, saying one first in the native language, then repeating it in their new one.

It was after one o'clock when they left for the train station, with high hopes of meeting Kate and Ben and leading two of the three ponies. It was 2:05 when they heard the train whistle coming up the valley. It arrived just minutes later in a cloud of steam and smoke. The 'iron horse' some had called it, though it hardly resembled a horse, just a great black beast of burden.

The engine trailed only a dozen cars, maybe less, one carrying either coal or wood to fire the boiler, two coach cars for passengers and their personal effects, several open gondolas with lumber and freight, empty ore cars waiting to be filled, two enclosed cars used for livestock or perishable freight, and a caboose where the train's crew lived and lounged when not on duty.

More than a dozen passengers were greeted by friends and family while several others disembarked and made their own way from the train before Kate and Ben stepped onto the landing. To Cady she still looked as young and beautiful as when he had last seen her, but Ben had grown a foot and now was just inches shorter than he. Ben had a big frame and would be a good sized man when he filled out, but now he resembled a colt, all arms and legs.

Shawna hung back allowing Cady to embrace them excitedly, until he turned, putting his arm around her and pulling her forward into the circle. They seemed to be all talking at once, smiling and laughing, giving details of their long trip. As the train began to move north toward the mill and the 'turn around', they each grabbed a handful of baggage and left the landing toward the waiting horses.

There were two larger wooden crates still left on the landing with Kate's name on them, which would be picked up later in the ore wagon. Cady first loaded the baggage, then the women onto the ponies, while he and Ben walked ahead leading them toward the boarding house.

The women struggled to communicate while Ben and his uncle chatted like schoolboys. Ben was full of questions, having never been out of the civilization of the city. He would be twenty in the fall, but he lacked the life experience which came with the western lifestyle.

At the boarding house, Kate and Ben were welcomed like family by both Catherine and Harless and escorted to their room where they deposited their baggage and washed off the dust of the day. Back in the sitting room together, Cady announced he had news to share as they accepted the coffee and cookies offered by Catherine.

Neither she nor Harless made any attempt to leave, anticipating the expected announcement. Cady became shy, almost boyish, as he slipped his long arm around Shawna's slim waist and blurted out their plan to marry. Kate seemed at first relieved, then overjoyed with the news, Ben just smiled ear-to-ear, hugging Shawna and pounding Cady on the back.

"When?" was Kate's question.

"Soon, maybe Saturday," responded her brother, "we've just been waiting for you to get here to share this with us. The parson has been helping us understand some things, and we have been attempting to learn each other's language a little better before we tie the knot."

"Maybe Ben and I should sit in on the language lessons too," Kate said, remembering the struggle she'd had visiting with Shawna.

"Good idea," Cady agreed, "tomorrow we'll introduce you to our mentors, then pick up your freight with the wagon." He continued, nodding at Harless and Catherine, "our hosts here serve us a fine meal both morning and evening that we'll not want to miss, but we still have time for a walk up to the church to meet pastor Ricks if you feel like stretching your legs. Or if you'd rather catch your breath, we can sit here and visit until supper, your choice."

Kate looked tired while Ben was eager to be off, so Cady took charge and suggested, "how about Ben and I take the ponies back to the livery while you relax Kate?"

She smiled weakly and answered, "that will give Shawna and I a chance to get to know one another."

Cady and Ben walked to the horses before Cady asked, "you ride?"

Ben answered, looking at the pony, "yes, quite a bit, but never bareback."

"Not much different walking here on the flat," answered Cady, "but quite a lot different in the mountains. You'll learn how to use your leg muscles rather than stirrups."

Ben followed Cady's lead, grabbing the mane and swinging his long leg over the small pony before sitting upright. Flashing a grin he said, "ready."

Cady smiled and led them down the muddy road toward the livery stable which sat beside the train station.

As they talked, Cady learned that Ben had finished school, all 12 grades, while working summers at a lumber mill just outside of St. Louis. For several years Kate had owned a sewing shop which made dresses and did alterations. Both had been eager to move west and start a new life when they had received his invitation.

Ben asked, "what will I be doing once we get to your mine?"

Cady smiled, "you'll be workin' hard, learnin', and having a great time doin' it. I haven't had a chance to speak with Kate yet about what her plans are, or if she wants to live out at the claim or not. I figure to take you there with us to begin with, then see how it all works out."

When they got to the livery, the horses were stabled and fed by a young red-haired boy with big freckles across his pug nose. As they turned to leave he said, "you are Mr. Miller, aren't you? The man that put the two troublemakers in their place?"

Cady smiled, then answered, "don't know about that son, but I know they are in the right place now. The Sheriff's taking good care of them."

On their way they stopped by the laundry and picked up the preacher's shirt. Ben and Cady were nearly at the boarding house before Ben spoke again, "What was the boy talking about back there?"

Cady answered, "seems as though folks are making a big deal outta nuthin'. A coupla fellas tried to do us a little harm but it come to nuthin', they're spending some time healin' up in the jailhouse. I kinda get the idea that city folks don't have much goin' on so they like to make a big thing outta what little happens."

The other guests were already gathering in the sitting room in anticipation of supper when they arrived. Kate, Shawna, and two women visited on one side of the room while the men gathered on the other. Catherine and Harless were ferrying food from the kitchen onto the waiting table as they seated themselves around it. Harless blessed the food, then began passing the it around the table.

As usual, there was little conversation in the beginning as all ate with relish, but after the pace slowed and seconds were dished, Catherine asked, "is the date set yet?" referring of course to the pending wedding.

Cady replied, "no, but we hope to discuss it this evening with the preacher and come to an agreement." Then, turning to Kate and Ben he continued, "we'd like to have you join us if you will."

Without hesitation Kate answered, "well of course, wouldn't have it any other way."

While the sun slid behind the mountains which surrounded the little basin, the temperature dropped rapidly as the evening turned to night. By the time they began to climb the hill to the church, the street lamps had already been lighted. Even without a breeze there was a chill in the air, making them all glad to have dressed warmly.

Cady had purchased a hot apple pie from Catherine before they had left the boarding house. She had wrapped it in several layers of cloth before putting it into a basket for them to carry. As they entered the small parsonage, Cady made introductions and was pleased to see Al and Linda there also. Sarah already had the coffee pot ready and wasted no time grabbing cups and cutting the pie. Orville blessed the food before getting right down to business with his fork.

After a well appreciated dessert of pie and coffee Orville began the conversation, going back over ground already covered, presumably for the sake of the new guests.

"Make no mistake about it, no man, no matter how hard he tries or how good he seems to us, will ever see or walk with God unless he first lets Jesus into his heart. He must ask for forgiveness for his past as well as future sins and agree to give control of his life to Jesus. That is a simple thing but not an easy thing for a man or woman to do. Simple to say the words, but hard to really give up control."

Linda quietly translated to Shawna as the others listened to Orville. She nodded often, and asked questions in Shoshoni from time to time, wanting to fully understand what was being said. Al, Linda and Sarah all nodded in agreement with each statement, while they watched the reactions on the faces of the four others.

Orville was looking Cady directly in the eye when he asked, "do you have any questions?" Then to Kate and Ben, "and you, do you know Jesus as your Savior?"

Kate spoke up first, "yes, I do. I gave my heart to Him as a young girl when our father passed away."

Cady was stunned, "you never told me," he said.

"No need to," Kate answered. "It is a personal thing that I did to find peace in my pain. It helped me a lot when I lost my husband too."

Cady's attention then turned to Ben, "and you son?"

"No, I never have, but I pray, I believe in God, I went to church with Ma went I was younger."

Orville stepped in, "that's a great place to start, Ben. Learning about Him from the Bible, learning to trust in Him when you pray, but it isn't enough. You have to give yourself to Him like giving a gift to a friend, without reservation."

Finally Cady spoke again, "I have been thinkin' a lot about it for the past few days and I think I want to do it, but what if I mess up later on and He doesn't want me anymore? I will try and do my best but I know I can never be good enough to please Him."

Orville smiled, "no, you can't, and we can't either, that's the whole point. None of us ever could, that's why He had to die in our place as a perfect sacrifice. And... once you have asked Him into your life, He has promised, 'He will never leave you or forsake you' no matter what you do. If you mess up, or when you mess up, you'll ask Him to forgive you and He will."

Cady nodded agreement, then looked over at Shawna who was still talking with Linda. Looking him directly in the eyes she nodded, then said, "yes, me too."

Ben looked a little nervous as eyes turned toward him. "Do I have to decide tonight? I think I'd like to think it over a little."

Orville took the reins once more, "of course you can, everyone needs to be sure before they make the decision. Only thing making it urgent is the fact that none of us know when our last day may come. If it comes before we decide, we will never have the chance. Your uncle here could have died when the two men attacked him the other night, if that had happened he'd never known salvation and would spend eternity in hell. For those of you who have made the decision tonight, please bow your heads and repeat the sinner's prayer after me."

As Orville led them, first asking for forgiveness, then asking Jesus to enter their lives, and finally closing with the promise to follow God all their days, tears of sadness and joy were shed. Cady felt emotionally drained, exhausted, while at the same time as though a heavy weight had been lifted off him. He wondered if the others felt the same. There were hugs, smiles, and laughter amid the tears of happiness.

Finally Ben spoke, "I did it, I did it too. I wanted to make sure we were all going to be there together."

Orville turned to Cady and Shawna saying, "now you know Who you are making your promise to, now I know you'll work hard to keep your vows. When do you want to have the wedding? Tomorrow is Saturday, we could have it in the afternoon, or Sunday after the service."

Cady looked at Kate and Shawna, "tomorrow or Sunday?" he said.

"Sunday," they said together.

"I personally like that best," said Orville, "the congregation can enjoy your day with you and the church will sponsor a pot luck. People feel more like a part of things if they bring something and eat together."

They continued to plan and visit until someone noticed the time had gotten away from them. By the time they entered the boarding house the lamps were out, save the single lamp in the entry.

Morning found Ben and Cady bunked together with Kate and Shawna each in their own rooms. Breakfast brought the guests together over hot muffins and crisp bacon with scrambled eggs and fried potatoes. The topic of the day was, of course, the wedding, with the women laughing and talking over one another like school girls.

Catherine volunteered to bake a cake fit for the occasion while Kate wanted to take Shawna into town to find a suitable dress. Several of the boarders pledged their intent to attend, offering help where it might be needed. Cady and Ben struck out for the blacksmith shop right after breakfast, with the intention of picking up the crates left at the train station. Al had completed the repairs and had the mules hitched up when they arrived. Cady attempted to pay for his services but was turned down, Al saying that he and Linda wanted them to accept it as a wedding gift. They left promising to see them at church the next morning.

At the station, the crates were loaded into the waiting wagon with minimal effort. Cady and Ben then stopped by the lumber yard to leave off a list of materials they planned to pick up before heading home the following week. Finally, leaving the mules and the wagon at the livery with the ponies, they stopped by the bank to replenish the money that had been spent during the week.

As they passed the mercantile, Cady went inside and confirmed that the provisions previously ordered would be ready to pick up on Monday. He left a sizable deposit with the woman telling her that the parson was free to use it in any way he saw fit, hoping that the church would benefit. Before leaving, both he and Ben bought new pants and shirts fit for the upcoming occasion. The woman was well aware, as was most of the town, of the pending wedding, pledging to be there to share in their event.

In their absence, the women had been busy... food was cooking, bows and decorations were being made, and they had been to the millinery and found a suitable dress and shoes for the bride. Kate had overseen the purchases, while Catherine had focused on the food. Harless had moved Cady's gear to a bigger room on the same floor with a double bed and additional furniture. He laughingly called it the 'bridal suite'. The portly pink-faced man and his wife had paid the room charge for them.

Everyone seemed eager to be a part of the event. Cady suspected the little church had not drawn such attendance as was expected the following day. Ben grabbed his uncle's best boots, spending a good part of the evening working to put a shine on them. After they had enjoyed another fine supper together and cleared the dishes, the women took Shawna somewhere to fuss over her and get her hair fixed. Cady would have been happy to see her just as she was, but they would have none of it.

Following an early breakfast, most went to their rooms to change into their Sunday best before filing to the church. Both Ben and Cady dressed in their new clothes as well, while Shawna remained behind closed doors with the women. At a quarter to the hour the men left on foot, making the short walk right on time. A few minutes later Al and Linda pulled up in a surrey, ferrying the women to the parsonage, arriving like nobility. Shawna was dressed in the dress that Catherine had given her earlier. She was carrying the wedding dress which she would change into after church but before the ceremony.

Orville began the service with a special prayer, asking God to sanctify His house and cleanse the hearts of those in it. He then made announcements including the wedding and pot luck which was to follow the regular service, with a delay of one hour to allow some to return home to bring back their food offerings. The congregation enjoyed several hymns before he began his sermon.

He began in Exodus, recounting the lack of faith among the chosen even after God's many miracles, then moved to the New Testament where doubters still refused to believe after witnessing Jesus' miracles. Hoping he had made his point about the heart of man and his stubborn nature, he spoke of God's grace and mercy, then closed in prayer.

Cady, Shawna, and his friends were immediately surrounded with new friends who had planned to share their special day with them. They were surprised at how easily they were accepted and welcomed into the community. As the crowd thinned out, many of them promising to return for the ceremony and dinner, Shawna was whisked away by Linda and Sarah to get ready. Catherine and several others began hanging bows and placing flowers in the church. Cady chose Al as his best man with Ben as groomsman while Shawna, likewise chose Linda and Kate.

Finally the hour arrived with guests in such numbers that left many standing along the back and sides of the small sanctuary. Benches and chairs were brought in until the supply ran out, leaving some still willing to stand. Cady and his two men stood in the area where Orville had been doing woodworking when they had first met, while Shawna remained in the parsonage until the time was right.

The small church did not own a piano, but one had been borrowed and brought up from the saloon for the occasion. Sarah played it beautifully. As Pastor Orville laid the groundwork, welcoming the crowd, he motioned the groom to the front where he stood with his supporters until Sarah began playing the wedding march. When the women entered from the rear, all heads turned and stared at them. Cady could not believe how beautiful Shawna looked and at how 'story book' it all seemed. Several times Linda leaned close and whispered to Shawna, urging her to answer the questions correctly when asked.

When it was over, they kissed amid applause, catcalls, and noisy congratulations, leaving by the front door and going to the parsonage. Cady had left a very generous poke of gold with a thank you note signed by both of them in one of the cupboards. It had been fun teaching Shawna how to write her name in English for the first time.

Hastily, many hands went to work, transforming the sanctuary to a dining hall, turning the benches sidewise while others brought in tables. A dozen table cloths of varying designs covered them before the food was brought in. Many faces Cady could remember seeing over the past week, without names attached, were seated at the tables when they returned to the church. The station master, banker, assayer and his wife and children, the clerk from the mercantile and her family, most of the guests from the boarding house, and even the Sheriff and his wife were among the several dozen who had returned to celebrate with them.

They were seated at the head of one of the two long tables, with Orville and Sarah heading the other. Orville stood and blessed both the food and the union before they all began eating.

Once the food was gone, Orville took the couple aside, suggesting that they may want to go early, rather than waiting for the guests to leave. Cady rose and thanked their guests, giving special thanks to the several notables, then nodded to the rest who had also contributed. Al had the surrey waiting when they left, dodging handfuls of rice on their way to it. As dessert and coffee followed, the crowd remained visiting, recalling memories of their own special day with jokes and laughter.

There was a light rain falling when Cady and Shawna stepped from the carriage and entered the boarding house. Cady felt uncomfortable and unsure of himself when they opened the door to their room, wondering what thoughts were in Shawna's mind. When she gently touched his cheek, as she had done when she'd been injured at the shack, and looked into his eyes, he knew nothing needed to be said. As they explored each other and became one, they knew joy beyond description, making silent vows to always be faithful. Cady had planned to leave town the following day but waited until Tuesday to begin the trip home.

– FOUR –

Tuesday morning, after eating a sizable breakfast, Cady brought their bill current, leaving a nice tip for Catherine and Harless for the kindness they had shown them, then went with Ben to the livery and did the same. Kate and Shawna stayed at the Merc, adding to the list of provisions they had prepared previously for Cady. The mules pulled the ore wagon to the lumberyard where it was loaded with two kegs of square nails and rough cut lumber, while trailing the three ponies behind.

Cady and Ben then picked up the supplies and the women, stopping by to see Al and Linda before leaving town. Cady drove the wagon with Ben riding beside him while the women rode on the ponies. As they went, Cady instructed Ben on the finer points of operating a heavily laden wagon over poor trails. Ben took the reins for a time with Cady riding shotgun before they started up the last leg of the trip that which was steeper and more precarious. He then moved to a pony. The women joined Cady in the wagon for the remainder of the trip.

Although it was only about fifteen miles, the trip took until late afternoon. The sun and the temperature were dropping rapidly as they began to unload the wagon into the cabin. Cady unhitched the team and staked them out in the meadow while allowing the ponies to roam on a tether line. Ben meanwhile stacked the perishables in the cabin to discourage varmints and predators. With all of this being hastily done, the cabin filled up fast. Without room to make four beds, Cady and Shawna gave up the cots to Kate and Ben, then made a place for themselves on the floor. It was immediately clear that the arrangement could not last for long as they worked to light the fireplace and begin supper. As he laid down to sleep, Cady wished he had worked harder to complete the new cabin before bringing them here, but nothing could be done about it now.

Cady doubted that anyone had slept much during the night and was up early trying to get a handle on where to begin his day. They left the crates and lumber on the wagon, having no reason to unload them yet, but pulled the supplies back outside so they could organize them and put them away as they went. Cady was pleased to find that Ben knew his way around a saw and hammer so they set about using some of the new timber to frame up some shelves and cupboards.

The women filled and organized them as quickly as they were hung. By lunchtime over half of the provisions were back inside with other items hung by ropes high in the trees away from coons and foxes. With a clear sky and no threat of rain or snow apparent, they made no effort to protect anything from weather.

Taking a break, Cady and Shawna showed their guests around the property, the mine, and finally the new cabin under construction. It was mutually decided that the new building should be two stories high, the floor of the second being the roof of the first story. Cady and Shawna had laid nearly six feet of walls before stopping when she was injured. That left only a couple more before they could put in the rafters and cover them, and move back to the walls again. Once they had the floor for the second story in, the first would become habitable although unfinished.

By that evening they had improved the living conditions a great deal inside the little cabin, giving each occupant a little personal space. They continued to make progress over the next week and began to install the rafters as the walls got to height. By the second week they had a routine, with each knowing and doing their job as the floor was completed for the second story. The women began gradually moving the sleeping accommodations from the old cabin to the new one while continuing to use it for cooking and eating.

By the first of June they were pulling up logs with ropes and pulleys using the mules, the boom having run out of reach. Cady could see that they would not be able to raise the rafters by hand and began to design a derrick crane to place them when the time came. He and Ben needed to make a trip into town to get more lumber and tin to roof it with. Both women, eager to get away from the routine also, looked forward to joining them. The hillside near the tunnel had begun to sport black-eyed Susans and wildflowers.

It was on the trip to town that Shawna and Kate brought up the subject of parenthood. Cady was driving the wagon with Ben riding alongside when they surreptitiously spoke loud enough that he could overhear them. He nearly lost control of the wagon before bringing it to a halt.

"What? Are you sure? How long have you known?" he blurted without thinking.

Shawna nodded, "sure, pretty sure at least."

Kate added, "It's not for sure yet, we should know within a couple of weeks, but I'd bet my best dress on it."

Cady beamed, as did they all.

Ben said, shaking his head, "uncle Ben," then laughed out loud.

From that point the trip went very quickly with everyone talking and laughing at once. Shawna was beginning to speak in sentences, and the others understanding more and more when she reverted to Shoshoni. Kate had become like a mother to her and Ben a big brother.

Even before stopping at the lumber yard or the Merc, Cady reined the mules through town toward the church. He was eager to share the good news with his friends. Broad smiles greeted them as they dismounted and walked toward the church. Both Orville and Sarah had heard their approach and walked out into the summer sunshine.

Once the hugs and greetings had subsided, Cady took on a worried expression, asking if they might send for Al and Linda before continuing their visit. Ben offered to ride down, giving his uncle a wink, before promising to return with them. Ben said little when he arrived at Al's but explained that they had an urgent matter to discuss at the church.

When they arrived in their surrey with Ben at their side, the two women could no longer contain their joy. Their smiles lifted the cloud as they gave the secret away with "we're pregnant!"

Then Kate amended the declaration, "Shawna's pregnant."

They were all smiles and congratulations as they shared lemonade and cookies in the parsonage.

Finally Orville turned to Cady and asked, "how are you doing with John?"

Embarrassed and caught off guard Cady answered, "not so good I'm afraid, been mostly working on the cabin. Haven't taken time to read."

Orville nodded knowingly, "understandable, but I'd like to read some of it to you before you leave, that might give you the information you need."

Cady nodded, "sure, maybe tomorrow after we get the supplies ordered, if you have time."

"You'll supper with us then?" asked Sarah.

"We'd be obliged, if you'll let us bring something to help out," answered Cady for them all.

Before Sarah could answer Al piped up, "we've got a garden bustin' with fresh vegetables and two fat chickens that have been growin' old just waitin' for your visit. Why don't you let your ladies sit back and enjoy our hospitality?"

Cady found it hard to accept from others what he would have gladly given himself. There's a lesson to learn about how to receive graciously without feeling guilty. Half embarrassed, he just nodded, "thank you, you are very kind."

Al slapped him on the back laughing, "'sides, when we come up to the housewarming we'll expect the same of you. Right preacher?" They all laughed again.

"And you'll be welcome," Cady answered."

They dropped in on Catherine and Harless, hoping they would have a vacant room for them. While the women stayed to share the good news, the men took the wagon into town. First stop was the lumberyard to leave a list to be filled, and then to the bank to pull some funds out to cover expenses. Finally, the list that Shawna and Kate had made was delivered to the mercantile. Everywhere they went they were greeted warmly. Just as they left the Merc the Sheriff came walking toward them, lacking his usual smile. Cady nodded and started by him but the Sheriff halted him.

"I need a word with you."

"Sure Sheriff, what's on your mind?" Cady questioned. The Sheriff looked over at Ben, hesitating before Cady spoke, "This is my nephew, Ben. Anything you got to say to me you can say in front of Ben."

The Sheriff relaxed. "In my office?" he asked as he turned and started down the boardwalk.

Ben and Cady followed him without answering.

He got right to the point. "Circuit judge sentenced them to ten years," he began without explaining himself. "But they killed the guard on the way to Boise and escaped," he added. "Thought you oughta know. Them's bad ones. I expect we'll see 'em again."

"Thanks," Cady said, "I'll keep an eye out."

"Better do more than that," responded the Sheriff again, "they won't be comin' atcha with a knife next time. You a hand with a sidearm?"

"Cady answered, "some, rather depend on the Henry in a pinch."

"I hear ya," said the Sheriff. "But it's not too quick in close and not always right at hand."

Cady just nodded.

"What about you son?" The Sheriff asked, looking directly at Ben. "Can you shoot?"

"Never have," Ben answered quickly, "never had a need to learn."

Looking Cady directly in the eyes the Sheriff continued, "wouldn't hurt to teach him some, if you feel the need, you might need a backup." The conversation was over; no more needed said, nothing was, but there was plenty to think about.

Cady was unusually quiet when they returned to the boarding house. The women seemed talked out, and had changed from their travel clothes, they were ready for supper at the church. They apologized to Carolyn, promising to enjoy dinner with them the following night, then left for the church in the wagon. That Cady had slipped the Henry in the boot before leaving did not go unnoticed by the three, however no one said anything.

Al and Linda had brought a bounty of food from home, easing the burden on Sarah who had made fresh bread and dessert. Baked squash, fried chicken, new potatoes, fresh snapped green beans with bacon, and cold milk made its way around the table after being blessed by the preacher. They talked as they ate, asking and answering questions about the cabin and the claim, before returning to the subject of the expecting mother.

"It might not hurt to see the doc as long as you're already here," offered Sarah. "He's a good man who can answer your questions." Then looking at Ben, "been a while since Kate had a young one."

They laughed when Kate replied, "that it is, but you never forget the delivery."

The small talk persisted through dessert until Cady stopped it with a raised voice. "Friends, I need to share something with you all, bein's how you are all so important to me. I need your opinions and advice."

They just stopped talking and turned to him as he repeated what he and Ben had been told by the Sheriff. They talked long into the night, never getting around to hearing Orville read from John. Each offered advice, asked questions, then paused while another did the same. In the end it was Orville who spoke, using the Scriptures as his guide.

"An eye for an eye..." he recited from memory. "A man was given the right to protect himself and his family when it becomes necessary. We sometimes have to do things we'd rather not do to accomplish that. I'd follow the Sheriff's advice and hope you never have the need to use it," he finished.

When Ben looked at his mother, she nodded with a tear in her eye. The mood was somber when they said goodnight and headed back to their homes, the joy gone out of the evening.

Next morning, right after breakfast, Cady kissed Shawna and Kate before leaving for town with Ben in tow. At the Merc they were sent down the street to the gunsmith whose shop abutted the hardware store. The smith greeted them, sizing them up with a single look, and asked how he might help them. He was a small man with bushy eyebrows and grease under his nails. His dark eyes were always moving, never making contact with theirs, giving him a nervous and untrustworthy feel. Cady disliked him immediately but asked questions and prices while looking over his merchandise. The man bought and sold guns and repaired them as well.

When they left without purchase Ben asked, "didn't he have what you wanted?"

"Maybe," answered Cady, "but it is hard to trust a man who won't look you in the eye. Let's visit with the Sheriff a minute while we are here."

The Sheriff confirmed Cady's feelings, "he's new to town, don't know a lot about him. He's got the look of a man who'd rather be usin' a gun than fixin' one."

Cady nodded.

"Whatcha lookin' for exactly?" the Sheriff asked.

"Just taking good advice from a friend," Cady quipped. "Need another pistol." My partner Tom left me with a Colt 44 when he passed, makes sense to me to stay with the same caliber. No sense in having to sort out which round fits which gun."

The Sheriff thought a minute before taking a ring of keys from his desk. "Let's see what we may have," unlocking a door into the back room. "I get stuck storin' quite a number of pieces for one reason or another. Sometimes the owner goes to boot hill, sometimes prison, sometimes he can't pay his fine. Can't sell 'em though, but I can take donations to help feed widows and orphans."

Cady and Ben had followed him in to the little room and were impressed with the assortment of weapons they saw. A half dozen rifles, a couple of double barreled shotguns, and ten or twelve handguns lay on shelves. The Sheriff picked up a Colt, much like Cady's, checked the cylinder and handed it to him. Cady noticed it was one of a pair and had nice leather with it. He handed it carefully to Ben, pointing out the features that a man should look for in a good gun.

The Sheriff smiled and handed him its mate saying, "ironically this used to belong to a man you know, a man who found himself overmatched in a knife fight."

Cady missed the point for a second, then caught the joke, the gun had belonged to the man from whom he now sought protection.

The Sheriff lifted a shotgun off the shelf, taking the pistol from Cady. "This little fella'd kill a grizzly up close, easy to shoot, hard to miss. Make a nice cabin gun for the women when you are in the mine or away."

Cady broke it open and looked down its tubes. They were large enough to stick a man's finger in them. "Take 'em both, Cady said, "where does a man leave the donation?"

"Best to leave it at the Merc, just tell them it's for the Widows Fund, they'll keep track of it," answered the Sheriff. "They come with some ammunition too," he said, pushing several boxes toward them.

Cady and Ben thanked him, shaking his hand before leaving for the Merc. Cady left several ounces of gold dust with the proprietor, as instructed, before returning to the lumberyard. At the yard they had already begun stacking his order, assuring him that it would all be ready by Saturday. More nails, lag screws, heavy hinges, and four real glass windows filled out his order. They had totaled the order, which he promised to pay in full when he picked it up, at just under six month's wages. Cady promised himself to get back into the mine as soon as he could after the construction was done.

Before returning to the boarding house, they stopped by Al and Linda's house and found them sitting on the porch drinking lemonade. Without hesitation they accepted glasses and sat, filling them in on the morning's accomplishments. Al walked to the wagon with them while Linda stayed, nodding as he looked over the weapons.

Al was looking right at Ben when he offered, "they can be a man's best friend or his worst enemy, remember that son."

Ben nodded, saying nothing.

At the boarding house Cady asked Catherine if he could pay extra and invite Orville and Sarah to join them for supper, if there was enough.

"No need," she said, "there's always plenty for our friends."

As they joined the women in the sitting area, the men told of the morning's events, which brought sense of dread with it. Leaving Ben and Kate at the boarding house, Cady and Shawna took the wagon to the church and gave invitation to the Ricks for dinner, which they accepted with smiles. Before returning, they stopped by the Merc and looked in the catalog at baby clothes. Both Kate and Shawna would no doubt want to make most of the things themselves but they found it exciting to see them first in pictures.

Cady took the weapons to their room with him when they returned, cleaning and oiling them before sitting them aside. Shawna said little while she sat quietly watching him. She loved the gentle spirit that had drawn her to him, but feared the man she knew was capable of protecting his family. She had not lead a sheltered life, knowing well the savagery of the times, both from her own people and the white man. Death was a necessary part of life.

Cady could see the fear in her eyes when he looked up. He smiled in an attempt to allay her fears and said, "probably won't need them, just better to be safe. I'm taking Ben out tomorrow to show him how to shoot, I'd like you and Kate to join us too."

"This one," he said, hefting the shotgun, "will be left in the cabin for your protection if we are away. Simple to use, but you need to know how to use it."

Cady cut a short length of leather shoelace from his boot, then proceeded to tie it tightly across the double hammers, making it easy to cock them both with one thumb. The shotgun had two triggers and two hammers, giving the operator the option to use one or both. He then removed the bottom screw from the butt stock, allowing the metal plate to be slid sidewise with a thumb. Harless had loaned him a brace with a bit equal in size to the shot shells. He slowly and carefully drilled a pair of holes in the butt where he placed two loaded shells before covering them with the butt plate, as Shawna watched.

He broke open the breach once more, then pointing at each tube said, "two here, two extras there."

Shawna nodded but said nothing.

The Ricks arrived early for supper, wanting time to visit with their friends and make new ones of the guests. Orville was always alert for opportunity to bring sheep into the fold. No mention was made of the discussions of the night before, but Orville did say that he had changed his sermon to include Scripture from John and Matthew concerning baptism.

"Might be a nice refresher course for others of the flock who have accepted the call but have delayed their public confession of faith," he offered.

They all enjoyed a fine dinner of beef liver and onions, hot baking powder biscuits, corn on the cob and fresh green salad followed by peach cobbler with thick cream for dessert. The men retired to the front porch to smoke while the women cleaned up the dishes. The pink faced man lit up a cigar while two others rolled their own. The rest were content just to visit and enjoy the cigar's aroma.

Finally Ben asked Cady, "what are our plans for tomorrow?"

Cady thought before answering, "Saturday. Well, I thought we'd drive out a ways and get you familiar with the .44 and then go to the lumberyard and load up the lumber and supplies so's we can head home Sunday right after church service."

Ben nodded in agreement.

Orville interjected, "I'd hoped you'd be open to a visit to the hot springs at the edge of town 'fore you left. I'd like to finish what we started last time you visited."

Cady turned to him, "let us hear the sermon and then each can decide on their own."

"Fair enough," Orville answered with a wink, "we'll let God help you decide."

Morning came early, bringing with it warm sunshine and blue skies. Cady, Ben and the women left in the wagon right after filling themselves up on biscuits and gravy. As they headed south out of town the mood was somber with little conversation until Cady pulled the wagon to a halt. He'd chosen a narrow draw with no sign of human presence.

He pocketed two boxes of cartridges and buckled the holster around him while handing the gun to Ben. The women followed behind them as they walked up a game trail that followed a small stream to a clearing in the trees. A large yellow pine had fallen across the creek providing a nice place to sit and lay down their burdens.

Ben, Kate, and Shawna seated themselves while Cady stood facing them. Unbuckling the gunbelt, he removed it and laid it on the log beside the shotgun. He removed the boxes of ammunition from his pockets, taking out several cartridges and passing them around.

"These fit the handguns and only the handguns," he said clearly. "They will not hurt you unless they are fired or damaged by fire or crushed by something." He then proceeded to hand them the revolvers, "and these will not hurt you unless you load them first with the right kind of ammunition."

He took time to show each feature of the guns, how to load and unload, cautioning them to never point at anything unless they intended to kill it. He explained that the single action meant that the hammer must be pulled back each time before the gun could be fired. Simply loading the gun and pulling the trigger would not cause it to fire. In the same way he showed the shotgun to them, showing how to break it, load it, cock it and fire it.

At this point he asked each to load and unload both guns. Then he showed them how to point at a target, making no effort to teach them to sight. Cady took a large piece of bark off the downed pine and walked several yards away, leaning it against the hillside.

"That is your bear, cougar, or intruder which has a mind to harm you," he offered. "What will you do?"

He took a small piece of cotton batting that he had brought and showed them how to plug their ears, then took the Colt and loaded a single round into it, carefully handing it to Ben. Ben cocked, then pointed and fired. The gun bucked up, the slug kicking up dirt high and right of the target. Cady took the gun, loaded it again, and moved in behind Ben before giving him the gun a second time.

Reaching around him he held the gun, his hands over Ben's, before cocking the hammer.

"Don't close your eyes," he instructed, "look right down the barrel and center it on the target, then squeeze the trigger gently."

The gun went off, jumping straight up again but this time putting a large round hole in the bark. Cady loaded the gun with six rounds and stepped away, instructing Ben to keep it pointed at the target and to empty the gun. Four of the six hit the target, with two missing to the right. Cady cautioned Ben, "you are pulling the gun right by not squeezing gently, don't be afraid of the noise." The next six all hit their target in various places.

Kate was next, and finally Shawna, who shook nervously with each report of the gun. Cady was patient and complimentary, helping them to gain confidence. Finally he took the shotgun, loading both barrels, explaining both the similarities and the differences of the two weapons.

"This is for up close, when you fear for your life. Don't even pull back the hammers unless you have decided to use it, then don't hesitate. We'll keep it in the cabin or you will take it with you if you go off alone. It holds two shells which you may shoot together or one at a time by pulling the triggers. I've put two more shells in the stock for backup."

He slid the butt plate aside showing the extra shells. Cady turned to the target and pulled one trigger. The bark blew into dust. The short little gun had bucked several inches upward, even in his strong grip. He released the hammer on the other cylinder gently before handing the gun to Ben. Cady tore off several more large pieces of bark and placed them along the hillside before returning to his little family.

He showed Ben how to properly hold the gun, his one hand on the pistol grip and the other on top of the barrels to resist the buck of the barrel. When Ben finally shot, the bark blew in half, the recoil nearly tearing the gun from his hand. One by one they took their turns until Cady was satisfied that they had the skill to defend themselves in a pinch.

They arrived back in town before noon, the two women leaving the men loading lumber into the wagon, while they walked on toward the Mercantile. Kate, having seen the windows, wanted to look for material to sew into curtains. At the livery, the red-haired lad greeted the men once again, with a huge white dog at his side. When they made comment on the dog's size, he said it was a sheep dog, big enough to hold its own with wolves. She had three new pups, if they'd like to see. Great Pyrenees his father called it, the dogs had come over from Spain with the Basques.

It was after two o'clock when the men stopped to pick up the women and load the order from the Merc onto the wagon. The women had elected to walk on ahead and were waiting at the boarding house when they arrived. With several hours at their disposal, Cady suggested they might enjoy the bath house, catching a look from Shawna as he spoke. Both Ben and Kate loved the idea, and Cady promised Shawna that there would be no more trouble.

They had the pool to themselves when they entered and settled back to enjoy the warmth. Cady could hear Kate and Shawna visiting beyond the curtain as he watched Ben swimming back and forth across the steaming water. The water having relaxed their muscles, they struggled to stay awake after enjoying Catherine's fine meal. One by one they excused themselves and went to bed early.

Getting up early after a great night's sleep, the foursome enjoyed a final meal with Catherine, Harless, and the other guests before paying their bill and loading into the wagon for church. They arrived a few minutes before service began and took their seats as others filed in.

Orville and Sarah greeted them, then stood at the door greeting others as they arrived and were seated.

Cady was surprised at how many took the time to walk over to he and Shawna to wish them well. The wedding of two months ago was apparently still fresh in their minds. He could see Shawna and the others were enjoying the fellowship as well.

Near the pulpit Cady noticed the addition of a piano. He wondered if the saloon lent it to the church every Sunday now. They began the service with a prayer and several verses of "How Great Thou Art" before Orville started his sermon. He thanked them all for coming and pointed out the return of the newlyweds and their family, asking them to rise. Embarrassed but honored, they did as requested as those around them clapped.

"Now, two pieces of business before we get into the Word. A great big thank you to the Millers for their generous donation which purchased our new piano," the pastor proclaimed. Applause and pandemonium took over.

"And second," Orville shouted, trying to calm the din, "I think they may have some good news to share with us."

Clearly unprepared, Cady assumed they meant the baby and replied, "why don't you tell them for us, Pastor?"

Orville smiled and nodded, "they are expecting."

Once again Orville let the noise go on for several minutes before restoring order. This was the first time in his life that Cady could remember really feeling a part of something.

The little Miller group were as much a part of the community as if they had lived there all their lives, at least that was how they felt inside.

Orville began his sermon by reading from the book of John slowly and clearly, making points and giving clarification along the way. When he reached 1:29 he hesitated, then read through verse 33, stopping again. He then read Matthew 10:32-33, solidifying his point.

"Many of you already know the Lord Jesus, while some are still searching, of those who know Him many have been baptized by water, giving public declaration of their faith, while others have not. I'd like to give invitation to all who feel the calling of Jesus to come forward today and receive Him now, while Sarah plays our new piano. After the service, I'd like all who feel called to join me at the warm springs for baptism."

To the surprise of many, the couple from the boarding house went forward and received salvation amid hugs and congratulations from the congregation. Several more hymns followed before Orville closed the service in prayer.

Cady quickly called a family meeting as the crowd filed out, attempting to see what his family was feeling concerning baptism. Both Shawna and Ben were eager to declare their faith. Kate had been baptized before, but agreed to do so again in support of the others. Cady was apprehensive but committed, making it unanimous.
As their turn came to shake hands with Orville and Sarah, Cady joked, "show us to the water."

Orville smiled and nodded to Sarah, "we'll need a few more robes it seems."

The church owned a dozen or so robes for such occasions which had once been white bed sheets, although Orville had assured all that the robes were optional, and any clothing was fine. When they arrived at the springs, the water was giving off steam and looked inviting, regardless of the occasion. It appeared to Cady that most of the congregation and also many of the town folks had gathered to observe the event.

The springs were just north of the bathhouse in a natural setting, little more than a deep pool in the stream. The bathhouse owners were church members and allowed public use of their changing rooms for these special occasions. Orville spoke to those gathered, explaining the ritual and symbolism it represented to all who cared to listen. One by one each entered, was asked the same personal questions, then was submerged in the clear warm water before being assisted upward again by the pastor. Each time friends and family would clap and shout encouragements.

Cady watched as first Ben, then Shawna, and finally Kate went before him, feeling happiness and pride in their commitment. When he came up from the water to the cheers of the crowd, all he could do was smile. He felt like the smile might last a lifetime. The event took no more than a half hour but was a significant milestone in the lives of all participants.

Some of the wives had the forethought to have brought picnic baskets full of whatever had been at hand. They openly shared, until their generosity was exhausted. Cady was grateful to be leaving town on a full stomach, in that they were getting a late start. They told their friends goodbye, inviting them to visit, and left a crude map and instructions of how to find their home. With the warm clear June weather it would only take a couple of hours with the wagon, where it had taken twice that in the snow and mud. A single rider on horse back could easily make it in an hour if pressed.

There was little conversation among the four, with each seemingly happy to dwell on the events of the day, forgetting any dark cloud that could be gathering on the horizon. Ben rode the pony, sometimes riding ahead then coming back to join them, gaining experience and enjoyment from it.

They had not found time nor seen the necessity to visit the doctor while in town since Shawna appeared to be doing well. Cady could hardly see any change in her appearance with the possible exception of the twinkle in her young eyes. He was very grateful for Kate's presence and the confidence she gave Shawna, acting both as a mother and a friend. He also loved his nephew and the innocent excitement he had about him, the eagerness to learn. Cady felt, in Orville's words, "blessed."

They arrived home without incident, unhitched the mules and parked the wagon alongside the new cabin. They then retied the ponies to the picket line in the meadow beside the stream with hours to spare before dark. Cady felt relieved that there was no sign of intruders either at the mine or in the cabins. His mind went back to the livery stable, a dog of some size might be a valuable asset to announce an unwanted visitor or discourage one when they were away.

The morning routine quickly came back to the four once they realized that Catherine would not be calling them for breakfast. But, their short vacation had refreshed them all, giving them new resolve to finish the work at hand. Kate and Shawna had started coffee and were cooking grits and bacon by the time Cady and Ben began cutting lumber with the new crosscut saw.

While less convenient, it had been decided that an external stairway to the loft was more practical and would allow more living space on both floors. They began by cutting, then framing the stairway, hoping to get it finished so they could cut in a doorway as an access to move the lumber and tin to the second level. By early afternoon the stairs were usable, making it possible to begin the task of cutting in the door.

They'd been in a hurry to get the walls up and the rafters in place.

It was Cady's oversight that made it necessary to cut it now. The men took turns with the heavy saw until the task was finished. They took a break, calling the women to admire their accomplishments, before beginning to ferry lumber up. Cady found he could stand in the wagon, handing one end to Ben who was then able to slide it through the door-way onto the floor.

When they were called to supper, both men were bone tired and hungry, more than ready to quit for the day. The oil lamp added a warmth to the interior of the dark cabin after the sun had set. Cady said grace in their new home for the first time, blessing not only the food but thanking God for His salvation.

It was nearly a month later when they began covering the cabin with tin roofing. Shawna was clearly showing her motherhood and claimed to have felt movement from the baby. Ben had fallen in love with Cady's big mare, spending his leisure time riding in the surround-ing mountains. He had also found time to practice with the .44, several times proudly furnishing a fat grouse or two for their next meal.

Cady worried that fall might bring early snows, thus spending most of his time working on the cabin. In the evenings he would often read John aloud to any who would listen while making comments and asking for opinions. Kate and Shawna spent much of their time sewing and talking. Clothing and curtains appeared, blankets of both fur and cloth, even baby clothes were stacked on new shelves.

Ben and Cady had begun at the eves, stringing the cross timbers over the rafters, then using them as a ladder to work their way upward to the ridge from each side. The tin required both men for installation, therefore it seemed to go on very slowly. Cady had found that both sides of the roof needed to be worked alternately to keep the weight of the materials from racking the rafters.

The four agreed to observe the Sabbath as God's Word commanded, but found it hard to be idle with work waiting to be done. It was late in July before it stopped freezing at night and they were forced to take their perishables into the mineshaft. By mid-August the roof was on and windows installed in the upstairs at opposite ends of the single large room. The women were eager to hang the new curtains but found they needed to leave them open most of the time for light.

Before beginning the task of chinking the logs, they agreed to take a break from their labors to spend a day in town. Purposely, they chose a Saturday, leaving right after breakfast, riding the three ponies rather than taking the wagon. Cady rode his mare, leading a mule behind, while Ben followed. Shawna and Kate shared the pony which had been hers when she had first had come to the valley. Both men wore sidearms, while Cady had his Henry in a scabbard that Shawna had made him from buckskin leather, hung across his back.

The trip went quickly, finding them dismounting at Al and Linda's place by mid-morning. Their friends welcomed them warmly, making comment of the tummy which now plainly showed on Shawna's slight build.

"What a nice surprise," Al offered as they walked to the barn to stable the horses. "We had intended to come up your way before now but summer's gotten the best of us. Linda has been canning from the garden and I've stayed busy helping her. 'spect that it will be worth it this winter when we are hungry."

Cady nodded his approval. "If things ever settle down at the claim, we'd appreciate a few pointers on this gardening thing ourselves."

"How's it going?" Al asked, interested in their progress.

Ben finally spoke up, "we got the roof on now and the windows in."

Cady added, "sometimes it seems to go so slow you wonder, other times you stand back and marvel at how much is done."

It was Al's turn to nod, "hear ya there."

"How's the smithin'?" Cady asked.

"Not bad," came the reply, "not gettin' rich, but doin' okay. Oh, reminds me, got a present for ya." Al added smiling. "Dog!" he yelled, "here Dog." A huge white pup bounded in from the back of the barn, half as big as one of the horses. "Got him from the freckle-faced kid at the livery, said you took a likin' to him. Was eager to give him to ya, his Dad said he couldn't 'ford to keep feedin' him."

Cady and Ben appraised the dog before saying, "'spect not, looks like he could eat."

Al nodded then said, "they come from my homeland, good loyal animals, you can trust them with your life, but they do eat a bit 'til they are grown. This one is about two-thirds grown already, the food bill will taper off in a couple of months. Probably cost you a couple of extra deer each year to keep him."

Cady smiled, "Truth is, I was thinkin' about how good it would be to have a dog to give notice of critters or trespassers before they got too close. How'll he do with the young one?"

"Protective, he'll mother it and not let any one or any thing near it," laughed Al. "He'll protect your livestock as well."

A call came from the house inviting them to join the women. At the house Cady told the women about "Dog" as they came out on the porch to see him. At Al's call, "Dog" came right up and sniffed their hands. He stood nearly shoulder height next to Shawna, with a big smile on his hairy face. Kate's look of concern passed as Al explained to them what he had already told the men. Ben and Shawna seemed delighted and played like children with the brutish animal.

"What're your plans?" inquired Al, looking at his wife, "for this trip, I mean."

"None really," Cady answered, "we're just takin' a break from the work for a visit with our friends. Maybe stay the night and head back after church in the mornin'. The women kind of missed havin' Catherine wait on them when we got home," he laughed.

Kate and Shawna gave him 'the look' but laughed with him.

They visited for another hour before heading toward the boarding house, accepting Al's offer to leave the animals in his barn. He laughed, saying it was the least he could do if they'd take the dog off his hands. They had packed light and had no trouble carrying their change of clothes and few possessions on the walk through town.

The boardwalk took them right by the Sheriff's office where Cady and Ben paused and said hello, then to the millinery where the women looked around, leaving with a handful of sewing items. Passing the saloon without interest or interference, they came to a door with a sign saying 'the doctor is in'. Both Kate and Cady took this as a message from God to stop, so they did.

Once inside, the doctor, having been alerted to their presence by a little bell over the door, greeted them warmly. He was a graying man with an easy smile and friendly disposition, and whose eyes missed nothing. In a few seconds, and without conversation, he noted that three of the four were healthy, the fourth was two, maybe three months pregnant.

"Doctor Adrian Smith," he said shaking hands with them, "most folks call me Doc or Smitty. How can I help you?"

Cady began to speak, but Kate took over before he could, "Shawna is about ten weeks, we just want to make sure everything is going well." The other three nodded their agreement.

"Well, Shawna, have you felt any pain or sickness?"

"No pain, a little sick sometimes after I eat and before I take my herbs."

Cady was shocked, he'd known nothing of her sickness. "What herbs?" he asked, a little too loudly.

Shawna looked surprised at his question, as though everyone should have automatically known. "These," she said, holding out a pouch of ground leaves and seeds toward Cady and then the doctor.

The doctor smiled saying, "of course," then naming off the ingredients which he had immediately recognized. "Why don't you men have a seat while the ladies come with me for a few minutes."

It was less than fifteen minutes later when Kate and Shawna returned with smiles across their faces, the doctor in tow.

"She's doing fine, baby is fine, don't see any problems, might not be a bad idea to come back in three or four months just for a look-see," Dr. Smith offered, "or any time if things don't seem right."

Cady thanked him, paid him, and then asked, "the herbs?"

"Native medicine, good stuff, she knows what to do. Must be passed down from mother to daughter when they are of age," was the reply.

Their last stop was the Mercantile where they were warmly greeted, as usual. The proprietor, whom they had come to know now as Sally, offered her congratulations first to Shawna and then Cady, seeing the dress beginning to tighten across Shawna's stomach. They gave her the list which included lamp oil, soap, salt, sugar, flour, and several larger items including cartridges for the .44's and for the Henry, promising to pick them up later that day.

Harless met them at the door, resting his eyes jokingly on Shawna's midsection, then yelling over his shoulder at his wife. God had placed them in the perfect place to serve, their friendliness and hospitality fit well with their occupation.

Before even asking the obvious question, Catherine volunteered, "come right in, we have rooms all ready for you."

Cady knew if she hadn't, she would have made arrangements somehow for them anyway. He continued to marvel at how such strong bonds had grown between them and the townspeople so quickly. The four dumped their meager belongings in their rooms and returned to the sitting room to visit.

The plump, pink-faced man and his wife had taken permanent residence elsewhere, now operating a small cafe in town. The two single men were in a few days a month to sell their gold and frequent the saloon, but were out now. A young single man and his sister were staying while he worked at the telegraph office. Catherine was unclear if he had replaced the previous operator or was filling in for him temporarily. She promised to introduce them over supper. She laughed when she heard about 'Dog' but wasn't at all surprised since it was a small town and he was a 'big' dog.

They had a full table at supper, with the married couple from their previous visits still in attendance, the four in the Miller clan, and the young man and his sister, and a carpetbagger who had arrived after them. After blessing the food, Harless began introducing them by name, leaving personal information for them to share as they chose.

The salesman was eager to speak and took opportunity to state his business, which was selling cookware. He motioned to the wagon tied up out front. Cady was surprised to learn the other man worked in the assay office, while his sister worked at the bank. They looked to be in their early twenties. The young man introduced himself as Thomas and not Tom, and his sister as Penelope who went by 'Phil'.

They all laughed at the contrasts, not just in name but also in stature. He was slight and short, she not heavy but sturdy and well over five feet. She had long auburn hair and light blue eyes which engaged Ben across the table, much to both his joy and discomfort. The conversation continued between bites of summer squash, whole wheat muffins, mashed potatoes, and roast beef, then and on into dessert.

With several hours yet before dark, Cady determined to return to the Merc to pick up their order and asked if anyone might want to join him. Kate declined, preferring to visit with Catherine and rest up, but Shawna and Ben accepted his invitation.

Phil spoke right up. "I'd like to go too if you don't mind," she said without consulting with Thomas.

"Sure," Cady answered, "anyone else?"

No one replied. Naturally Cady led, with Shawna falling in by his side, leaving the younger couple walking behind them. Cady took Shawna's hand but made no attempt to talk, content just to be with her. In fact he was eavesdropping on the younger couple who were having quite a time getting comfortable with their situation. There was an obvious attraction between them that encouraged but also confounded their efforts to communicate.

Cady was amused by the one word questions followed by the one word answers that he could overhear. Once inside, Sally began gathering their order together for them, taking notice of the youngsters across the room. She kind of smiled and then raised her eyebrows at Cady and Shawna, who returned her smile. Each, including Phil, had an armload on the trip home, with Cady balancing 50 lb. sack of flour on his shoulder, with his arms full as well.

The sun was fast setting, hanging just above the mountain tops, while the moon had just begun peeking over them from the east when they laid their burdens on the front porch with a sigh of relief. Several hanging swings decorated the porch, amid flower pots sporting wild-flowers and geraniums. Phil occupied one without hesitation and invited Ben to join her. His eyes met Cady's, who took opportunity to usher Shawna inside without comment. Glancing in Kate and Thomas' direction, he answered the unasked question nonchalantly, "kid's are on the porch." One by one the guests excused themselves, adjourning to their rooms until only Cady, Shawna, and Catherine remained visiting.

"You and Harless ever get away?" Cady asked.

"Not much," came the answer, "beds need made, people fed, no one else to do it."

"So you never close down?" Shawna inquired.

"Haven't," she said, maybe a little wearily, "goin' on four years now. We've talked some about trying to hire someone but there ain't enough in it to pay someone full time." She laughed and continued, "you lookin' to change occupations?"

"No, can't see myself in town regular anytime soon," Cady laughed. "'sides, we're still building our first home. Just askin' mostly, we invited Al and Linda to visit, thought you and Harless might come up too."

Catherine brightened noticeably. "You know, maybe we could manage a trip like the one you are takin' now. Might could get Sarah or Sally take over for a night. Got room?"

"Will have," Cady replied, "before snow flies. I expect to bring down another wagon of ore August or September and maybe take back an iron cook stove like the one you have. It'd be a nice time to follow us up the canyon." Cady had not discussed any of this with the others, it had kind of come together in his head just now. Fortunately, Shawna nodded an enthusiastic agreement.

"Harless and I'll talk it over, sure'd be nice to eat someone else's cookin' for a change," Catherine said as she dreamed.

The light was out under Kate's door when they passed, but the youngsters hadn't come inside before Cady and Shawna joined Catherine in saying goodnight. They lay together, husband and wife, holding and gently touching one another when Shawna gasped and jumped.

"Did I hurt you?" Cady said, concern in his voice.

"No, it moved, the baby moved," she said excitedly, placing his big hand on her swollen stomach.

Cady could feel nothing but the soft warmth of her bare skin, "what did it feel like?" was his question.

"Like the flutter of a butterfly's wings," came her soft voice. Several minutes went by before she said, "there, did you feel that?"

Cady thought he had but was not sure, not knowing what he should expect. "Maybe."

Finally they drifted off to sleep, his hand still resting over his child.

Cady, Shawna, and Kate were up, dressed and downstairs finishing their second cup of coffee before Ben joined them, looking tousled and tired. Although no one said anything, Catherine winked and smiled at them when he seated himself late. Sourdough pancakes, fried eggs, and fried salt pork made a filling breakfast. Harless had come up with some apple cider from the previous fall to share with them as well. Phil seated herself across the table from Ben, looking beautiful and well rested, with Thomas to her right. The entire table enjoyed the non-verbal conversation the kids were having as they ate.

Finally Kate broke the ice, "how many are planning to join us in the church service this morning?" she asked innocently.

The salesman made excuse, while the other couple nodded their agreement, Catherine and Harless said "of course," leaving just Phil and Thomas to answer.

Thomas began, "we never have been much on church, except when our folks took us as kids."

"Your folks still alive?" Cady questioned.

"No sir," said Thomas, "they's killed in the river at the crossing when the wagon turned over."

"Sorry to hear that son," Cady continued, "Kate and I lost our folks too when we were still in school, makes it hard."

Kate offered, "it was the reason I found Jesus, I needed someone to take away the pain I felt after Dad was killed."

No one said anything for several minutes, then Phil spoke, "I think we should, Thomas. Let's give it another try." Thomas looked unconvinced but shrugged and nodded.

Orville was already shaking hands at the door when they arrived, nearly doubling the attendance. He smiled, greeting them warmly before turning his attention to Phil and Thomas.

"Welcome, nice to see you. I'm Orville and this is my wife Sarah," he said turning to her.

"I'm Thomas and this is my sister Penelope, we're glad to meet you," Thomas said, taking their hands.

Following the opening hymns and announcements, Orville led them in prayer, then went right to Exodus. The sermon showcased God's patience, love, and faithfulness in contrast to His chosen people. Pointing out how they complained, broke their promises, and abandoned Him time after time for idols.

Following the service, folks stuck around to visit and catch up, enjoying the sunshine. Many came up to the Millers, greeting them and giving their pledges to pray for the baby. The pink-faced man and his wife were jovial and seemed especially glad to renew their relationship, inviting them to dine with them on their return visit. Two young couples were gathered around Thomas and Phil visiting, while Ben stood awkwardly nearby.

Al and Linda moved into the circle and began to visit with Shawna and Cady, as Orville and Sarah did likewise. They quickly caught up on the events of the past few weeks, with Cady announcing his daily Bible reading routine with pride. He quickly added that there was much he didn't understand and many questions from his family he could not answer. Both Orville and Al urged him to be patient and stay committed.

When Al offered to give him a ride down in the surrey to pick up the ponies, Cady jumped at it. Leaving the rest of the family behind to visit, he went down and got them. When he left, having given them each a warm hug, Dog was following faithfully behind. It took another thirty minutes to break free of the group still remaining at the church who had to admire Dog and say their good-byes before they could return to the boarding house and load up for home.

– FIVE –

With the mule loaded heavily and riders on the ponies, they made good time getting home as dusk neared. They unloaded their mounts and put them out to pasture while the women began the task of lighting a fire and starting a stew with elk roast, adding vegetables from town.

When the men joined the women inside, the first thing Cady did was to check the cabinet with the false front, making sure the double barrel had not been moved. He had chosen to leave the weapon handy, but hidden, in the event the women needed it quickly. There was no sign that anyone had been in the cabins in the short time they had been away. Dog personized every tree while he chased every rabbit and squirrel in the meadow, playing in the creek and beaver ponds.

The break in the routine had given them all a lift, renewing their commitment to the projects at hand. They began by gathering large amounts of moss which hung dark like horses manes from the pine trees. In the washtub they made a slurry of the natural clay that lined the stream banks, then added the moss. The result was long strips of moss covered with white clay that could easily be pushed into cracks and dried hard.

They began at ground level, working their way around the cabin, then higher and higher until they had to use the wagon to stand on, and finally they were forced to construct ladders. It took nearly a week before the daylight stopped showing through, by that time their hands were raw and red from their efforts. The family continued to cook and eat in the smaller cabin but moved their bedding and personal items now to the second floor of the new cabin, where they enjoyed both the light and the ventilation that the windows provided. Blankets on ropes were hung as dividers, allowing some privacy, with the thought of permanent walls to come at a later time.

Cady took a break from the construction, returning to the mine with Ben, while the women worked to make and fill mattresses. They would someday cover the beds that Cady had promised to make. After a long week in the mine, both he and Ben had developed a routine and a bond that only men who sweat together can understand.

They began to anticipate each other's moves, working efficiently together with little conversation. Ben proved to be a quick learner, asking questions and accepting answers without debate. By the second week the wagon was filled with ore that showed good promise, ready for the mill.

Down the center of the meadow, following the stream, were stands of aspen that grew up from the roots of others nearby. The beavers chose them rather than pine or fir for their never-ending dam construction. Cady also chose them to build the new beds. Their smooth white bark made it unnecessary to peel them as would the evergreens, and their grain was less likely to crack and split as they dried.

August and September proved unusually hot and dry, the mine being a relief from the sun for the men, while the women sought the shade of the trees or the refreshing coolness of the beaver ponds. They continued to read the Bible in the evenings and observe Sundays as a day of rest. Ben had become quite effective with the carpenter tools, first making a new table, then one by one, matching chairs.

He and Cady discussed putting in a wooden floor in the down-stairs living area but found they lacked finished lumber to do so, having already fit the support poles into place. While the floor lowered the headroom almost a foot, it gave them a step up that kept dirt, mud, and water out. They filled in between the lodge pole floor joists with the tailings from the mine, which gave them insulation and minimized space for varmints to live.

Shawna was now clearly with child, finding it hard to do some chores and suffering in the heat. Ben, always full of energy, coaxed Cady into teaching him how to pan gold, spending most evenings on the stream. Not a single visitor entered the little valley, although Dog watched vigilantly every day for a reason to bark. Kate was quiet and efficient, working behind the scenes to make sure things got done. It was she who reminded Cady that the doctor had suggested they visit again before the snow came. They made plans to leave Friday of that same week so that they may enjoy a couple of days in town with their friends and Sunday at church.

Leaving early in the morning, with Cady and Shawna in the wagon and Ben and his mother on two of the ponies, they left Dog to protect the homestead. They arrived well before noon, leaving the ore at the mill before meeting at the livery to board the animals. The boy asked about Dog and was pleased to hear he was doing well and had now filled out to full size.

Both Ben and Cady had worn side arms on the trip to town, but expecting no trouble, had left them at the livery with their clothes. The Sheriff tipped his hat to the ladies as they passed where he was sitting outside his office, and nodded to the men. They entered the doctor's office and were greeted by Dr. Smith, who left with the women while the men walked next door to the new café.

Inside, their pink-faced friends, who were obviously suffering from the heat, offered them lemonade while they bustled around serving other customers their food. Finishing their drinks, Ben and Cady left, promising to return with the women to have lunch with them.

The women had just finished with the doctor when they arrived and received the welcome report that both mother and child were doing well. Dr. Smith estimated that early February still looked to be a viable date for delivery.

Having run out of batting for the mattresses, Kate and Shawna were eager to get to the Merc. Ben also seemed eager to get to the assay office to check on the ore. So, once again they parted ways, promising to meet back at the café in one hour. They were greeted at the assay office by Thomas, who had just finished testing their ore. They were given a voucher to tender at the bank before Ben asked, "is Phil working today?"

Thomas nodded saying, "you should see her when you get there." On the walk next door, Ben held out a poke in a buckskin bag, "Uncle Cady, I have been saving my dust from my panning to surprise you, I want to do my part for the family,"

Cady, who had been wondering how the boy had done but had not asked, replied, "well, let's see how much you got there."

They entered the bank where Phil greeted them with a huge smile before asking how she could help them, in a very business-like tone.

Cady led, "need to tender this voucher and keep some back for supplies and lumber. Ben here needs to have this weighed," he added, tossing the bag onto the counter.

When Cady had finished his business, he stepped back nodding Ben ahead. The boy lost himself in the sparkle of the big blue eyes and found himself unable to talk. Phil carefully poured the contents on the scale, making careful notes on paper as she went.

She removed a large nugget then said, "fifteen ounces of dust and a nugget," then more quietly gave him the value at current rate. Before they left Phil had suggested they meet later to visit.

Passing the lumberyard, Cady stopped and left a list of lumber he needed before moving on towards the café. "Ben," he said, tossing the poke to him, "you been doing more 'n your share since you come, with the cabin, in the mine, all of it. You keep what you get in your spare time for yourself."

"But," Ben answered, "it's too much. We spend all you make without you holding anything back."

Cady's heart swelled with pride. "Son," he said, "you're doin' a man's job every day, you don't complain, you don't quit. I figure we are partners in the mine, the four of us. Take your dust and spend it any way you like."

Evan and Betty, still showing their pink complexions, seated them right up front where they could watch the cooking and visit with them. It turned out that they had come from down south just before the war started, where Evan had been a barber. When they got to Idaho City there was already a barber and no need for two, so they decided to stay and do what they enjoyed, cooking and eating.

The food was good, and served in large portions, but lacked the homey atmosphere Catherine provided at the boarding house. They paid and left, gathering their things from the livery on their way to get a room for the night.

Catherine greeted them with a smile, "heard you was in town, hoped you'd spend the night."

Kate answered, giving her a hug, "two if you have room. We're going to stay through for church on Sunday."

It was mid-afternoon with little to do, so the men sat on the porch catching up, while the women stayed in and visited. Harless raised an eyebrow toward Ben while looking Cady straight in the eye, "there's a barn dance tonight out by the springs," he stated. "Lotsa folks'll be there, might be a good place to see your friends."

"I imagine Orville and Sarah and Al and Linda will be there sure," Cady replied. "Sounds like fun, don't know if Shawna is up to it though, what do you think, Ben?"

Ben smiled, "sounds good to me. Mind if I take a walk into town and look around?"

Cady answered, "Nope, but you might check what time Catherine is gonna serve supper so's you're not late getting back."

Ben went inside then came out, walking purposefully toward the center of town, with a spring in his step. Harless and Cady exchanged smiles without making comment.

Ben stopped first at the Merc where he visited, a little uncomfortably with Sally, concerning his idea to have his gold nugget put on a chain to make a necklace. She showed him several chains from stock and pointed out others that he could order from the catalog. She then offered that the watch-maker would be the man to put them together, since the town lacked a jewelry store and a full time jeweler.

Ben, being unsure of himself, showed her the nugget and asked her opinion of which would be the best choice. She weighed the nugget, then chose an especially sturdy chain, advising that the lighter ones would not hold up under the weight. Ben left with the chain in a small box after paying Sally with gold dust.

Art, the watch-maker, looked old by Ben's standards with grey hair and thick glasses, but retained a twinkle in his eye and a ready smile. That smile filled his face when advised of Ben's plan. After looking over the chain and the nugget, he advised drilling a hole in the gold where the gold had some heft, then using a jump ring to carry the weight on the chain. The jump ring would be made of a harder metal and wouldn't wear out as quickly as the gold.

"How long?" was Ben's question. "Will it take long?" he said asked excitedly.

"Well, let me see, I got all these people waiting on me," he offered pointing around the empty shop. "Might take a while, when do you need it?"

"Well," Ben began, "there's a barn dance tonight..."

Art interrupted him, "just joshin' ya, I can do it right now, take only a few minutes."

Ben forced Art to take a few grains of the dust from his poke and left the shop walking about a foot off the ground. At the bank he tried to act nonchalant when he asked if Phil was working. He found out she had left for the day to get ready for the barn dance.

Back at the boarding house there were a few looks exchanged when he entered, but nothing said as he joined the group seated at the table, just in time to say grace. It was not only the good food that Catherine served, but also the pleasant environment in which it was served, that made her guests come back.

Everyone ate with relish, sharing the events of their day, passing the food, and speculating on what tomorrow might bring. Of course, the pending birth gave the women cause to share their own experiences and offer unasked-for advice to Shawna and Cady.

Dusk was quickly approaching as they dressed for the dance. While some had their own transportation, Harless and Catherine offered their surrey to others not wanting to walk the distance to the barn. Several women accepted, while Cady, Ben and some of the other men chose to walk.

The revelry had already begun by the time they arrived, with the fiddles and guitars bringing energy to tired feet. As is the way with people, they began to gather in clusters or groups of similar interest or age. The old, the young, the marrieds, singles, mothers with children at their sides, men with a flask in their jackets, the rowdies, and the church goers... birds of a feather flocking together.

Orville and Sarah were in a center of a group with Al and Linda and other faces Cady knew from Sunday mornings. Most were dressed up, eager to enjoy the music and the dancing. The Sheriff and a woman who Cady presumed to be his wife were present to keep an eye on the others. As the night wore on the music grew louder and faster, the swings and kicks higher and wilder. The Sheriff quietly and discreetly broke up a couple of arguments before they became fights.

Cady asked Shawna to dance when a slow song came along, allowing them to learn while they held each other close. Ben saw Thomas and Phil with a bunch of young adults standing near the band but hadn't any idea how to approach her. She finally spotted him across the room and pointed to the open door, while moving towards it. Outside they met under the stars, ignoring others around them. She spoke first, "I heard you came around the bank looking for me, sorry I missed you."

"Yeah, I was hoping that you might be coming here and wanted to invite you," Ben answered.

"Do you dance?" Phil asked straight out, looking right through him.

"Some, well not for a while, not too well," he stammered.

"Well, let's go see," she said turning toward the barn, "no sense just talking about it."

"Wait!" he said too loudly, then lowered his voice. "I have something I want to give you."

Ben was sweating now, he could feel it running down his lean back, under his shirt. When she stopped and smiled at him, he found it hard to breathe. He fumbled the small box from his pocket, almost dropping it, before finally handing it to her.

"Panned the gold myself, had it made for you," he mumbled.

As Phil held it up before her she exclaimed, "Oh Ben, it's beautiful, I love it." Then before he knew what was happening she kissed him square on the lips. Not missing a beat, she turned her back to him handing him the necklace, "here, fasten it for me."

Ben's hands were shaking as he fumbled with the clasp, finally closing it around her long white neck. She took his hand and literally skipped onto the dance floor holding out the necklace for all to see.

Dancing, clapping, whirling and stomping to the music, couple after couple took the floor, being replaced only when they tired. Kate found her way out more than once, looking beautiful in her green dress. A widower from the mill in a white shirt and overalls seemed to make a point of asking her often. In one corner of the barn the younger ones were bobbing for apples and playing mumbly peg. Finally the band took a break, finding both hard and soft cider abundant and fellas with jugs around back.

Some of the women from the church had brought cakes and pies to auction off for the Widows and Orphans fund, they were on tables well supervised and protected from hungry hands. When the pastor started it off with a bid of $2 for a peach pie, others quickly offered up a bid. As each was sold, it was quickly cut and consumed by the winners' friends or family, mostly with their hands.

By the time the band returned, the alcohol had worked it's way into the crowd, making the crazy even crazier and the sedate a little more spunky. The Sheriff keep a keen eye out now for trouble, knowing it to be inevitable, but wanting to keep it to a minimum while everyone had fun. Ben and Phil danced and danced, hardly noticing anyone else was in the room. It was plain to Cady they had an attraction for each other, he said as much to Kate who had also noticed.

She laughed, "I was younger than him when I fell in love with his father. He's twenty in three days."

As Cady looked at Shawna, radiant in her motherhood, he felt old. He'd be forty in two months.

Suddenly the band stopped playing causing Cady to look up. A tall husky man dressed like a logger had a hold on Phil and was looking down on Ben who he had pushed to the floor. Both Thomas and Cady started forward but stopped as Ben gained his feet and the Sheriff crossed the floor. It was broken up, with hard looks and harder feelings the only result. Cady found out later that the big logger had tired of watching Ben hog the pretty girl to himself and had a rather ungentlemanly way of cutting in.

Phil and Ben joined Cady and his group, Ben still angry, feeling humiliated. Phil bubbled with happiness showing off her necklace, having already forgotten the incident. Thomas walked over and offered his support, slapping Ben on the back, saying he got the best of the deal after all.

It was after midnight when the couples started drifting off for home, leaving the hardcores and drunks behind, still dancing. A dozen of them walked together, first dropping off Al and Linda, then Thomas and Phil, and finally Orville and Sarah at the bottom of the hill, before returning to the boarding house.

Morning came early, as it always does when one keeps unusual hours. Most of the guests were content to eat, speaking only when spoken to, as they struggled to wake up. Cady had planned to pick up the lumber today in preparation for leaving after church on the morrow, with further intentions on showing the women the cook stove that he hoped to take with them. He and Ben left the women curled up in the sitting room, visiting over a cup of coffee, and walked toward the livery to reclaim the mules and wagon. As they passed the saloon they heard a shout, bringing them to a halt.

"Hey kid, sorry I hurt your feelings in front of your little cat."

The logger and two older men laughed as they stepped from the saloon. Cady appraised the situation quickly, noting that all three where packing sidearms. He also noticed that unknown to them, the bartender had come out behind them and skittered down the street to the Sheriff's office.

Ben was about to speak when Cady took the lead, "you boys keepin' late hours, up all night?"

With a sour look the big man answered, "none of your business what we do, I's talkin' to the kid."

Behind them Cady could see the barkeep and Sheriff coming up.

"Ain't no kids here," he said, "only a young man ready to kick your butt if I'd let him."

"Big talk for a man not carryin' a gun," was the quick reply.

"No, way I see it, the big talk is from the man with two backups who is carryin'", Cady said coolly. "Maybe you'd like to unbuckle and step into the street, and give it a go man to man, or the three of ya if you need help."

The Sheriff was leaning back now against the building behind them, taking it all in but saying nothing.

"Well Red," said one of his the cronies, "looks like we gonna have us some fun this mornin'."

The three had set their belts aside and stepped down onto the hard clay street as Cady turned to Ben with a wink, "don't hurt him son."

The men were still circling one another trying for advantage when the Sheriff retrieved the guns and sat down to watch. Ben was a shade over six feet, lean and wiry but lacking body weight while Red was six two or three and outweighed him by forty pounds. Red was muscled and strong from hours in the woods but walked stiff legged and slow. He growled something and rushed at the boy while the other three stopped to watch.

Ben waited until the last second and stepped aside, sticking out his boot. Red fell like a yellow pine but was quick to regain his feet as the boy circled him without a word. As Ben stepped in closer, Red swung but missed by a mile as Ben stepped back quickly. Ben hit him with a good left in the side of the nose before moving away again.

Knowing that he'd just made the bear mad, but hadn't hurt anything but his pride, Ben became more careful as Red's buddies egged him on. They had stopped worrying about Cady and were intent on watching the game at hand. A crowd had gathered on the boardwalk, watching and offering their opinions.

When Red swung again he anticipated Ben's movements, missing his head but hitting his shoulder hard enough to knock him backward to the ground. Red rushed him, intent on throwing his weight on the boy, then hammering him into the dirt. Ben waited as he charged then put his boot into the bigger man's stomach, letting his own momentum carry him up into the air and over, finally crashing into the hitching post.

Ben was on his feet and ready as Red started to get up slowly, moving right into the punch. Ben ended his swing right where Red's adams apple turned into a chin. The sound of Red's teeth coming together from the blow evidenced it's power. He never regained his feet, instead he toppled backward, slamming his head into the now broken hitching rack.

"Looks like it's over to me," the Sheriff offered to the crowd, then to Red's friends, "you boys want to spend a few minutes learnin' from Mr. Miller?"

They declined his invitation and helped Red to the step.

"I'll keep these for you boys until you've paid for the hitchin' post and are ready to leave town," the Sheriff said, holding their guns.

Ben and Cady turned to leave among smiles and affirming nods from the crowd when the Sheriff said, "always nice to see you Mr. Miller, you too Ben."

They loaded the wagon at the lumberyard before going by the boarding house to pick up the women. Catherine had given Cady a couple of names to consider when looking at cook stoves, Majestic and Monarch, but he couldn't remember now which had her recommendation. He also took time to look over the installation of the chimney and piping. At the Merc they found only one brand in stock, the other would need to be ordered, arriving most likely after snowfall.

It being both awkward and heavy, three men worked hard to load it and secure it on top of the lumber already in the wagon. They purchased several lengths of metal stovepipe and bags of mortar to build a chimney outside of the cabin. Both women were excited at the prospect of cooking and eating inside of their new home.

Returning to the boarding house, Cady, Shawna and Kate used the afternoon to relax and visit with Orville and Sarah who had dropped by. Ben spent time on the porch swing with Phil, lost in laughter. Eventually the conversation got around to the subject of the fight with Orville complementing Cady on keeping a cool head. Kate, as mothers will, worried that the event would not put an end to the affair and voiced her concerns.

Before Cady could attempt to assure her, Orville, with Sarah nodding agreement, spoke. "'Trust and obey,' as the hymn says. We must all be wise and use our best judgment while relying upon God for His protection. Trusting not in ourselves but in Him."

The truth of the statement rang true with them but failed to take away Kate's fear. "It's so hard to totally trust, having lost my parents and husband and not knowing why," she said.

Orville and the others nodded in agreement, "maybe the hardest thing God asks of us is faith, and that faith comes only from Him and in His own time. Don't feel alone when doubt and worry creep in, just pray."

As evening neared, Catherine and Harless invited Orville and Sarah to join them for supper and set extra plates. Orville was asked to bless the food and they began to eat. Thomas and Phil, with Ben beside her, sat across from Cady and the women, the other guests spread out around the large table, enjoying the bounty set before them. The mules and horses were allowed into the small pasture beside the house where Harless kept his own team after being unhitched from the wagon. The Ricks excused themselves and returned home, Orville saying he needed to prepare for the morning's sermon. The guests, a few at a time, retired for the night, leaving only Ben and Phil to shut out the lamps behind them.

Following Catherine's now famous breakfast, the guests readied themselves for church. Cady and his family, in anticipation of leaving for home straight from the church, loaded all their gear in the wagon before paying for their board. They were just climbing the little hill when surprised by the peal of bells from the church, calling all to worship. The little church was filled to over-flowing as they arrived with others still coming up the road. When he mentioned it to Orville, while shaking his hand, Cady received a big smile.

"God doth provide. We may need to do two services soon if we aren't able to find a way to add on to the building," he said.

From their first visit to now, it had been less than six months, and yet it appeared to Cady the attendance had more than doubled. The room that Orville had used for his woodworking the first time they had met was now filled with guests on chairs and benches. Younger children were on their parents' laps. The small church seemed to be bursting at the seams. While he felt at home, he felt a little guilty to be dropping in, expecting to have a chair when some of the regulars were standing along the walls.

With the first two hymns finished, Orville addressed the assembly with updates and church business. He announced births, deaths, and coming events for the next week, thanking those who donated of their time or resources. Before beginning the day's sermon, he noted and apologized for the crowding and came right to the point.

"I met with the bank and our deacons this week concerning the possibility of enlarging our sanctuary," he offered. "We were told they would loan up to half of the cost of materials but none of the labor." He continued, "what I'm going to ask from you today is your prayers for God's direction and guidance in the matter, then wisdom to hear and follow it. In the meantime, and temporarily, you will hear our new bell's call to worship next week at 9:00 and then again at 11:00. We do not intend to begin a building fund until God has made it clear to us that it is His will to do so."

He fielded no questions and went right into the sermon on faith. Beginning with Hebrews 11:1 he walked his willing sheep through the meaning and source of our faith. To Kate it must have felt like he was talking directly to her after last night's discussion. But to each the Spirit of God gave it special meaning as it applied to their lives and circumstance. Orville closed by tying the introduction concerning the building to his faith that God would provide.

Following the closing hymns they filed out into the sunshine, taking time to visit with friends, both new and old. Cady and Shawna renewed their invitation to Al and Linda, Orville and Sarah, and Harless and Catherine to come and visit them, giving Orville a hand drawn map with directions to their claim. Cady said he expected that the place would be ready for guests by first snowfall, adding that by mid-October the trip often was slow and difficult.

– SIX –

Shawna and Kate registered alarm when, as they left town, Cady handed Ben his sidearm and buckled on his own. The Henry in the boot nearby, Cady attempted to downplay the necessity for weapons.

"Never know when a guy might get a shot at a fat deer, elk, or have the need to scare off a mama bear with cubs," he quipped.

Neither woman was fooled, but said nothing. Just before they turned off the main road heading north onto their own little lane, Cady pulled the mules to a stop. In the road in front of them stood Red and his two friends, their horses nearby. Cady noted that the Sheriff had given them back their sidearms, and their posture indicated hostility.

Cady quietly asked Shawna to go to the back of the wagon then spoke, "Mornin' Red, fellas. You're up kinda early this mornin' aren't ya?" as he stepped down into the road. Behind him Kate and Ben had dismounted with Ben moving forward to Cady's side. "What's on your mind?"

"What is on my mind is to shoot you dead and have my way with the women," Red bragged for the sake of his men.

Cady kept his voice low, "is this about yesterday, Red? I thought that business was done."

"Not by half," Red sneered, "not by half."

"I'm sorry to hear that Red, I was hoping you'd let things go," Cady continued. "There's a couple of things I'd like to tell you before I kill you, Red, that alright?"

"Big talk from a man and a boy, out numbered and alone," came the response, followed by laughter.

Cady ignored the attempt to worry him and continued, "We went to church this morning, Red. You ever go to church? The preacher was speakin' to us about faith, about how we need to have faith that God will provide for us. God helps us not to worry by giving us His strength to do what we need to, that make any sense to you?"

Red growled, "enough of your talk, let's get on with it."

Cady continued to ignore him, "one more thing, Red. Then if you want I'll shoot you, okay? Thing is, if you should beat me, I go to Heaven to be with the Lord, but if I beat you, where do you suppose you'll go for all eternity? Have you thought about how long forever in Hell might be?"

Red cursed again, "you don't worry about me, miner, you worry about your little family here after I shoot you."

"I'll tell you what Red, last chance before I shoot out your eyes. I gotta idea, how about you and I empty our guns, while your two and Ben here keep theirs loaded. Then we draw down on each other to see who is the fastest? That sound okay? We can always reload and go again."

"Damn you miner," Red said, uncertainty clear in his voice now. "All you want to do is talk. Okay, have it your way, we unload and slap leather."

"Good choice Red,' Cady said evenly, unloading his pistol. "You go for it when you're ready."

As Red reached for his gun, Cady pulled his own and said "bang, you're dead," before Red cleared his holster.

Red just stared, saying nothing.

Cady spoke, "We can go for real if you still feel the need but I'd rather buy you a drink next time we are in town or have you sit with me in church."

The men stared at each other for a moment, then Red spoke, "never seen nothin' like it. You coulda got all three if you'd wanted. I'll take the drink and think on the other. Sorry to bother you."

"Good day to you Red, fellas" Cady said.

Nothing was said for a long while as they turned up the lane headed to the mine.

"Good sermon today," Kate offered. "Learned a lot."

"I think we all did," answered her brother, "faith is what helps us do what needs doin' and shows us the right way to do it."

Dog heard them coming far before they saw him. He welcomed them like they'd been gone a month, cuffing and smiling as he greeted each personally. Ben put the ponies and the mules out to pasture after leaving the wagon up close to the front door. As he began to untie the ropes to begin unloading, Cady laid his big hand on his shoulder stopping him.

"It's the Lord's day son, let's enjoy it."

That night they ate and read the Word, talked about the trip in detail, but nothing about the ride home or Red. They teased Ben until he blushed red, then some more. Cady, Ben and the women carefully discussed placement of the stove and the chimney, trying to foresee any problem or difficulty in advance. It was agreed it would occupy a place at the end and centered in the room, the chimney going up outside past the peak of the roof. They ate and went to bed early.

While Shawna and Kate started breakfast, Cady and Ben moved the boom into place and sat the stove down on the ground. Right after the last bite of biscuits and gravy was washed down with black coffee, the last piece of bacon swallowed, the men began cutting and installing the plank flooring. The planking varied in width from six to eighteen inches with lengths from twelve to twenty feet, so careful planning was necessary to utilize them most efficiently. They began at the door, working their way inward, fitting but not cutting or nailing them until they were satisfied. The lumber was mostly still green and could be expected to shrink as it dried, making it necessary to place them as tightly as possible together while over nailing it to prevent cupping later. By noon the flooring was approaching the midpoint of the room when they stopped and enjoyed an impromptu lunch, using Ben's table and chairs for the first time. As darkness overtook them, they stopped just a few boards short of completion, unable to see well enough by lamp light.

Morning came with the men tired and hungry while the women were eager to occupy and use the new space. Both women were bouncing off the walls with excitement as they began to see all of the hard work coming together. When they pressed to get the stove inside, Cady warned that it required proper venting before it could be used. It took all four of them to coax the stove in through the doorway and situate it along the inside wall opposite the stairway.

Ben and Cady brought the remaining rough cut inside to dry, stacking it to allow air movement between the planks. On the third day, which was both hot and humid, Cady was ready to return to the coolness of the mine, but the women would have none of it. They were eager to begin baking and cooking on the new stove without having the understanding of the amount of labor ahead in constructing a chimney.

Cady and Ben acquiesced, scrounging rocks, using the wagon to haul them in. Most of the ore from the mine was not suitable to use, forcing them to travel to find sufficient quantities to begin construction. Digging down several feet, they filled the hole with fine tailings from the mine, packing them as then went to form a crude footing. Next they began mixing mortar in the wash tub, then brought the chimney up to a height of four feet as a solid column. Cady cut the access hole in the log wall through which the stove pipe would pass, leaving room to surround it with stones and mortar, while the base was allowed to cure.

It was several days and several more trips to bring in more stone before they began actually enclosing the stove pipe, which came through the wall, then made a ninety upward. At about nine feet the women could see no reason not to build a fire and, over Cady's objections, did, smoking up the house.

Things moved ahead well until they could no longer reach the chimney from the wagon, being forced then to work from ladders. Each rock then had to be taken up individually and mortared in place. Cady remembered in St. Louis where scaffolding would have been available and sought to devise a man-lift using the boom, but found it unstable.

Instead, they used the boom to lift multiple stones at once, allowing them to choose size and shape before mortaring them into place. Both Cady and Ben found this tedious and painfully slow as they moved higher and higher toward the peak of the roof. They were well into September before they finished and cooked their first meal on the new stove.

Much to Kate and Shawna's delight, the stove worked very well once they had become accustomed to it. The men returned to the mine, working hard there during the day, then spending evenings accumulating firewood and grass hay from the meadow for later use. By now they had stripped the original cabin of it's meager amenities, leaving only the fireplace intact. They were still undecided rather whether to continue to use it for storage of supplies or to convert it into a barn. The small lean-to against it was filled to the roof with firewood and kindling, with more whole logs dragged in as their time permitted.

The first frost made everyone aware of the urgency of preparation, reinforcing their anticipation of the winter snows. The bed frames had been completed before they had gone into town, and the mattresses had been finished for all three when the men labored with the chimney. The original cots from the old cabin became extras, now available for guests. They however, had no mattresses, just skins and hides supported by ropes across them. On Cady's long list of things to do were to replace them with beds like the three they now enjoyed. At this point all he could manage was to cut and store the materials in the old cabin for use later.

As October approached, the higher mountains around them became dusted with snow that initially melted in the sunshine, but now had begun to stay and accumulate. Cady began to feel the pressure of responsibility that he hadn't felt since he assumed the role of raising Kate. He now learned more and more to depend on Ben as he felt crushed by the weight of it. Ben accepted both the responsibility and the training well, while gaining confidence in himself.

One day, while taking a break from the toil in the mine, Ben asked, "Uncle Cady, can I ask you something?"

"Sure son, anything," was the man's reply.

Ben continued, "When Red and the other two stopped us on the road, how did you know you could outdraw him?"

"Didn't," came the one word answer. " I hoped it wouldn't come to that. Truth is, I had been thinkin' on pastor Orville's sermon about faith just before we saw them. It just seemed natural at the time to trust in God." Cady went on, "I might have been bluffin' him a little too I suppose, but what I told him I believe to be true about the dyin' part. I'm startin' to see how takin' a life, if there is another way, is wrong."

Ben nodded, thinking. He then asked, "have you ever killed a man?"

"Shamed to say I have. Lookin' back I wonder now how many were necessary and how things might have been handled another way," Cady answered him. "When I was your age I pretty much was able to do what I wanted. Until I met Tom, I didn't have anyone to teach me much about the important things in life, I kind of steered my own course. Tom was older'n me, had been around some when we hooked up. He talked me into coming out here and showed me how to mine," Cady reminisced. "He talked to me like I'm talkin' to you now."

Ben nodded and the two went back to digging.

Cady spoke up as they ate supper together, "I think maybe I need to make a last trip to town with the wagon before the weather closes us in. Don't know how you feel about that."

Kate spoke up first, "we need a few things, but don't see reason for me to go unless Shawna's going and wants my company."

Shawna shook her head, "I've got plenty to do here and the wagon ride doesn't sound appealing."

Then Ben said, "I'd go, unless you would rather I stayed and looked after the place."

Cady listened before speaking, "I kinda hoped you'd all feel that way. I figured to make it down and back the same day. That's a lot of ridin' without much time to enjoy the trip. Ben, I hoped you might take the Henry and see if you could start laying us in some meat while I'm gone. It's cold enough at night now to keep through the winter."

"Sure 'nuff Uncle Cady, when you plannin' on leavin'?" Ben answered.

"First thing in the morning if the ladies here can get me a list to-gether of what we need," Cady said, smiling at Kate and Shawna.

Cady was hitched and left right after eating breakfast. It was cold out, a stiff breeze was blowing with sunrise still a promise as he headed out toward the basin. He expected this might be the last trip to town with the wagon before spring. Fall rains brought mud, making it slow and difficult, and later snow made the trip impossible. In less than three hours he'd dropped the ore off at the mill and was headed to the Mercantile with quite a list to fill when he spied Red leaning on a post in front of the saloon.

Cady pulled the team to a stop, "mornin' Red," he offered, "is it too early to buy you that drink?"

"No need," Red answered cordially, "but I'd jaw with ya if you have the time."

"I've the time, how about coffee here at the café then?"

Red nodded.

As they walked the few feet down the boardwalk, Cady said, "gimme a minute to drop a list of supplies off at the Merc?"

"Sure," Red replied.

The men sat inside, warming their hands on the coffee mugs for a few minutes before Red spoke.

"I wanna apologize to you and the kid," he said matter of factly, "I had no cause to start trouble." Cady nodded and Red continued, "when I let the drink get ahold of me I get mean, know that. Most times I'm not in town and don't cause no trouble. Out in the woods, guys can fight and it don't mean much. I give up drinkin'. Ain't had a drink since I saw you last."

Again Cady said nothing, just nodding in agreement.

"Been thinkin' 'bout what you said, 'bout the other too, 'bout dyin'. You'se the first who told it to me so's it made any sense. I'd like to hear more 'bout it."

Cady finally spoke, "I'm not sure I'm the one to explain it to you, Red. I'm still learnin' it myself, but I'll tell you the way it is with me."

Cady spent the next few minutes giving his testimony, talking about the way he felt before and the way he felt now. He told about how he had done what was wrong, but now had been forgiven and wanted God to help him to do better.

Red listened quietly, nodding as Cady had earlier, then asked, "So how does it work, what do I have to do to be forgiven?"

Cady smiled, "The way it was explained to me, you just say you are sorry and ask. The same way you did to me, only this time to God. The preacher told us, God's just waitin' and hopin' that we'll do that because He loves us. All of us, the good ones and the bad ones. Would you like me to walk up to the church with you while you talk with the parson?"

"Do you think I need to?" said Red, "I mean, do I need him to tell God that I'm sorry and ask him to forgive me?"

Cady answered right away, "no, you don't, you can do it here right now or do it in private if you'd rather. But Orville could maybe answer other questions better 'n me if you have 'em."

The café was empty except for the two men, cook was somewhere in the back.

Red said, "Let's do it right now, 'fore I lose my nerve. Will you show me how you dun it?"

They bowed their heads with Cady doing the best he could to remember how Orville had lead them to Jesus, stopping now and then to let Red pray. Finally, after he heard Red say 'forgive me' Cady said amen.

Red offered quietly, "this is just between us?" seemingly a little embarrassed.

"No," answered Cady, "this is between you and God, but I'll let you share it with who you want."

They shook hands and left the café, Cady returning to the Merc to pick up the supplies.

Time had gotten away from him so Cady did not take time to see his friends. He stopped at the assay office, then took the voucher to the bank. At the bank Phil deposited the voucher for him, then took a minute to write a note, asking Cady to deliver it to Ben for her. Cady noted the time, concerned that the women would be worried when he arrived home after dark, but could do little about it except to pick up the pace a little on the way back.

As he rode, he contemplated what had transpired in the last few hours, feeling grateful to have been a part of it. Through God's grace, an enemy had become a friend and that friend now had assurance of eternal life in Jesus. He swallowed, trying to rid himself of the lump in his throat, feeling tears in his eyes.

A half mile from the cabin Cady heard Dog bark a welcome, as darkness threatened to obscure the wagon tracks in front of him. A lantern shining from the cabin window revealed three faces looking out into the darkness, anticipating his return, as he pulled the wagon to a halt. Before unloading the wagon he went to the cabin to reassure them with a big smile and hugs all around.

Later, the supplies safely stowed away, Cady relaxed over coffee and berry pie, fielding their questions. Reluctant at first to break a confidence he did not speak of Red, but as they pressed to know why he was delayed, he told them the whole story, cautioning them to keep it private. Amazed and overwhelmed described their appraisal of the story. Especially Ben, who had been struggling with the faith versus common sense issue, could clearly see now God's hand at work in the world.

They celebrated Cady's 40th birthday while watching the first snow fall in the valley. Large soft flakes fell, continuing well into the night. Morning light evidenced six inches in the meadow near the house and progressively more as one looked up the elevations above them. Cady was grateful for the progress they had made through the summer and into the fall, as he reminisced about how far he had come since the previous spring. With Shawna's help he oiled and repaired his traps, showing Ben and Kate how they worked, in preparation for the season at hand.

The trap line would often provide not only income but also food and pelts for clothing, with almost no financial investment. Under Cady's tutelage Ben learned quickly, while they laid out the string along the stream. The layout depended upon the quarry, predators needed bait while others required expert placement along a trail or near a watering hole.

Ben was excited to show Cady the buck he had taken the previous day, hanging now in a tree near the cabin. Shawna had shown him how to dress, skin, and care for the animal. The horns had been taken off with a portion of the skull still attached. Once nailed to the wall it would provide a lasting memory and a nice hat and coat rack. Shawna would find use for the remainder of the skull, possibly for fasteners or buttons. The Indians wasted very little of nature's bounty, finding utility in many parts which the white man would often discard. Cady sometimes had to remind her that Dog was part of the family and needed fed also.

The first snow lasted only a few days before melting, but the chill in the air promised its return soon, with a vengeance. By mid-month the snow was there to stay, accumulating more each week and bringing to their attention to the first design error of the cabin.

They had positioned the door on the side rather than the end, causing the snow that slid off the roof to accumulate in front of it. After shoveling snow away several times only to wake up to more, Cady set about building a second door. With the door finished, they chose to cut another doorway in the end, positioning it under the protection of the stairway landing. This turned out to be a blessing disguised, cutting considerably the distance from the door to the stairway and up toward their bedrooms. They lacked a second set of hinges making it necessary for Cady to rob Peter to pay Paul, removing the set from the door on the old cabin and replacing them with leather.

Somewhere in modern generations mankind came to identify with their occupations, precipitating the question "what do you do for a living?" Cady was a miner by occupation but lived for a living, by necessity and for enjoyment and pleasure. The four of them just enjoyed living, watching the child grow within Shawna, battling nature's fury, caring for their animals and each other. The men still frequently struggled in the cold mine, but mostly tended their traps, split firewood, and enjoyed the new cabin.

Cady improved the interior, finished the new beds, and began to lay out the framework for the interior walls upstairs with his remaining lumber. Sometime in December they heard a commotion and found that a cougar had been stocking the ponies who were forced to forage in the meadow. While Dog held it at bay, Cady returned with the Henry and reduced it to a fine pelt to cover their bed.

As Christmas approached, each of the four became secretive as they worked on little gifts for each other. Cady spent hours in the old cabin working on a baby bed to give Shawna, Ben was carving some wooden spoons and hair decorations for Kate, while Shawna was doing some fine bead work on another shirt for Cady from the leather she had tanned. She was also making warm fur hats and gloves for each of them. Kate was quietly sewing, often until late at night by lamp light, in her little bed chamber.

The snow was now shoulder height, forcing the animals to be fed from their small larder of grass hay, while foraging also in the denser stands of trees where snow had not accumulated. Dog slept quietly in the corner of the kitchen, looking for opportunity to go outside with anyone and play in the snow. When the snow stopped falling it became unbearably cold, often falling below zero during the day, making work in the mine impractical. They were forced to melt ice and snow for water or use the mineral water from the hot springs. The water was unfit to drink due to high sulfur content but worked well for bathing and watering the animals who seemed not to notice.

The four developed a regular routine that included eating, sleeping, Bible reading, and caring for the animals and each other. Each privately praised God for allowing them to have finished the cabin. Cady, having spent several winters in the old one, knew they could not have all survived the ordeal there. When one of the ponies became sick, it had to be put down with no other options available. It's carcass became a blessing for Dog while helping stretch the meager hay for the remaining animals.

Not quite sure of the day of the month now, they celebrated Christmas day with a nice breakfast of sour dough pancakes and the last of their salt pork, before exchanging gifts and singing hymns together. They had misjudged both the severity of the winter and the amount of food it took to feed them and were quickly being forced to a repetitive diet of meat, beans, rice and potatoes. While elk and deer were the mainstay, an occasional rabbit or grouse from the traps were a welcome treat.

They continued to trap but the volume of pelts diminished as they were forced to travel farther and farther to set up new lines, losing more and more to hungry predators who beat them there.

While the kitchen area was warm from the stove, the bedroom area was cold enough to freeze ice at night, raising concerns about the coming baby. Cady drilled holes in the floor above the cook stove, forming a grate that allowed heat to rise through it. His intention was to buy an iron one in town when spring allowed. It worked well, although lowering the kitchen temperature several degrees, it raised the upstairs comfortably.

Finally January came, bringing with it warmer daytime temperatures but also more snow, forcing Ben and Cady to shovel the roof of the old cabin to prevent collapse. It finally became impossible to find the traps, forcing them to be left behind until spring thaw.

As February neared, they were down to a half bag of flour, twenty five pounds each of rice and red beans and half an elk, no vegetables. Shawna's time was near, making it difficult for her to climb the stairs. Cady brought one of the extra beds down to the lower floor, allowing her to rest during the day.

Cady became concerned about the shortage of provisions and began considering a trip to town. Knowing that it most likely would be on snowshoes, the amount of food he could carry back made it almost counter-productive. He decided to wait and see what weather February brought. If necessary, a rider on a mule could follow the stream bed where willows and brush minimized the snow, first to the valley, then on into town. With the fear of running out of firewood a possibility, Ben and Cady found a 'buckskin' standing not far from the mine. They cut it and used the mules to drag it to the tunnel, where they were able to saw and chop it into firewood.

The weather continued to warm as temperatures during the day caused snow on the south and west to settle and melt, refreezing at night. Drifts in the shade and on the north and east remained frozen and would until May or June, depending upon their elevation. Kate kept an eye on Shawna, for signs of labor or distress with the baby during the day, while Cady watched over her at night. Ben had taken over responsibility for the animals, spending a great deal of time outside with Dog, making sure they had food and water.

Early one evening, about the tenth of February by their estimate, Shawna's water broke before she had gone up to bed. Kate had prepared clean cloths in advance and had a pot of water heating on the cook stove within a few minutes.

She took control, instructing Cady and Ben what to do and where to stand out of the way when they finished doing it. Though it seemed like forever to Cady, it was just over six hours before he heard the cry of his baby daughter. Shawna had done well and smiled at them as the child was placed into her waiting arms.

With Shawna nursing on the bed nearby, the three sat at the table recounting the miracle of birth to one another, reliving the highlights and worries that had came with it.

"Faith," Shawna said, referring to the baby.

Cady and the others instantly knew what she meant, Cady concurred, "Faith Katherine Miller."

It was decided to bring the cradle downstairs where Faith and Shawna could sleep close to the fire, food, and one another for the next several days. After they had taken inventory of their remaining supplies, Cady decided to try a ride partway down the little valley to appraise the viability of a trip to town. Having to skirt several beaver ponds and fighting the brush as well as the snow, he was able to make it almost to the basin and back after six tiring hours. It was clear that it would be a two day trip at minimum and also that waiting longer may cause the stream to flood, making it impossible to follow along it.

In preparation for the grueling trip Cady feed both mules well, dressed warmly, and left at sunrise the following morning with a long list of needed supplies. He took with him extra food, rope, and canvas for protection should he need to spend the night out.

The sun was high in the sky by the time he reached the basin and found the main road untraveled. Cady changed mounts, leading the one he had ridden, still the last five miles took three hours and used up the remaining energy of both mule and rider. Before leaving his mount at the livery, Cady took time to go to the Merc with his list, asking that they fill it so that he might leave early the next morning.

With that done, he gave orders at the livery stable to feed and water the mules and grain them both. Grain cost a premium but would give them the energy to fight their way home with their burdens. Exhausted but with light spirits, Cady stopped first at Al and Linda's to share the good news. Al offered a much appreciated ride in his buggy as Cady made the rounds first to Orville and Sarah, then finally to Catherine and Harless, where he enjoyed a hot meal and went right to bed.

Catherine had let him sleep in a bit before she sent Harless to wake him for breakfast. Over a filling breakfast, Cady told and retold of the birth and of the events of the winter at the claim. Catherine rolled several sour dough pancakes around the left over bacon and pork sausages before handing them to him for the ride home.

Cady found the Merc still filling his order as he walked toward the livery. As he approached Dr. Smitty's office, he stopped and went in to announce the good news. Doc asked several questions before congratulating Kate on her midwifing abilities. He then, writing instructions with each, gave Cady several bottles of medicine in the event of future complications.

At the bank Cady withdrew funds and told Phil of the new addition to the family, before paying the liveryman and returning with the mules to the Merc. It was almost nine o'clock on the 12th of February when the loaded mules, with Cady astride, left Idaho City for home. The weather was clear and cold, with high clouds that showed no threat of snow. Both mules were heavily laden but had seemed to have enjoyed the good feed and rest as they retraced their own tracks up the valley.

The first leg of the trip was nearly flat and the going was much easier, having no snow to break as on the trip down. At the trail to his claim, Cady dismounted, letting the mules water in the stream while eating a handfull of hay that he had brought with him. With a silent prayer he asked God's blessing on the food Catherine had prepared for him, then asked for God's protection on his return home.

The trail back up the little stream was steep and rocky, with both mules struggling under their loads. Cady had to stop several times to lead them around pitfalls and snowdrifts. By late afternoon Cady and the mules were spent, but still several miles from home, when he stopped to rest. Trying to evaluate the best course to pursue, whether to continue or hold up for the night, Cady prayed, asking the Lord to give him direction.

Both mules stood heads down, shivering and wet under their burdens, with Cady feeling much the same. He made his decision to lead them a little farther while looking for a stand of trees which would provide protection from the night's cold. There he would make camp and build a fire. Using the last of his energy, he unloaded the mules and covered them with the canvas tarps he had brought.

As they foraged among the trees for scant pickings, Cady built a fire from pine needles and small dead branches nearby. The provisions on the ground, he leaned back against them, enjoying the look of the fire more than it's meager warmth, as he finished off the remnants of Catherine's breakfast. He was chilled, not because of the temperature or lack of warm clothing, but because of the water from the stream and his own sweat under his clothes. He had coffee in the pack but no means to boil it, not having taken a pot with him.

Tying the mules to a tree, then tying on the canvas to prevent it falling off them, Cady returned to the fire and placed several larger limbs across the glowing embers. He lay down against the packs, covered himself with a fur and leaned the Henry next to him before drifting off to sleep under a scrap of canvas.

He was awake at once and reached instinctively for the rifle, having heard the sound of movement in the brush nearby. The fire had all but died down, with only red embers fading at his feet, the faint light of the moon behind thin clouds gave an eerie dimension to the scenery. The noise repeated itself, hoofs in the snow coming down the stream.

Cady peered into the darkness without success, then he chambered a round in the Henry while holding his breath. All at once a moose was on top of him, almost before he could fire. It dropped a few yards away, a yearling cow, foraging in the dark for food. One of the mules broke free of its tether, running up the trail while the other strained at its rope, frightened by the report of the rifle. Cady, too tired to gut the huge animal, cut its throat, then moved his bed over against the warm carcass which promised to stay warm the rest of the night.

At first light Cady was awakened by Ben's voice calling out to him from up the trail. Apparently, having heard the gunshot and then finding the mule without a rider, he had set out early, fearing the worst. Riding on the big mare, Ben was a welcome sight. He brought with him warm clothes and makin's for a fire, and food for breakfast.

Cady changed into dry clothes while Ben restarted the fire and put on coffee and elk steaks. They caught up as they ate, then turned their attention to the moose, gutting and quartering it. Lacking the second mule, it was decided that they should first take the supplies to the cabin before returning for the meat. It turned out to be only an hour walk leading the animals behind them, less than four miles they reckoned.

It took as long to tell the women of the trip and unload the animals before heading back, hurrying to beat any predators to the moose. The mule was left to rest and eat with it's mate, they took both ponies, loading two quarters on each as they lead them back to the cabin.

The mood was festive, the five of them enjoying the evening together with vegetables and fresh moose roast for supper, grateful for Cady's safe return. Faith was doing well as was Shawna, much to Cady's relief, showing their strong native heritage. Cady, who had heard stories of Indian women giving birth and then continuing their normal routines without rest, was beginning to believe them.

The days blended into each other until, by their count, it was March. March brought with it infrequent light snows, occasional rain, and increasingly more sunshine. With little to do, they scrounged more firewood, retrieved some of their traps from the snow, and searched for places where the animals might forage. By mid-month, it only froze at night, while melting during the day, increasing the stream flow. Cady and Ben were able to return to the mine, at first feeling the lack of exercise from their long layoff, but then relishing the sense of accom-plishment the labor brought with it.

By April there were many bare spots in the snow, with only the shaded areas remaining covered. The wagon was loaded with ore ready for the mill from a new vein that the men had found. The vein seemed to be growing in size, giving them renewed energy to pursue it. Shawna and Faith took their first bath in the hot springs, previously having had only the wash tub inside. Ben was back at stream-side now in the evenings with his pan, finding more and more powder that had been unearthed by the swollen waters. Even Cady enjoyed time in the sunshine working alongside his nephew. Song birds and deer began to return as did the spruce grouse, providing them with an occasional change of diet. One evening, after supper and Bible reading, Kate brought up the subject of town.

She said what had been on everyone's mind, "when will the trail be passable enough for a trip?"

Cabin fever the flatlanders called it, and they all had it bad. Ben offered to take a ride on the mare and access the feasibility of a trip, to which, with some reservation, Cady agreed. He was to ride down the valley to the main road, making sure the horses and mules could make it. There was no thought of trying the wagon this early in the year.

Shawna had sewn a fur-covered pack board for her little 'papoose' to ride in, sheltering her from the elements, while leaving Shawna's hands free to ride the pony. Ben returned, announcing his success, while describing the two or three areas which may present difficulties due to high stream flow.

Thinking it to be a Thursday, they left after an early breakfast, taking with them extra gear in the event of encountering problems. Their intent was to stay in town until Sunday, enjoying a visit and church service before returning home. More than once they had to ford the stream to avoid downed trees or brush that had washed down, blocking their way. They did so with difficulty but without incident, finally making it to the main road in the basin well before noon. Cady had made many mental notes of areas that would require considerable labor before the wagon could follow. He expected that he and Ben might spend as much as a week with shovels, picks, saws and axes to reconstruct the trail.

The main road showed evidence of traffic in its rutted surface. Avoiding the deep mud, the horses walked along the side of the road in the snow. They rode straight to the boarding house, depositing their gear before returning to the Merc, then stopping to see Dr. Smitty. The good doctor pronounced her in robust health with a like verdict for her mother, much to everyone's joy. Everywhere they went, friends had to spend time ogling Faith and commenting on her.

Ben disappeared for a time before returning from the bank, all smiles. While none commented, all noted his new sunny disposition. It turned out to be Friday the 24th rather than Thursday but that had no effect on their plans – except to shorten the visit by a day or have them leave Monday rather than Sunday. They rode to Al's next, spending a great deal of time visiting and catching up before leaving their animals at the livery and returning to the boarding house to go through the entire ritual again with Catherine, Harless and their guests.

By supper time word had spread, causing other friends, including Orville and Sarah, to join them. The Miller group enjoyed the company of friends and the change of atmosphere, having nearly forgotten how much they had missed them.

Gathered in the sitting room following a sumptuous meal and dessert, Orville spoke to Cady directly.

"I spoke to Red," he began. "Told me quite a story."

Cady had little to say so he just nodded.

"He spoke quite highly of you."

Cady hesitated, then answered. "He's really a nice guy now that he's given up the bottle."

It was Orville's turn to nod before continuing. "He's been a regular in church every Sunday since the snow shut the logging down. I hold a Bible study Wednesday evenings at the church, he never misses one."

"I am grateful to God for the change in him," Cady replied, "and for the changes in me."

"Amen to that, aren't we all?" agreed Orville, nodding.

Hesitantly Cady asked, "do you think I told him right? Do you think he has salvation?" "

Orville smiled, "as certain as anyone could be, you did just what the Lord asked of you."

To those who had not heard the story, Orville gave his version, looking to Cady for correction if needed. None was, it was close enough, and just the way Red had told it to Orville.

Thomas and Phil had joined the group, hearing the story for the first time, amazed at all that had transpired after the incident at the dance. Of course none but the Miller group had been aware of the confrontation on the road.

"God's hand was certainly in that," was their comment after hearing of the showdown.

Pastor Orville quoted, "the way that seems right to a man leads to death," adding, "but the road to God leads to eternal life."

Thomas turned to Orville and asked, "can anyone come, I mean, is the Bible study only for those who have already accepted the Lord?"

"Anyone is welcome of course, many want to know more about Jesus before moving forward," Orville answered, "women are welcome too," he said looking right at Phil.

They all visited until Shawna excused herself to nurse the baby, everyone then taking notice of the time, and began to leave.

The next morning, Saturday, found the Miller family, Thomas and

Phil, and several others eager to enjoy the hot springs, following a hot breakfast. Catherine had taken Kate aside, mentioning that a man at the mill had asked about her after the dance. Ignoring the wink, Kate smiled and asked if she knew him or anything about him.

Catherine knew that he'd been widowed the second winter in town, influenza, she thought. He owned a small whitewashed house at the edge of town and kept to himself. She'd seen him in church upon occasion but never with a woman.

She turned to Harless, "do you know his name, the widower who lives at the edge of town? Works at the mill."

"Steven or Stephen, I think," Harless responded, "pronounces it with an accent, kind of European sounding. Nice quiet sort of a fellow."

Following a relaxing soak at the hot springs the women returned to the boarding house while the men went about the business of the day. Ben and Cady were walking toward the Merc when the Sheriff hailed Cady, "got a minute?"

"Sure Sheriff, what can I do for you?" Cady replied.

"It's private for now," he said looking at Ben, "no offense."

"None taken," said Ben. "I'll be at the Merc."

"'Tween you and me, I'm getting along in years, be fifty in the summer, and startin' to get arthritis in my hands," the Sheriff offered, "my wife'd like me to step down."

Cady just nodded, listening.

"I been lookin' you over since we first met," he said matter-of-factly, "and I like what I see. What are you now, forty?"

Cady nodded.

"Mining is a hard life, a man can't do it forever, and there's the family to consider now. I been thinkin' on a proposition. How about movin' into the job kind of gradual, taking time to learn the ropes? You work the claim when the weather is fit, stay in town and Sheriff when it ain't."

Cady was overwhelmed, his mind going places he'd never considered. It was not often he looked beyond the next season.

"Takes a level head more than a fast hand," the Sheriff offered, "you've got that. Little more than using common sense when others have lost it," he continued. "Red shared his story with me after you left town last time."

Cady answered, "I'll think on it, talk it over with my family, if that is alright. Where'd we stay? Couldn't stay all winter with Harless and Catherine."

"I've discussed that with the Mayor. Since me and the wife have a place already it hasn't been a problem, but for someone else the town is willing to provide the land and materials for a house. I suspect that the community would furnish hands to put it up. The job don't pay much, but you don't do much either. Most of the time you just keep an eye on things and keep people from causing trouble, but it ain't without it's challenges and dangers either. In five years, I've only had to use my gun once, threatened to more times than I can count, though. A little like your face-off with Red and his friends."

Cady nodded, "only as a last resort."

"Yup, that's about right," agreed the Sheriff, "you carry a gun with the idea that you never want to use it."

Cady asked, "is even carrying it necessary? I mean, doesn't it sometimes cause things to get cross-wise in the road?"

Again the Sheriff agreed, "I see where you are goin' and I agree, once in a while a fella wants to try your hand just because you are packin'. You can't avoid that. But it also gives others a reason to respect the badge, and you, when he's feeling a little big for his britches. Then too, sometimes there isn't time to strap one on. The one I shot was going to hold up the bank one way or the other, might have killed someone in the attempt. I couldn't talk him down and owed it to my wife to protect myself."

Cady said, "Let me talk with my family first, then maybe we could all sit down together. I'd like Shawna to have time to talk with your wife about it before we decide."

"Fair enough! I'd want everything out in the open too. You could try it and see how it works out for you first without a long term commitment."

They parted ways, with Cady meeting Ben at the Merc to see how things were going with the supplies. Of course Ben was curious but hesitated to ask straight out, instead he asked, "trouble?"

"Not at all," answered Cady, "we'll talk it over as a family. He wants me to consider the job of Sheriff during the winter months. But, keep it under your hat for now."

They were told that the supplies would be ready later that day and pledged to return later to pick them up. Cady was quiet and introspective on the walk back, speaking only when Ben initiated the conversation. At the boarding house they found that Kate had gone to town with Catherine in the surrey, leaving Shawna and the baby to rest.

When the women returned from town, the men learned they had enjoyed lunch with Kate's dance partner Stephen, at the café. They chided Kate about the glow she had and about the 'beau' who seemed interested in her. After a lot of joking around, they learned that his parents were first generation immigrants from France, accounting for the accent still evident in his speech. He and his wife were married for twenty years but had been childless when she died the previous year. They too had come west from St. Louis to make a life together. To Cady it seemed that Stephen was a man with integrity and substance.

Shawna and baby Faith had joined them in the sitting room while Catherine and Harless had excused themselves to prepare for the supper meal to come in a few hours.

Cady spoke, "I'd like you all to join me this afternoon for a visit to the Ricks' home." Everyone laughed, then wondered why the formality of the invitation, until he continued. "I've an important decision to consider which involves all of us and I'd like to include Orville and Sarah in it also."

Ben smiled knowingly but said nothing. Everyone nodded their agreement without asking the obvious question that was foremost on their minds.

"We can leave whenever you like," was Shawna's answer.

Cady asked and received permission of Harless to use the surrey. They arrived at the preacher's home and were warmly greeted as was usual, before Cady opened the conversation.

"I think you all know what happened at the dance last time we were in town, then afterward between Ben and Red. I think also Orville and Sarah are aware of the events which came later, ending with Red coming to salvation in Jesus." Having brought everyone up to date, Cady hesitated before continuing.

"Today, the Sheriff approached me with a proposal. He asked me to consider acting as Sheriff during the winter months when the snows made life at the claim difficult." Again he paused looking at his friends and family before continuing. "I told him I'd think about it and discuss it with my family... and you are my family."

Everyone seemed to be absorbing the news and reluctant to begin, finally Kate said, "Why you?"

Cady responded quickly, "before I go into the details let me add, I did tell him that if we agreed to go father with the idea, I'd want us to all sit down with he and his wife to ask just those sort of questions directly." He added, "he did say that he sees something in me that he believes makes me right for the job."

Orville spoke next, "I'm not surprised at all. What I see in you are those qualities that would make you a good Sheriff. Those who are willing to be led are often the best to lead others. You are learning to follow Jesus and accept where He leads. You have already shown with Red the heart for that. A less godly man might have already sent him to Hell rather than pointing him toward Heaven."

Shawna asked, "would you stay here and leave us up at the mine?"

Cady assured her, "no, of course not. We'd all be down here together, making life easier on us all, when the weather makes it unbearable."

Then Kate spoke again, "but, where would we stay?"

Again Cady answered, "we'll go over that with them in more detail, but he proposed that the town furnish a place for us. Said that he and the Mayor had discussed the land and materials for it but not the labor to put it up."

Then Ben spoke, asking the question which had been on the women's minds, "is it dangerous?"

"I don't see it any more dangerous than the life we lead now, alone in the mountains," Cady said honestly. "Different dangers, but not more dangerous than getting hurt in the mine, or lost in the snow, or running out of food. The same kind of 'bad people' wanting to do bad things, only in town, not out in the mountains. It might even be easier to deal with them with other good people around you."

"Don't forget, God is in charge," said Sarah, "here in town or at your claim, His will will always be done."

They all nodded in agreement, then Cady spoke. "We seem to over-look that a lot, thinkin' that we are in charge. I am beginnin' to think that God may have provided this as an opportunity to raise Faith in the best of both worlds."

Again nods of agreement.

Shawna agreed, "I may worry about you more because this is new to us, but I'll try not to, because it is not new to God and I know He loves us."

Ben seemed to be warming up to the idea too, "I could spend more time with Phil and we could all come to Bible study." It was noted, but not mentioned, the order of his young priorities.

Kate, always to the point asked, "could you shoot someone? Has the Sheriff had to kill anyone?"

All eyes were on Cady when he replied, "I hope I'd let God guide that. I have, and think I could again if necessary. The Sheriff said he had been forced to shoot a bank robber who gave him no other option, in the five years he's had the job."

Orville spoke, "I remember that. Two men, I think, were holding up the bank, threatening to shoot the banker for refusing to open the safe. As I recall, the Sheriff shot one after he had already been shot at, the other gave up. God gave us specific rules for taking a life. Very detailed. There is a difference between killing and murder in His eyes."

– SEVEN –

As the afternoon wore on, they took time to pray together, asking that God direct their decisions, before leaving for the Merc and boarding house. They agreed not to discuss it with others until they had spoken to the Sheriff and his wife and made a decision. Supper, as always, was a feast. Catherine had killed a couple of her chickens who refused to produce for her and was serving them with homemade dumplings. They enjoyed home canned peaches and cream for dessert. They all chose to go to bed early, but spent much of the night considering the events of the day before drifting off to sleep.

Sunday morning brought hot biscuits with sausage gravy, eggs, and coffee with an apple crisp as a treat, followed by the peal of the new church bells, calling them to worship. They quickly cleared the table but then left for the early service, leaving the cleanup for later.

The town folks had already developed a new Sunday routine to deal with the two services, while the Miller group had to adjust to the new time. They arrived just as Al and Linda were stepping down from their buggy. The church being about half full, the congregation seemed more relaxed and less anxious about seating than when they last came.

Cady noted some new faces and introduced himself and his family while renewing older friendships. Faith was the center of attention among the women and a point of pride to Cady. Sarah began the first hymn on the piano, signaling for the congregation to find their seats before they began singing. When Orville began his sermon, after the second song, Cady noted that the room was about three-quarters full. He wondered if the second service would be likewise.

Both Kate and Shawna gave knowing glances to Cady when Orville announced the subject of his sermon... murder. He took time to explain the difference between killing and murder, also explaining that in translation the two had become synonymous, but never should have been. As they went from verse to verse for enlightenment, it was easy to see the difference.

God prescribed stoning as punishment for certain offenses but never termed it as murder. As the sermon continued, Cady's mind went back to the time he had shot the three claim jumpers. He was glad to have been given forgiveness, when he was saved, because he felt now he should not have done it.

His mind was filled with questions, unanswerable except by God. It now seemed to him that a threat to property did not justify killing, where a threat to life may. Confusing. It made his pending decision about the Sheriff's job all the more complicated.

Orville finished up the sermon with emphasis on the sanctity of human life based upon the value God gave it, keeping it short and sweet like the peal of the church bell. The very fact that He was willing to give His Son to die for us gave strength to the argument that man had no right to end it.

Following the service, the air was clear but cold as the spring breeze penetrated their Sunday dress, minimizing their visitation time outside. His passengers loaded, Cady was about to turn the surrey toward home when the Sheriff stopped them.

Tipping his hat to the women, he said, "John Day, and this is my wife Helen," before continuing. "If your time permits, we'd like you to join us for peach cobbler and hot coffee." Then, turning to Cady, "I hope I have not put the cart before the horse. Did you all have a chance to visit concerning my proposition?"

Cady nodded, "we did, but have not made a decision yet."

The Sheriff continued, "I had not expected you to, nor was it my intent to push you. I would like to let the women have opportunity to ask questions and get all the facts before you leave town for home."

Cady smiled, knowing that he had been outmaneuvered.

Turning around toward the women Cady asked, "ladies, how does cobbler and hot coffee sound?"

Everyone nodded with enthusiasm, eager to get out of the brisk wind.

Cady answered, "thank you John, Helen. We are pleased to accept your offer. May we follow you?"

"Please do," came the reply.

Sturdy, that was the term for the small white house with the fence around its front yard, lying at the edge of town. Out behind was a barn, privy, chicken coop, and a corral with several head of horses in it. Cady looked over the operation with an appraising eye, nodding his approval.

John, Cady had trouble not calling him Sheriff or Sheriff John, stated simply, "built it from the ground up."

"The horses?" questioned Cady.

"Oh, mostly just a hobby now, I fancied myself a cowboy once. Don't get much chance to ride anymore. I sell one now and again to make room for a foal."

Inside, the house was neat and clean, everything in its place, but small and plain. It became evident that they lived comfortably but not in luxury. John brought up a couple of extra chairs, arranging them around a small, round kitchen table. Helen had just brought the coffee with cobbler and fresh cream to the table when Shawna excused herself to nurse Faith.

Kate broke the silence, turning to Helen, "how long have you been here?"

Helen answered, "Six, almost seven years now. We were here before the rush. John used to ride herd for one of the bigger ranches down south 'fore that. Leavin' me alone a lot."

They could tell from her voice that loneliness had been a problem between them at one time.

John continued for her, "moved here to be together, hoped to raise a family."

Again, they could feel the pain in his voice which held the disappointment of no children.

"Good move," said Cady, hoping to lighten the mood, "couples need to invest in their marriage."

It was Ben's turn to speak, "how'd you come to be Sheriff?"

All heads turned toward John as he spoke. "Funny how things work out. About the same way they are now." He went on to explain, "used to be there was just a U.S. Marshall that traveled the whole territory once a month, no local law enforcement at all. Folks just did the best they could with the bad ones doin' what they wanted. As the town grew, some of the peaceable folks tired of the rowdies and got together for protection. At first they hired a gunfighter. Turned out he was just as bad as the ones they paid him to protect them from."

"When he got shot in the back, they come lookin' for a better answer, someone who shared their values. Guess that was me. They say I got what they call 'policeman's eyes', like Cady here, kind of naturally see stuff other folks miss. Head off trouble most times, before it gets outta hand."

It was Cady's turn to nod. He'd never considered that he was different than other folks, expected that others had the vision to see what he saw. He could see now that thinking ahead and through a problem was better than trying to fix one later. Helen had left the table to spend time with Shawna. Cady could hear them talking softly in the other room.

"A deputy?" Ben asked. "Have you ever had a deputy?"

John answered candidly, "in the beginnin' the town was too small, couldn't pay enough to split it up. Now that the town can afford more, I never got around to askin'."

Cady thought before speaking, "I have an idea that might give us all a chance to see if this is the direction to go. I can see myself as your deputy, available when I am in town full time, but only part time when I'm at the mine. It's two hours riding time in good weather, if you need me. Down the road, who knows, maybe we're here more and there less. I might take over as Sheriff – you as my deputy.

Helen, Shawna and Faith rejoined them, forcing Cady to restate his case while Kate, Ben, and John listened. Cady could sense that Helen was ready for John to quit now, with no strings pulling him back as deputy. He could also sense that John wasn't ready to let go of the reins to a town he called his own. They would have to work that out themselves.

Kate, who had been quiet to this point, spoke again. "What do you think Shawna, Ben?" Cady felt sorry for her, he could tell that she was over-whelmed by it all and too new at decision-making to speak her own mind in front of strangers.

Ben, on the other hand nodded in agreement. "I like it."

"Me too," Kate added, "it's been a long first winter."

"When would you start?" Shawna asked, giving her assent.

John took the reins back. "Lots of little details to work out. I'd have to get the Mayor to agree to pay your room and board, make sure Catherine has space this first winter, and board your animals until you return to your claim in the spring."

Helen looked enthusiastic, like she was seeing a dream come true. Years disappeared from her face as she smiled and offered seconds of coffee and cobbler.

Cady took stock verbally of where they had left things at home. "The horses and mules are here with us, Dog can easily take care of himself for a few days, and the cabin's locked up tight. Not much chance of anyone trespassing with all the mud and snow this time of year. If you all agree, let's move one step forward, but without burning any bridges behind us."

They stood to leave, giving and receiving hugs, handshakes, and smiles before John said, "I'll set up a meeting with Mayor Fitch in the morning, let you know what time."

Cady nodded. As they found their way to the boarding house, all were surprised to find it had become late afternoon. Cady parked the surrey in the barn, feeding and watering the horses before joining his family inside. The women were busily talking to Catherine when Cady entered. He interrupted the conversation, asking that she keep the news between Harless and herself for the time being. Taking Ben aside, he asked him also not to share the news with Phil until after they had spoken with the Mayor and had a firm agreement.

Beef brisket, potatoes, cabbage, and onions brought the Irish out in the guests as Catherine added fresh rolls and hot tea for those who declined coffee. The Miller family reveled at the change of menu, giving compliments and smiles to the cook.

After the plates were cleared, several guests stayed on playing 31 until bedtime. Cady, Shawna and Faith retired early, leaving the others playing cards. With Faith asleep in her mother's arms, Shawna and Cady discussed the events of the day in more detail. She voiced her concerns and worries while he did his best to answer her questions honestly and guess what tomorrow might bring for them, with or without the Sheriff's job.

Cady was afraid to paint too rosy a picture to anyone, but could see God's hand guiding the circumstance. Long term he could see Kate withering and dying old and unfulfilled at the claim, while he had seen her blossom at the mention of Stephen. Ben, loyal to the end, needed to be around people of his own age and have a chance to start a life with someone like Phil. Little Faith needed to grow up in a culture where she would eventually have to live, and Shawna needed to have support from Christian friends to learn how to live in a world filled with both love and prejudice. There were valuable lessons to learn in their mountain home and as many more to learn in town.

The day dawned behind low gray rain clouds, while moderate weather throughout the night had left the ground soft and muddy. As Cady walked to the Sheriff's office after a fine breakfast of grits, eggs and country bacon, he reminisced over the events of the past twelve months, amazed at the changes God had brought.

John, Sheriff John, greeted him, then ushered him out and down the street to a small office which the Mayor shared with the only lawyer in town, himself. Mayor Fitch was unimpressive, squat, stoop shouldered, nearly bald, and wearing heavy glasses. However, Cady soon found, hidden under the surface, a man of intelligence, faith, humor, and dedication, hardly a usual portrait of a 'lawyer-politician'.

Cady immediately liked and trusted the man, finding him easy to talk to and understand. He allowed John and Cady to speak first, making notes but not interrupting them. He answered their questions, making more notes, then began asking Cady questions about himself, never offensive, but often blunt and to the point. The man did not beat around the bush. Cady guessed him to be a good attorney who would have made a great judge.

The Mayor, having asked and received permission, lit up a pipe, enjoying its aroma, while he further listened to the men.

"You fast?" Fitch asked out of the blue, referring to Cady.

He thought before replying, "I'm alive."

All three men laughed, enjoying the humor and appreciating the answer. Cady was a humble man but also confident, which came across in the statement.

Fitch turned now to the Sheriff, "you'd not have brought him here unless you believed in him, John. You got any doubts or other comments to make?"

"I think we said it all, Mr. Mayor," came the reply.

"Mr. Miller, when are you leaving, heading back to your claim?" Mayor Fitch asked Cady.

"Gotta get back to work," Cady said with a smile, "just depends on where I work."

The Mayor stated, "I'll call a meeting of the town council tonight, should have an answer for you in the morning. You fellas want to attend?"

John shook his head first at Cady, then at the Mayor. "No need to keep everyone up all night jawin' and goin' over the same ground, is there?"

Mayor Fitch smiled and nodded, "no need unless you want to see democracy in action."

Back at the boarding house, Shawna and the baby were napping, while Kate was reading in the sitting room. Ben had gone into town, likely to visit with Phil, leaving Cady to relax and contemplate the recent events. He made sure the horses and mules were ready for the trip home in the morning, whether it be one or all of them. Then, taking some time for himself, he rode the big mare up to pastor Orville's house.

There alone, he confided in Orville about the turn of events and prayed for God's will to guide them. Cady was surprised to find that Orville was already aware of the situation and sat on the town council. They were all volunteers, most of them business men, who had organized to give direction to the growing town. Many, if not most of the members, willingly taxed themselves to provide funds for the necessary services.

Upkeep for the school and jailhouse, salary for the Sheriff and school teacher, food and medical care for the prisoners, and a special charity fund for widows and orphans in need, were among their funded projects. Originally, the city had owned all the land within its borders and had sold off much of it to private ownership, providing the initial funds. The church became central in assessing need and administering charitable help to the community following a fire or untimely death of a breadwinner.

The more he learned, the more Cady liked the town and its people. He could see why John had remained Sheriff in spite of its danger and small financial rewards. Much like Orville, he had felt a 'calling' to serve. There was no town hall, therefore the church served as a gathering place for meetings of importance, both to the council and the town at large. After talking with Orville, Cady changed his mind about attending the meeting, vowing to return at 6 o'clock.

Upon his return, Faith was rested and bright eyed, Shawna, Kate and Catherine were fussing in the kitchen, and Ben had not returned yet. Cady was feeling more and more interested in the job as Sheriff, although not just as law enforcement, but more as a public servant. God seemed to be grooming him for a change of service.

With little to do, he helped Harless feed the animals, then set the supper table. Thomas, Phil and Ben entered together laughing, enjoying some private joke, just as the guests began to be seated around the table. Kate gave him a halfhearted frown, then smiled and reminded him to wash his hands, like a mother would.

White beans and ham in abundance, corn fritters and dessert filled the cold and hungry stomachs to near bursting. As the table was cleared, Cady took Shawna and Kate aside to bring them up to date on the quickly changing events regarding the Sheriff's job. Indicating that he would be attending the meeting, he gave no invitation for them to join him, rather, he discouraged them by saying it was a Council meeting.

When he arrived, about ten minutes early, Cady was surprised and relieved to see many familiar faces. Nearly everyone with whom he had business dealings was already there or arrived in short order.

Orville opened the meeting with a prayer asking for God to guide discussion and decisions to be made, then Mayor Fitch assumed control. The Mayor did not seem surprised to see Cady, nor did John when he arrived a few minutes later.

Apologizing for the short notice, he got right to the heart of the matter, going quickly over the ground that the three had discussed earlier in the day. Keeping control, without pausing to answer questions, he asked John to say a few words. John was straightforward as he had been with Cady, outlining his reasons and needs to step back, if not down, from the Sheriff's office. He also gave testimony of his appraisal of Cady's ability to fulfill not just the duties but the intent of the job.

Nearly all of those present knew Cady in some respect or had heard stories of his ability to maintain order with a minimum of violence. Cady was surprised and a little embarrassed when Orville gave testimony of his spiritual appraisal of him as a man. Heads nodded agreement, including Al and Dr. Smitty. Up to this point Cady had not spoken a word, nor had he been asked to.

Mayor Fitch got to the matter of finances, always a difficult subject, by declaring that they had abused the current Sheriff by not providing for him sooner. Acknowledging that their budget was small, he asked for council input for ideas how to provide long term funding for the growing town. Sarah, the only woman in the room, took copious notes as the men, one after another, gave their proposals.

After nearly an hour of discussion, the banker asked for the floor and proposed a 'transaction tax' that might be collected from buyers and sellers by each business. He indicated that it would bring revenue from many who did not live in the town but relied upon it for their goods and services. Of course, a tax in any form always brings heated debate, both for and against it. This forum was no exception, many speaking out against it, mainly as the reason why they had moved west.

Mayor Fitch tried to restore order more than once before the gavel quieted the debate, then he said. "So, in the absence of some form of community support, you are agreeing to continue to provide ongoing support for the town indefinitely?"

The businessmen, who knew they had been flanked by the shrewd lawyer, were more willing now to consider alternative ways to share the growing burden. All of a sudden, some form of tax became more acceptable to them. The Mayor let the discussion go for a time before calling for order.

"Now," he said, "to the business at hand. We can work out the details in a future meeting after we have had time to think about it. Today, I propose we make arrangements to provide for Mr. Miller and his family room and board for the remainder of the spring and until he returns to his claim. Do I hear a second?"

The second was made by Al and the vote was unanimous.

"Further, let me suggest that we double the current Sheriff's salary effective immediately."

Again, the measure passed.

Fitch continued, "and if there's no more pressing business before our regular meeting next Tuesday, I propose we adjourn and get home to our families."

That measure also passed with smiles and nods.

John strode over to Cady taking his hand. "Thank you," he said, "when do you want to begin work?"

Cady hesitated a moment then replied, "I need to make a trip home, get the dog, and secure things first. If I leave early, I should be back late tomorrow afternoon."

"We'll start Tuesday then, getting you acquainted with the job and the town," the Sheriff stated.

After several of the council joined them, introducing themselves and wishing Cady well, he returned to the boarding house where friends and family awaited his return. He answered their questions as briefly as he could, still having no details about the pay or the job itself. The family seemed relieved to be staying in town and set about making a list of things for him to bring back with him. When Cady saw the lists, which included Faith's bed, he included a mule in his plan for the trip.

Following a filling breakfast, Cady loaded the big mare with supplies in the event of problems, and rode out leading both mules behind him. Catherine had promised to make good use of any perishable food or left over meat he could bring back. That amounted to most of the moose and a little elk, more than one animal should carry over winter trails. Ben had offered to go along and help, but Cady felt he needed the room to haul, more than he needed the help to load it.

Cady made good time over the frozen main road and then up the trail to the cabin, getting there before noon. He inventoried the lists which the family had sent with him, loading them on to the first mule, then tying them securely. Next he positioned the second mule below the meat hanging in the trees and let the quarters down one at a time, until the sturdy animal began to show the strain. The final quarter and a portion of the elk rode with Cady on the mare with clothes and a few personal items. He buttoned the house up tight, attempting to foresee and prevent problems while they were in town before heading out.

By early afternoon, the sun had made its presence known, increasing the volume of runoff in the stream and turning the earth back to mud. Cady moved slowly, attempting to choose the easiest and least risky route for the mare, with the mules and Dog following behind. More than once one of the animals lost footing momentarily, causing him concern, only then to recover before falling or being injured.

Several times he was forced to dismount and retie the loads more securely to the pack saddles on the mules. Gradually they reached the flat of the basin, watching the sun as it diminished in the afternoon sky. It was 3 o'clock when he pulled up at the boarding house, where he was greeted by Harless and Ben, who immediately began to help unload. The women took the clothes and personal items to their respective rooms, as Catherine instructed where and how to place the windfall of fresh game.

It was nearly time for supper by the time the animals were rubbed down, fed, watered and stabled. Cady washed up and changed clothes, then relaxed while the women fussed in the kitchen. Brimming with excitement, Kate joined him and began telling of the possibility of a teaching job at the school. She had found out that the current teacher was in poor health and needed immediate help, which, depending upon her recovery, could turn into full time work. Unknown to Cady, Kate had taught in St. Louis while Ben was still in school.

Shawna whisked into the room, like a spring breeze, giving Cady a peck on the cheek, then placing Faith in his arms. Amused by the change in his family, he relished the infrequent times when he could hold his daughter.

When Catherine literally rang the supper bell, none lingered, all ready to see what she had created. Ribbons of elk strip steak, layered with homemade egg noodles, butter and sour cream, formed the entree as carrots, kale, and fresh bread finished it out. While the Millers had eaten their fill of wild game over the long winter, they found her recipe a treat, eating it with relish.

Following dinner, the Miller family and several guests rode with Harless and Catherine to the hot springs where they enjoyed a long hot soak, lingering well past sunset. The water had taken the energy out of them and most went right to their rooms upon their return, finding sleep easily.

Tuesday morning came early, with Cady refreshed and eager to begin the day at his new job. After a filling breakfast of pancakes and eggs, he excused himself from the table and walked briskly to the Sheriff's office where he found John waiting.

"Mornin' Sheriff," John said with a grin.

"Mornin' to you Sheriff" Cady answered smiling. Cady continued, "we gotta figure this Sheriff thing out. I figure you as Sheriff and me as the deputy or trainee. I think other folks will feel better 'bout it if there are not two Sheriffs in town."

John nodded agreement. "Makes sense, I'm full time Sheriff and in charge until you learn the ropes. You answer to me but are free to ask questions and offer suggestions as we get into it. That suit you?"

"I see it no other way, Sheriff," Cady said with a grin. "What's your plan for the day?"

John answered, "I brought us a couple of mounts, got 'em hitched outside. I thought we might start by riding the town, seeing the area you'll be responsible for, meeting a few people along the way. I don't see your gun belt."

Cady smiled, "do you expect I'll need one?"

John answered easily, "no, 'spect not, but it might be a bit embarrassing if I'm wrong and you do. People respect the man, but they also respect his ability to handle situations as they present themselves."

Cady nodded his understanding.

"I got a nice .45 here in the back. Save you a trip back home."

Again Cady nodded.

Although they did not speak of wages, Cady assumed at some point they would, that he'd be paid a salary. He was also quickly coming to the realization that he'd do the job for free if it came to it.

It took most of the day to ride the perimeter of the town, stopping and chatting as they visited with people they met along the way. John offered commentary and history about those he knew, both good and bad, asking Cady to make mental note. It just so happened that they were pulling up to John's house at right about the time Helen was taking something out of the oven.

"C'mon in," said John, motioning Cady down from the horse, "smells like she's burnin' somethin'."

Cady joined them in the house where Helen had the table already set and was busy slicing hot roast beef and fresh bread. John blessed the food, then they ate quietly for a few minutes before Helen asked, "your women folk all settled?"

"Yes, and they are enjoying the comforts of town," was Cady's reply.

Helen nodded, seeming pleased at his answer.

Then John asked, "how do you like your mount?" referring to the big roan gelding that Cady had been riding.

"I like him fine, John, though a saddle takes a little getting used to. He's got a lot of depth, you raise him?" asked Cady.

"I did, he's just over four now. His mother's the red dun you seen out back, his daddy is an appy from down around Silver City," he answered. "I used to ride for them 'fore moving here, most of the folks there like the appy's, they're tough with a lot of heart."

John continued, "I'd like to give him to ya, if you'd take him, saddle and riggin' too. It'd save me feedin' him."

Cady was surprised and embarrassed. "John, I appreciate that but I can't let you do that. Let me buy him from you."

"No, son," the older man said, "I expect you'd do the same for me if the shoe was on the other foot."

Helen nodded, adding, "Let us do this for you."

John had been right, it was just the kind of thing Cady would have done, but he'd always found giving was easier than receiving. Cady struggled to accept the gift with gratitude, as offered. Finally he just said, "thanks, it's the finest gift I ever was given."

John laughed, "you're forgettin' your salvation, your wife and baby.

It's not much considering what you already have."

Cady felt a lump in his throat and did not try and answer, he just nodded. The more he knew about John, the more he liked him.

Finally back in town, they walked the streets as the lamps were lit and shopkeepers closed for the day. John tried doors, making sure they were locked as they went, telling Cady what he knew about each proprietor in a factual way. Cady was impressed, it seemed John withheld judgment of those whom he served, content to keep it to himself. He told what he knew, not what he thought. Cady remembered reading something similar in the Bible, though he couldn't remember it word for word. They returned to the office where John began to lock up.

Cady asked, "what about at night? What if there is trouble at night?"

John smiled before answering, "usually is, that's when the devil does his best. They'll come and get me, always do if it gets outta hand. Man can't be everywhere all the time."

Cady nodded, noting that they had been at it twelve hours already.

"Summer's the worst, folks stay up later, days are longer. Gives 'em more time to get into mischief," the Sheriff mused.

They locked up and parted ways, Cady riding his new roan one way, John the other. In Harless' barn, even by lamp light, the gelding was beautiful, and of course everyone had to come admire him. Having missed supper, Cady ate leftovers which Catherine had saved for him, fielding questions from the group.

The days ran together, each bringing new opportunities and adventure. Ben began working part time at the mill where he was being mentored by Stephen, Kate was filling in for the school teacher, and making new friends, while teaching their children. Cady had fallen into a comfortable routine and was beginning to earn the respect of his position as he came to know the townspeople.

John began taking mornings off, spending time with Helen, but returning to the office later in the day to catch up and enjoy a visit with Cady. Shawna spent most days caring for Faith and learning a great deal from Catherine about cooking. A group of women met once a week at the boarding house to sew, quilt, knit and swap advice on a variety of subjects. Linda would often join them, as would Sarah and several of the other local women, exchanging ideas for bazaars and fundraisers.

By the time Faith celebrated her first birthday, wildflowers had replaced the snow in the valley, now lingering only at higher elevations. Chancing the unpredictable spring weather, the ladies in the church combined the birthday celebration with a pot luck charity benefit.

Tables were assembled out of doors for the food, while inside the church blankets, knitted items, and hand crafted clothes were put up for auction to raise money for charity. The men added carvings and handmade furniture, while some of the shop keepers donated their wares.

The Millers had each, in their own way, made the town their home. There seemed to be a cloud on the horizon in the form of their home and mining claim demanding their return. Cady could see that none, including himself, looked forward to returning full time, and yet their finances demanded that it be given attention.

He was still struggling inside when Shawna asked simply, "when will we go home?"

He could have hugged her, realizing that she, of them all, understood that their permanent home was in the mountains and not the town. "Soon," was his answer.

He and Ben had made several trips to the cabin to work on the road, staying overnight, then returning the next day. In town he had borrowed a fresno which, when pulled behind the mules, made the task much faster and easier. It was shaped like a flat bottomed bucket about four feet wide, used to move soil and level it. By the end of the third day the road was restored, ready for wagon travel.

Cady had not seen Ben and Phil together lately and wondered if their interest in each other was on the wane. At the same time, he could see the spark growing between Kate and Stephen, who had become her regular escort to church and other local events. As Cady became a familiar face around town, sporting the badge of authority, most seemed to accept him in his new role without question. He took care to refer to himself as deputy when the need for a title became necessary, not desiring to undermine or challenge the Sheriff's authority.

If not for the newness of the job, it might have become boring with little to occupy the majority of his time, except for vigilance. One night he thought he had caught a burglar, only later to find out he'd apprehended a drunk who had entered the wrong house in error. A night in jail and the ongoing ridicule from his neighbors served as punishment for his crime.

– EIGHT –

On the first of June, Cady and Ben returned to the claim and brought the heavily-laden wagon back with them, depositing its ore at the mill. The four then held a family meeting regarding the return to the mine. Kate elected to stay in town longer, since school had not yet adjourned for the summer, but Ben and Shawna, with the baby, joined Cady on the return trip.

The trip home with supplies, clothes and horses was uneventful and was made in two hours. Faith was beginning to walk and found the open space in the cabin a new world to explore, keeping Shawna busy. The men worked in the mine long full days, enjoying the labor and feeling the muscle tone return.

They all felt a distinct loss at the absence of Kate; her wisdom, help, and especially comradeship with Shawna and the baby. As they sat, three around the table, eating or reading the Bible together, there was a feeling of incompleteness, felt, but never mentioned.

Ben resumed riding the big mare in the evenings, shooting game of opportunity, and panning gold to keep busy. Shawna had her hands full trying to cook, watch the growing child, and keeping up on the housework that she had shared with Kate. Cady helped as he was able, often taking Faith outside with him as he did chores and cared for the animals. Dog became Faith's constant companion and protector. She was often found asleep on him as they both lay in the sunshine, having tired of watching Cady split firewood or care for his tools.

One morning, a small party of Indians followed the creek, just inside the tree line on the far side of the meadow, moving up into the high mountains, without making contact.

The cabin had wintered well, needing no repairs, much to their surprise. Cady and family discussed the wisdom of a roof over the outside stairway in preparation for the coming winter, and the viability of an escape exit from the upstairs in the event fire might block the stairs.

The meadow along the stream was lush with new meadow grasses, yellow buttercups, purple lupines, and animals both large and small. Sometime about mid-month, the wagon had been filled while a second load of ore waited, also to be freighted to the mill. They ate fresh venison, fried potatoes with onions, and squaw bread baked in the oven. On one of his evening adventures, Ben found a bee hive full of honey, but lacked the knowledge necessary to harvest it. He and Shawna went back the next day, using smoke and guile to bring home a few combs, with only a few stings to show for it.

Eager to reclaim Kate, see their friends, and deposit the ore, they returned to town, finding a warm welcome waiting for them. With Cady driving the wagon and trailing the roan, Ben rode the big mare, leaving behind the two ponies in the care of Dog, who patrolled the claim. After unloading the ore, Ben deposited the voucher at the bank, while Cady delivered Shawna and Faith to the boarding house. Leaving the wagon and mules, he then rode the roan to the Sheriff's office to visit with John.

At a glance it was apparent that John was not well, an unhealthy pallor replaced his normally tanned complexion. In an attempt to downplay his condition, he tried to joke, but without success. Cady found that the Sheriff had been stricken with stomach problems over a week ago, finding it difficult to hold down food or rest well. Dr. Smitty had not been able to provide much help, except to say it "had to run its course."

Immediately Cady made arrangements to stay and take over the Sheriff's duties. While John pretended to have everything under control, he eventually saw the wisdom in giving his deputy keys to the office and went home to rest. With some reservation, Cady spoke to Ben about the viability of him returning with the wagon and bringing down the second load of ore. Ben was eager to prove himself equal to the task, accepting responsibility for its safe return. They figured a two and a half day turn around, which included a full day to load the big wagon by himself. They decided to wait.

Cady made the rounds of the town, reacquainting himself with the routine. As evening neared, he called at John and Helen's place to check on his friend. John was still sleeping, as he had been since lying down mid-afternoon. Helen had a worried look about her but showed relief at Cady's presence and concern.

The town, with the exception of the saloon, was quiet by the time Cady closed the office and went home to eat. Ben had shared the information with Shawna and Catherine regarding John, explaining Cady's absence. Kate returned home from school to hugs and stories of missed opportunities at the claim, while she countered with stories of her students and interaction in their lives. Everyone saw the pride she took in her part of their education.

Following supper, Shawna asked Cady if they could visit the Sheriff and his wife, ostensibly to deliver them a meal which Catherine had prepared for them. When he agreed, she smiled, then went to her room to retrieve her medicine bag, leaving Ben and Kate behind to visit.

At the Days' home, Cady and Shawna got out of the borrowed surrey and knocked on the door. Helen answered and showed them inside, where John sat looking much the worse for wear.

"He's just been sick again, I'm afraid. I doubt that this good food will stay in his stomach," she offered.

Shawna quietly moved toward John, speaking softly and encouragingly as she did. Helen started to speak but was quieted by Cady who raised a finger to his lips.

Finally John nodded weakly, and looking to his wife he said, "do you have water on for tea?"

Helen nodded, then poured a mug full of steaming water, to which Shawna added a pinch of herbs from her bag. No one spoke as the water breathed new life into the dried leaves, their aroma wafting across the room. Cady could discern the scent of wild peppermint, sage, and other earthly smelling leaves and twigs, having previously been ground into a potpourri.

Shawna let the mixture steep for a few minutes while it cooled and settled before urging John to drink it all. Several times he attempted to stop before finishing, only to be admonished to finish. Shawna patiently explained to them all that this need be repeated three times a day just previous to eating. She also suggested eating small amounts at a sitting but on multiple occasions during the day. This was the native remedy for food poisoning and also what she had used during her morning sickness.

Days followed nights, with the Miller family finding their rhythm. Cady decided to delay the trip to retrieve the ore until they could determine how long they'd need to remain in town. As well, John was recovering his strength daily. By the third day he had to be told to go home and rest after dropping by the office for a visit. Both Dr. Smitty and Shawna were delighted at his quick recovery. Orville and Sarah and their Bible study group had been praying for John and looked at Shawna as God's provision for him.

Friday morning John arrived at the office right on Cady's heels, looking strong and robust, claiming he could not stand even one more day at home. He begged Cady to let him work. By 10 o'clock Ben and Cady were on the way home with the mules pulling the empty ore wagon, and by noon they had finished a quick lunch and were reloading the wagon. It pleased Cady to see how well the improved road into the property had held up, making mental note to purchase a fresno for future maintenance. The sun was still well above the mountains when they arrived in town and deposited the voucher for the ore at the bank. Ben asked Phil to join him for supper, only to find that she had other plans for the evening.

Over supper that evening, Cady remarked at how easy the new road had made the trip to and from town in the wagon, the same as what it had been before on horseback. Discounting snow or heavy rain, it was now an easy two hour trip. Kate brightened considerably, feeling less trapped and stranded than she had felt during the long winter months. With school in recess until fall, she chose to rejoin her family during the summer months, committing to return when they did.

Harless, looking first at Catherine, opened discussion about making the long delayed visit they had planned. The Millers voiced excited approval, Cady promising that the surrey could easily make the trip now while providing them comfortable transportation. Quickly, a plan was hatched for them to follow Cady and family home on Monday. It was contingent, however, upon finding a willing replacement to run the boarding house in their absence.

A great deal of the day Saturday was spent in preparation, with

Cady and Ben first loading the materials to build the roof over the stairs, then loading supplies and food. Early vegetables were available from the Merc, while supplies of fall ones were nearly exhausted. What few spuds they could find were already beginning to sprout and soften, with cabbage, carrots, and onions faring only a little better.

Cady and Shawna spent some time in the afternoon visiting with their friends Al and Linda, inviting them to join Harless and Catherine for a short visit. They delighted in Faith, watching her antics as though she had been their own family. They promised to discuss the trip and let them know the next day at Sunday's service.

Before returning to the boarding house, they reigned their horses in, stopping at the Sheriff's office. John greeted them warmly with a smile on his face, that a twinkle had returned to his eyes was noted by the Millers. They made him aware of their plan to return home Monday but made him promise that if his illness returned he'd send someone to let them know. Cady stressed that he could be there in a couple of hours anytime if need be.

Next they stopped to see Dr. Smith, who gave a cursory check over mother and child before pronouncing them "healthy as a horse." He asked if Shawna could leave some of her herbs with him and if they could be easily replaced. She left what she could and promised to harvest extra to leave with him as they became available, some were only available in late summer and fall.

During service the next morning, pastor Orville verbally noted John and Helen's attendance, giving praise to God for answered prayer while looking right at Shawna. His sermon was on God's faithfulness and the wide variety of tools used to accomplish His purposes. He urged the congregation to try and see God in all things, not taking things at face value. To those involved, his sermon was self-evident.

Following the service, the Millers brought Orville and Sarah up to date, having not had opportunity to do so since they arrived. Al and Linda confirmed their commitment to join the troop the following day as Catherine and Harless announced that the storekeepers at the Merc would take care of the guests at the boarding house for them. In return, they had agreed to do the same if they wanted to get away in the future.

By 9 o'clock a caravan left town with Cady and the ore wagon and supplies leading, followed by Harless with the surrey, Catherine, Shawna, and Kate aboard. Al and Linda in their own buggy were next, while Ben on the mare came behind with the other horses and Dog.

The townspeople laughed and called out to them as they passed, looking for all the world like a small wagon train. The day was clear and perfect, with just a hint of dew to keep down the dust from the many wheels as they traveled. Everyone's mood was cheerful, enjoying the adventure and excited as they arrived.

Dog sniffed out the area, pronouncing it intact as they unloaded and were shown around. The women began at the house, the men at the mine, explaining things as they went along. It turned out that Harless had some mining experience in the past, making it easy for him to assess the mine and its potential. Al was more drawn to the cabin and it's design and function, making observation here and there as he was shown around.

With the supplies unloaded and stowed in the house, the women began early preparation for supper, cleaning and straightening as they went. The men unloaded the lumber and tin from the wagon before returning it to the mine and unhitching the mules to join the horses in the meadow. Cady was amazed at how, in just a few days, the meadow grass had grown.

Sleeping accommodations, even with the two cots from the old cabin in use, were short. Ben volunteered to take the floor, allowing a couple to share his bed, making it all work out. Al looked over the old cabin, now a barn of sorts, pronouncing it suitable for Cady's cow. They all laughed until Al, now serious, began telling of saving it for them. Scratching their heads as how to gather and where to store hay for the growing number of animals, Harless suggested a scythe for cutting, the wagon for hauling, and a crib for storing the hay.

Cady had never considered taking the operation to this extent, but then had never considered himself a family man, or a Sheriff either. They continued discussing the placement of the crib near the barn, but under the trees for protection from the snow and sunlight. Al argued it should be roofed while Harless said it would be easier to leave it open for filling from the top. The open design of the crib would provide for air movement, allowing the green grass to season, while preventing both wild and tame animals from eating it.

Cady looked to his friends for guidance, having little knowledge about the amount of hay necessary to keep an animal, wondering if it was viable at all. The two Indian ponies were used to foraging and demanded much less than the two mules or the new roan would. The cow would need to be fed nearly all winter, not being able to produce milk on a limited diet.

It was decided to set four poles upright to a height of 12-15 feet forming a square, then to lattice it on three sides with smaller poles, leaving spaces between them, then enclosing the fourth side as the crib filled. As he emptied it, he would remove one side as the hay declined, reversing the process. His two friends agreed to help him select and set the four posts during their visit. Cady made a mental note to purchase a scythe on his next visit to town, then to begin laying in hay for the winter.

As the men washed up for supper in the creek, Al commented on the viability of a trap line in such close proximity to the house. To him this seemed like paradise, but as Ben quickly reminded him, "you haven't wintered here, yet."

Inside the house the discussion continued, drawing the women into the conversation as they enjoyed the food and friendship. Their friends from town, while dealing with a fair amount of snow, weren't isolated and alone and found it hard to imagine what the Millers had experienced during the winter. Part of the experience had been the newness of their situation. Four being thrown together, building their home alone, facing the birth of the baby, and finding answers to questions they'd never dreamed of asking.

Cady stated that he felt confident that they were in a much better position to endure the ravages of the coming winter than they had been. His family agreed, but still showed a lack of enthusiasm for the adventure, its memory still too fresh.

Following supper, with the sun setting, the men checked the livestock a final time before leaving them in Dog's care. True to their custom, Cady read from the Bible, stopping often for discussion and comment. The only small moment of anxiety occurred when eight people had only one privy available for use at bedtime.

The next morning, Catherine and Kate had arisen early, the rest were awoken by the smell of fresh coffee and cooking bacon. The Miller clan could tell by the relaxed expressions on their faces that their guests were enjoying the change of scenery and short vacation a great deal. Cady made a note to give a repeat invitation to both Orville and Sarah, and John and Helen.

While the women were finishing up after breakfast, Ben and Harless took one of the mules, a saw, hand-ax, and heavy rope in search of just the right crib poles. Cady and Al set to work measuring and digging, after agreeing on the placement of the crib. The first two feet went quickly in the soft topsoil, but when they came to the clay hard pan, things slowed considerably for the men. The holes were ready when the mule stopped, behind it were four 8" diameter poles, nearly twenty feet in length. Ben and Harless had limbed them and now measured and cut them to length at Cady's direction.

The four men had little trouble raising the poles, eyeballing them for vertical before tamping the soil in place around them. The whole project had taken just over an hour. They rested and visited over fresh lemonade while the women and Faith joined them out in the sunshine. Then, taking the second mule and hitching it also to the wagon, the four left together to find some smaller poles for rails.

Several hours passed with the men in the forest carefully measuring and selecting each pole, with the women going to the hot springs to bathe and visit. The wagon now boasting upwards of three dozen 3"-4" poles, the men returned with a feeling of accomplishment and comradeship. After tying the uprights together, top and bottom, with rails to keep them square, Cady persuaded the men to leave the remainder for another day.

They all noted the afternoon sun fading quickly in the west as the two buggies were loaded and headed back to town. When they told their friends goodbye, they each made a promise to repeat it in the future. Ben, using the excuse to ride, followed them down until they reached the main road. At supper that evening, Kate commented that the last few days had seemed like a holiday, to which all agreed.

Over the next week, Ben and Cady alternated time between the mine and the hay crib, enjoying the labor and the change of scenery each brought with it. The women got a scare one afternoon while the men were in the mine when Dog barked a warning.

A black bear and her two cubs had followed the creek up and were in the yard trying to find a way to get the hanging game out of the tree. As Shawna quickly pulled Faith inside the house, Kate discharged the shotgun into the air, mistakenly pulling both triggers in her excitement. By the time the two men surfaced and ran to the house, the women were inside laughing, and the bears long gone. Kate was already sporting a black eye and swelling on her cheek from the kick of the shotgun. She had not held it tightly against her shoulder, multiplying the damage done there also.

– NINE –

July brought with it temperatures approaching a hundred degrees, making the lure of the beaver ponds hard to resist. By Independence Day the wagon was loaded with ore and the foursome and child were on their way to town once again. Upon arrival, they repeated their routine, first leaving the ore, next securing a bed for the night, then making a circuit of the town to visit friends.

It was fortuitous timing which brought them. The Chinese contingent in town, famous for their fireworks, would be using the occasion to display their skills, as darkness fell. Many had arranged to meet at the church on the hill above town, to sit on the grass and watch the display. Sarah and her woman's group had organized a pie social where pies were sold, then to be shared with friends and family.

Cady was able to purchase both a scythe and a hay fork at the Merc and replenish their store of perishables, requesting they be ready for pickup when they left town. They had run out of spikes with which to finish the hay crib, but bought more at the lumberyard, before joining John at the Sheriff's office.

"Glad to see you, Cady," John said, "might find I need your help later on tonight."

Cady asked, "trouble?"

"No, none yet, but fireworks and whiskey often bring out the little boy in men," John continued.

Cady nodded understanding. "I didn't wear my belt," Cady he said, "only brought the rifle with us."

"No harm," answered the Sheriff, "still got the .45 you can wear and the star is in the drawer."

Again Cady nodded, "be here right after supper if that works."

"Be fine, and thanks," John said, "usually things don't get stirred up until after dark, then it's hard to be in more than one place at a time."

At the bank Ben found Phil eager to spend time with him, finding out later that Stephen had also missed Kate's company and had asked her to the social as well. Shawna was completely unaware of the meaning of the 4th of July and had never seen fireworks before.

As Cady explained it to her, he could see the little girl in her come to life, mirroring little Faith's innocent face. Catherine was overjoyed to see her friends and made room for them in the house which was already almost full due to the celebration. The town seemed overrun with miners, loggers, peddlers, and folks just wanting to be part of the celebration. They ate a sumptuous meal, but refused dessert in favor of pie later at the church. Cady explained his situation to Harless and the women, asking if Shawna could ride up with them, knowing that Kate and Ben had other plans, then left for the office.

As soon as Cady arrived, John slipped home to have a quick bite of supper and to bring Helen back with him to the church.

Cady had not brought the roan with them, so he elected to ride the big mare that Ben had ridden down, if he found he needed mobility. Putting on the star and buckling the .45 across his hips, he had a feeling of dread come over him. Alone, he went right to prayer, asking for direction and protection for himself and those he loved. But even so, the feeling persisted.

Twilight is brief in the mountains, shutting off the sun early and darkness following quickly. The town was fortunate that a huge orange moon appeared in the eastern sky just minutes after the sun disappeared in the west. On those nights without moonlight, the night is so dark that one cannot see their own boots.

When John returned to the jailhouse, he and Cady devised a strategy to divide up the town into sections which they could patrol on horseback. Using the main street as the north-south boundary with the mill to the east and boarding house to the west, they agreed to rendezvous every hour in front of the saloon to compare notes.

They walked Main Street on opposite sides, checking doors on the shops as they went, before mounting their horses and heading out into the darkness. Cady once again felt the uneasy feeling as he rode slowly along, with the bursts of the fireworks lighting up the night sky. Most folks were standing or sitting with their faces upturned toward the displays, which came several minutes apart. Tradition determined that they would send several up then wait a time before doing more, extending the time of the event over a longer period.

Occasionally a gun shot would drown out the report of the fire-works when some exuberant reveler would shoot into the air. As the night wore on, with the displays less frequent, the shots became more frequent, causing them concern. Cady arrived at the saloon just as John had broken up a fight, sending the men home without their sidearms. The faces of two from the watching crowd disappeared as they stepped back from the light leaving Cady to wonder where he had seen them before. The crowd dispersed and reentered the saloon as Cady and John met together, exchanging information before re-mounting to continue their patrols.

Cady felt the hot sear of a branding iron across his back as he had just turned in the saddle to look over his shoulder. Without thinking, he slid off the side of the horse farthest from the saloon, keeping the mare between himself and the shooter. As he hit the ground, the .45 in his hand, he surveyed the blackness without success. It was not until he saw John returning at a gallop that a muzzle flash located his assailants. Cady fired three times at the flash before turning his attention to the now riderless horse approaching.

John lay unmoving in the street in front of the saloon where onlookers were lined at the windows. Cady moved with the horse as a shield toward his friend, while watching the blackened shadows between the buildings for movement. When a sudden burst of an overhead display lighted the area, Cady saw two figures, one laying against the building and the other waiting and watching for opportunity. Cady emptied his gun into the man, watching him fall in the fading light. Reloading as he ran, Cady moved toward the fallen Sheriff as people poured into the street from the saloon.

John was hit hard in the ribcage under his left arm, bleeding badly when the deputy reached him. Cady yelled for someone to call the doctor as others gathered around, offering help and advice. Smitty had been up at the church watching fireworks and eating pie when he heard the shots and cries for help. In less than a minute the doctor arrived and had John moved two doors down to his office.

As they passed, the fallen forms of two men were revealed to Cady in the lantern light. The two, apparently dead, were the two he had seen earlier and also the two with whom he had had the knife fight the previous year after the altercation in the hot springs. After escaping from custody on the way to prison they had made their way back to town to seek revenge. The doctor's office was too crowded for Smitty to work so Cady escorted onlookers out with a promise to keep them advised.

"Missed the vitals," Smitty said as much to himself as to Cady, "but I think a piece of a rib punctured his lung. Bullet went clean through."

The Sheriff was moaning now but still appeared asleep.

Cady asked, "what can I do?"

The Doc answered, "wash your hands first, then hand me what I ask you for. I'm gonna have to go in between the ribs and see what is in there."

After 45 minutes, Cady looked like a butcher, covered in blood, bathed in sweat, and totally exhausted. A rubber tube had been placed in the wound to drain blood from the chest cavity, with Doc having sewed around it to hold it securely in place.

Outside, Helen, Sarah, and many from the church waited and prayed, hoping for good news.

"You can let Helen in now, if you will Mr. Miller, so's I can tell her that prayers were answered," said the doctor.

Cady asked Helen in, while he himself exited into the night air. He gave reassurance to those present as he had been given by the doctor but was unwilling to answer their many questions about a prognosis, deferring to Smitty. Orville led them all in a prayer of thanks and praise before attempting to send them home to their families.

Shouldering the mantle of responsibility which he had never sought, Cady asked Ben to garner help and have the two bodies moved to the undertaker a block south. Shawna and Kate, faces creased with concern and pain, drew his attention to the blood on the back of his shirt. For the first time he could feel the trickle of his own blood and the pain of the wound. As they reentered the office together, the women drew Smitty's attention from the Sheriff to Cady's wound.

Smitty turned over John's care to Helen and Sarah with instruction to call him if needed, then cut away Cady's shirt.

"Scapula," Doc said, identifying the bone showing through the skin, "he must have been turned sidewise to them. Slug hit the bone then cut along the surface all the way across."

"I just turned to look back," offered Cady, "then I felt it."

"Praise God!" the old doctor exclaimed, "you hadn't, you'd be dead now. Shawna, you got some medicine like you used on his stomach?"

Shawna nodded, clutching her ever present medicine bag to her.

"Let me give it a couple of stitches to bring the skin over the bone, then I'll leave him to you," said Smitty with a smile. Cady suddenly felt old, tired, and weak as realization of the night's events swept over him.

At 7 o'clock the next morning Cady awoke, hurting everywhere at once. Shawna sat in the chair nursing Faith, quietly humming to herself. She smiled as he, with some effort, raised himself onto one elbow and greeted them.

"Catherine saved us some breakfast," Shawna announced matter-of-factly.

Cady appreciated it as Shawna helped him on with a loose fitting shirt over his bandages. Harless and Catherine hovered over them when they finally sat at the big table, other guests having already eaten and gone.

"John made it through the night well," Harless offered, "Doc says he should make it."

"Thank God," came the response.

Ben was already at the jail when Cady arrived, sitting back with his big boots on the desk like he belonged there. Cady was grateful but instead said, "who told you you could open and put your boots on the Sheriff's desk?"

Ben looked crestfallen for a moment until he saw his uncle's smile. Cady continued, "thank you for looking after things. I'll speak with John when he is able and see how he wants to handle this, until then you are the deputy's deputy."

Ben brightened considerably, "do I get a badge?"

"Not yet," answered Cady, "but we'll see how it goes. Don't wear a sidearm or badge until I speak to the Sheriff or Mayor Fitch."

Cady moved like a man twice his age but found that movement and exercise decreased the pain so he forced himself to walk rather than ride. At Dr. Smitty's he found the patient sleeping but breathing well, with color in his cheeks. The good doctor brought him quietly up to date on John's condition before taking a look at Cady's back.

"Helen's just gone home, was here most o' the night. Maybe you could drop be later this afternoon and fill her in."

Cady nodded, "I'll make a point of it. Can he talk?"

Smitty nodded, "could if he wanted, no damage to his vocal chords, but he needs bed rest. I wouldn't wake him unless there was an emergency. He woke once during the night, and asked about you."

Cady was surprised before he remembered that the first shot had been at him, that John would not have been aware if it had hit or missed.

"Say Doc, you had any sleep?" asked Cady.

"Dozed a little now and then, why? Am I looking bad?" came the reply.

"How about I ask Kate to come and sit with John for a while, I know everyone is eager to help where they can," he responded. "We can call you if he needs you. You eaten?"

Doc answered, "Naw, wasn't no time for food, but I could eat a bite now."

"I tell you what, why don't you slip next door and grab a bite at the café while I'm here, then I'll go get Kate and give you a break?" Cady volunteered.

The doctor didn't have to be told twice, and with a wink and a smile he was out the door. While the doctor was gone, Orville and Sarah came by to check up on their friend. Cady told them as much as he knew, then gave them time alone with John while they thanked God and prayed for his recovery. When they finished, they volunteered to go for Kate on their way to sit with Helen.

Smitty took nearly an hour and missed the Ricks' by several minutes. Kate was pleased to have been asked for her help and listened carefully to the doctor's instructions before shooing him away to his quarters to rest. Rather than returning to his office, Cady walked down the street, first to the saloon where he was warmly greeted and pelted with questions, then to the Mayor's office.

Mayor Fitch greeted his guest, first with concern, then later with joy when told of John's improving condition. The Mayor gave Cady full responsibility as Sheriff and authorized Ben as deputy until John's condition improved, asking that he come by and be officially sworn in.

Finally, making the loop, Cady went by the undertaker where he verified the identity of his assassins before collecting their guns and valuables. One had been hit square and died of a single shot while the other had been hit twice before the third round ceased his pain.

At the jail he gave the news to Ben, sending him down to meet with the Mayor. Cady asked Ben to find out what to do with the valuables he had recovered. Several from the town stopped by during the afternoon to ask about John's condition and were pleased to hear the answer.

When Ben returned, he was wearing a star and a smile, looking all of seventeen with his goofy grin. Cady took his time impressing the weight of his position and the gravity of the choices he might have to make.

"The gun is the last resort, never draw it unless you have to, never shoot it unless you are ready to take responsibility for a human life," Cady said slowly. "It changes a man when he kills another, and never for the better."

Ben nodded solemnly, saying nothing.

"Another thing," Cady remembered, "accuracy is more important than speed. If you have to shoot take your time and make it count. There are some who may want to test you just because you are young. Keep your head, never get angry, angry will get you killed."

They talked through the afternoon until Kate opened the door and joined them. Doc had enjoyed a nice rest and was changing John's dressings when she left. Worry filled her face when she saw Ben's star, first beginning to object, then closing her mouth without a word.

Her brother looked into her eyes before saying, "It's just temporary, until we can get things under control. Mostly he'll watch the office and spell me when I have to go out."

She still didn't speak, fearful of crying.

Ben approached her. "I'll be careful, Uncle Cady has put the fear into me," he quipped.

Finally Kate spoke slowly and firmly. "It isn't right that a parent bury their child, ain't God's way. I want to live to be a grandma, you be extra careful."

Cady noticed she was holding back tears as she left to return to Shawna and Catherine. "Yer mom's right, she's already buried her mom, dad, and husband, she deserves to be happy," he said quietly.

– TEN –

Cady left the office riding the mare out to John and Helen's house, where several rigs were parked outside. Helen let him in where he found friends had brought food, hugs, and prayers to share with her. At their insistence he shared a quick meal and what news he could about John before returning to let Ben go to supper.

After locking up he made the rounds, checking doors and answering questions from both the curious and the concerned. Bone tired and hurting, he stopped by the doctor's office giving Smitty a few minutes off to eat and relax next door. While the doctor was gone, John awoke for a few minutes, speaking weakly and incoherently. Cady took notice that the tube had been removed and the hole had been closed with stitches.

Linda and Sarah showed up just before Doc, praying with Cady for John, then offering to spend a few hours while the doctor got some sleep. Both had brought their sewing baskets with intentions to stay, not accepting Smitty's weak attempt at playing the martyr. Doc finally acquiesced, gratefully accepting their help, and finding himself quickly asleep.

At the boarding house Cady accepted only pie and coffee, explaining his lack of appetite. Shawna and he went to their room early where she inspected his wound, applied some slave and reattached the bandage. He mentioned how good a soak in the hot springs might feel only to be informed that the water would slow the healing of the herbs. Shawna was insistent that he not bathe or soak for at least two more days. It was barely 8 o'clock when he drifted off to a sleep filled with nightmares and violence and nearly twelve hours later when he awoke bathed in sweat. The loss of blood, worry, and stress of the day had taken a greater toll than expected.

Cady was relieved to find that Ben had already opened the Sheriff's office. He made no attempt to rush to work, rather he enjoyed a leisurely breakfast and sponge bath from his wife before asking for a plate to take to the doctor.

Smitty had fully recovered from his ordeal, eating the offered food with relish and gratitude, while he filled Cady in on John's condition. Although gaining strength, John was running a fever, indicating the likelihood of infection. Doc asked if possibly Shawna might take a moment to come by as she had time. Cady promised to ask her.

Ben looked very grownup and professional, sitting up straight and alert as Cady entered the jailhouse. He wanted to laugh but felt it might hurt Ben's feelings if he took it wrong.

"Mornin' deputy," he quipped instead.

"Mornin' Sheriff," came the quick reply through Ben's big smile.

They talked for a few minutes, with Ben catching up on the news next door before Cady stated, "Ben, one of us needs to get back to the claim, check things out, make sure that Dog and the ponies are alright. I'm kind of old and stoved up right now, I's hopin' you'd like to take a ride today on your mare."

Ben did not miss the reference to the mare. "My mare?" he questioned.

"Yup," said Cady, "a deputy has to have his own horse."

Ben was all at once a little boy again, almost hugging his uncle before regaining his manly composure. "I'll need the roan too, if you'd bring him down with you."

Nearly a month went by before John, twenty pounds lighter and looking five years older, walked into the Sheriff's office sporting his gun and badge.

"Sheriff," Cady greeted him, before giving him a warm hug.

"Sheriff," came the amused reply.

"How you feelin' John?" Cady asked.

"Good," he answered, "no pain, but I haven't got my stamina back yet. Still get tired easy. It's been nice to be able to nap in the afternoons. I'm sorry to have messed up your summer's diggin'."

Cady laughed, "You took the second bullet meant for me, now you are feeling guilty about it?"

John laughed too, "hadn't planned on gettin' shot, just hoped to get there in time to help you out. How things been goin'?"

"Fine," Cady answered, "like you told me in the first place, most of the time not much to do."

"How's your back?" Sheriff Day asked.

"All healed up, only a scar to tell me it ever happened," Cady answered, "hurts a little when I stretch."

"How's Ben doin'?" John asked.

"Real well, so far, but things have been pretty calm since the 4th. Most folks have kept to themselves. Even the bar crowd remember the two lying dead against the building," came the reply. "I've tried to build into him a sense of the responsibility that comes with the badge, but he's just turned twenty-one, and hasn't been around much."

"I know what you mean," agreed John, "we seem to either get more than we can handle or less than we need when we are growing up. He's been lucky to have you and Kate and his faith to fall back on."

"Thanks," said Cady.

"When you plan on headin' back to the claim?" John asked.

"Not right away, at least not until you are feelin' 100% again," came Cady's answer. "I'd like to get away for a half day though when you're feelin' up to it. I need to get back up and bring a load down that's just been sittin' waitin' for me right out in the open."

"How about tomorrow?" the Sheriff asked.

"You really up to it my friend? You're still lookin' a little tired," Cady replied.

"Sure enough, take Ben with you, that way you'll be back so's I can take my afternoon snooze," John said with a laugh.

"Deal, we'll leave early, should be back by noon, God willin'," Cady said with a smile.

At supper that night Cady laid out the plan. He offered to let the women ride along if they wanted, but he emphasized however that it would be a quick trip to load the ore and then return to relieve the Sheriff. Cady suspected that John wasn't really up to the job yet. Shawna deferred, saying that Faith had the sniffles associated with teething and had been running a fever. Kate had already had made plans with the sewing group with little interest in a quick wagon ride. Ben, however, was eager to break the routine and get back home and to work.

They left after a quick breakfast, with the mules pulling an empty wagon, lunch in their ruck sacks, arriving two hours later. Both Cady and Ben gave the claim a once over before pronouncing it secure and undisturbed, then began loading the ore. Several times Cady felt the burn of adhesion's across his back where the scar had allowed the tissues to attach to the muscle incorrectly when healing. He forced him-self to work through the pain, finishing the job at hand in an hour. Both he and Ben could feel the effect of their recent lack of exercise as they shared lunch together, before returning to town.

Arriving in town, they dropped the ore at the mill, then stabled the mules before relieving John at the jail. While affable and alert, the lines in his face belied his cheerful disposition. He made no effort to dissuade Cady from re-assuming responsibility for the office as he left for his home to rest.

Quietly, Cady wrestled with the certain knowledge that the office of Sheriff was quickly becoming a full time job. Within the near future, whether he recovered completely or not, John, and especially Helen, was ready to step down from the responsibility and danger of the job. The important question loomed in his mind, was he the one to assume the full time position, putting his own dreams and plans on hold?

What would his family think? He was well aware that though he had given them opportunity to speak and voice their opinions, he had pulled rank, promising it as a part-time position. He had also down-played the seriousness of the risks involved. After the incident, that could no longer be done. Cady left the office in Ben's hands while he walked to the church to seek counsel from his friend Orville.

Other than Sunday mornings and a brief visit or two during his convalescence, he and Orville had not had spent time together. Cady badly felt the need of spiritual and wise mortal advice. While Sarah was gone to a meeting with Kate and others of the sewing club, Orville welcomed him, listening closely as Cady shared his heart openly. Cady attempted to lay out the dilemma impartially, pointing out what he saw as pros and cons. Orville proved to be a good listener, interrupting infrequently, while asking only pointed questions of his friend.

They had been together for over an hour before Orville finally asked, "what did God tell you?"

Cady was disarmed, finding himself without a response.

Orville waited, then continued. "Have you asked Him?"

"Well no," Cady admitted, "I haven't, not directly."

"And why do you suppose that is?" questioned the preacher.

"Why what is?" asked Cady, not understanding the question.

"Why you'd seek the advice of man rather than the counsel of God," was the quiet reply.

Cady was silent.

Orville let the silence fill the room before continuing. "May it be that you are afraid that you may not agree with His answer?"

Cady still had no answer, but searched his soul and found that he had already made up his mind and was looking just for affirmation. And yes, he was afraid that God may have other plans for him that he was unwilling to follow.

"So," Cady finally began, "by answering my questions with questions you are forcing me to seek answers elsewhere?"

"Exactly right," Orville answered, seemingly impressed that Cady understood, "answers from God, Who knows and wants what is best for you."

"You don't make things easy," Cady stated.

"Too many of us look for the easy way, ignoring the right way," Orville continued. "Jesus speaks to that in several places, most notably Matthew 7:13-14." Orville read the verses, explained it in context, then suggested that Cady also read it several times before praying for an answer.

"One last thing, try laying your heart out before your family as you have with me, then pray together for direction. No matter what the decision, you'll all be more at peace with it."

Cady returned to the office and spent the afternoon brooding, but without sharing it with Ben.

At the supper table, there was a notable lack of conversation among the Miller clan, that poured over on the others at the table as well. The mood was somber and quiet without anyone really knowing why or what had changed. Two days went by with the tension growing between them, before the women took matters into their own hands.

Cady was alone in the Sheriff's office while John was at home and Ben was making rounds when Kate and Shawna arrived, without Faith.

Alarmed, Cady asked, "where is Faith? Is she alright?"

The women answered as one, "she's fine, Catherine has her, but we're not. What is going on with you?"

At first Cady considered lying to them to avoid confrontation but knew all too well it wouldn't work. Then the book of Jonah came to mind and he found himself in tears. For the first time in memory he was crying. He knew at once that he'd been hoping God would come to him rather that he having to humble himself and go to God. Both women were alarmed at his strange behavior until he began to talk.

"I have always seemed to be able to figure things out on my own, to think through situations and see an answer. I see now I have been fooling myself. Where I thought I was making decisions on my own, God has been guiding my way. Like Jonah, I didn't like what God was telling me to do, so I tried to hide and ignore Him. It hasn't worked and it has made me miserable worrying about it," Cady confessed. His face red with shame and wet with tears he began to talk, just as Ben entered the office.

"Ben," Cady said softly, "please sit down, I want to share my heart with all of you."

The three listened carefully, much the same as Orville had, without interrupting him, nodding from time to time. As he continued to speak

Cady could see their expressions soften and their eyes fill with love. When he finished, he told them of his time with Orville and of his advice. He confessed that his pride had kept him from seeking God's direction and asked that they pray with and for him. They took turns praying for what seemed like hours as tears flowed and emotions filled their hearts. In reality, only a few minutes later, drained and cleansed, they said Amen.

No one spoke for a long time, as they soaked up the realization of what had just happened. God's Holy Spirit held them closely and comforted their fears.

Kate spoke first, "I think I'd like to stay in town and teach school. The other teacher is not well and has chosen to retire. Stephen and I are considering getting engaged."

While Cady had considered this possibility he had never directly asked. It seemed that others had things on their mind as well as he.

Ben spoke next, "Phil means a lot to me, although we have not talked about marriage, I think we may be headed in that direction eventually. One stumbling block to making plans has been the uncertainty of employment. I don't know what I want to do. I like it all, the claim, the mill, and the deputy job."

Shawna took Cady's big hand in her small one and spoke, "I want to be part of whatever God asks you to do, I want our children to feel love as we feel love. Sometimes I worry about you when I should not, I know that God will protect you until He takes you home, then He will care for us until we join you. We named her our daughter Faith because that is where she came from, our next child, who I think is already with us, will be Hope."

Cady's mouth dropped, then rounded into a big grin. "Another girl? How would you know that?"

Shawna smiled also, "it just seems right somehow. The one after that will be Charity."

Everyone laughed, but sobered to the possibility that she could be right.

Cady spoke again, "So everyone has been holding back a little, waiting to see what happens next. I'm going to ask if John and Helen will meet with us at the Mayor's office and talk things out, if you agree. We'll let God guide us from there."

There were nods and smiles all around as they locked up and headed home to supper.

Mayor Fitch's office was small and austere, barely providing enough room for the assembly to be seated.

"No need for the full city council, thank God, this is just a fact finding mission to see if we can resolve some issues" he began. "I think we can all be candid and keep this conversation to ourselves." He continued, "John, Helen, you mean a great deal to us and to the town, first and foremost we want to try and make you happy."

"Thank you, Mr. Mayor," John began, "the town and its people mean a lot to us too. We've had a lot of time to talk in the past weeks about things we should have talked about before, somethin' like what happened has a way of puttin' things in proper perspective."

Everyone nodded agreement.

"Helen and I are ready for change, just what kind, we're not sure. Maybe a little adventure without the danger."

Everyone laughed.

Mayor Fitch resumed control saying, "so it's decided that we need to be looking for a full time Sheriff?"

All eyes turned to John as he nodded while Helen put her hand on his arm. It was evident that he was saddened but resigned to the change.

"What'll ya do?" questioned the Mayor, in his best attorney voice. "Have you thought that through? You're not a man to just sit around and grow old."

Cady jumped into the discussion, "do you plan to stay in town?"

"The Sheriff answered, "ya, I guess. You got a thought?"

Cady answered him slowly, "well, maybe, I'm not sure yet. How'd you and Helen like to take a little vacation?" Questioning eyes were on Cady as he continued, "if Ben would watch the jail for a couple of days, Shawna and I'd like you to be our guests at the claim, a little get away."

They continued to visit with Fitch, making it clear the Sheriff's job was Cady's if he wanted it. He neither committed nor refused, rather saying thank you and asked if they could discuss it further.

At mid-morning, with Kate promising good care of Faith and Ben assuming control of the jail, Cady mounted the roan with Shawna on behind. John and Helen brought their buggy with a few clothes and provisions, following along behind. The summer sun was hot with while the earth below was dried and dusty as they left town. Before they had gone far, a light wind came down the canyon, trees lent their shade, and the stream chuckled beside the road. The closer they got to the cabin, the more relaxed and peaceful the scene became.

As Shawna opened up the house and began showing Helen around, Cady and John walked the property. Dog, filled with boundless energy, ran ahead, then returned to do it all over again. Cady noted the hay crib remained empty as it had been when they had taken a day trip almost two months before. John approved of its construction and commented on the abundance of waist high grass in the meadow, easily accessible to fill it.

Cady was surprised to find that John knew his way about a mine, having never mentioned having experience at it. Cady explained as he went, showing off their accomplishments to date and speaking of their plans to build a cover over the stairs. As John got a feel for it, he made comments and suggestions, just as Cady had hoped. The women had aired out the musty cabin, opening it to the outside. They spent the day together, enjoying a fine supper and visit before turning in to bed.

Cady arose early, letting his guests sleep, while Shawna started the coffee and prepared breakfast. He was just learning the cadence of the scythe, swinging a smooth level arc, when his friend joined him in the meadow.

"It looks like you've got the knack," John offered, nodding his approval.

Cady stopped, and turning to him replied, "have you ever done this before?"

John answered, "as a kid, helped my Pa some, but I was too small to keep it straight and level long. Let me give it a go."

Cady handed the tool to him and watched him wince as the muscles across his ribs came into play, but noted the grace and power of the arc. Laying the scythe aside, John commented that the exercise was just what he needed to get back his strength.

"A guy'd have to work into it, but it'd loosen up those muscles that'd not been used since the shootin'."

Cady nodded his agreement, recounting how loading the ore had done likewise for his back. Inside the cabin, Helen was amazed at the spaciousness of the rooms and equally impressed by the new stove. As they shared a breakfast of bacon and eggs with fried potatoes and onions brought up with them from town, they continued to visit.

"Could you two see yourselves livin' in a place like this part time?" Cady asked candidly.

"Oh, I'd love it!" Helen blurted. "How about you John?"

"It'd be a nice change, that's for sure, quiet and peaceful," he answered.

"Winter's hard," Shawna interjected, "I wondered if we'd make it last year."

"I imagine it takes a lot of planning, makin' sure you got all you need when the snow comes," agreed John.

Cady nodded. "T'was a real experience, that's for sure. All of us learnin' as we went, buildin', and the baby comin' too. 'Spect it will go better this year if I get the hay in and wood chopped before snowfall."

After supper they shared some time together at the warm springs before calling it a night. Helen surprised them in the morning by having the coffee boiling when they gathered in the kitchen. The smell of corn-bread wafted from the oven and gravy simmered on the stove. Cady blessed the food before they all ate hungrily. About noon, with Dog barking goodbye and running alongside the buggy, they headed toward town.

Beside Cady, Shawna was riding her pony, looking like a young girl again, her long black hair flowing down her back, with new life in her tummy. When they reached town they parted ways, with thanks and promises to do a repeat visit. On the way home Cady remembered a Scripture about planting seeds, he thought to himself that man may plant seeds but only God can make them grow.

Next morning John was at the jail early, he walked in right behind Cady, who noted a spring in his step. He wore neither his gun belt nor his badge, making it clear he had not come to work.

"Mornin' Sheriff," John said.

"Mornin' John," Cady replied, amused by his tone.

"Been doin' some thinkin', wondered if I might offer you a hand up at the claim. You know, helpin' you get ready for winter."

"That's a temptin' offer, John," said Cady, "but what about you and Helen spending some time together now that you're retirin'?"

"I was thinkin' maybe we might go up together, Helen loved it," mused John. "It's a real weight off me not having to worry about the town any more."

Cady smiled inside, "who'd take care of your horses and chickens while you're gone?"

"I kinda hoped you might," John answered. "You could stay right there, have the run of the place, treat it like t'was your own."

Cady could feel God's hand directing them when he said, "how long you figger you'd need?"

"Well, depends I guess," said the ex-Sheriff, "how long'd it take?"

"Gosh, John," began Cady, "I'm not sure there's still time before snowfall. You might find yourself snowed in and spending the winter." He continued, "It moves slow when a man's working alone. There's the roof to put up over the stairs, the hay to bring in for the animals, the timber to cut and drag in, then cut and split for the fire. I wonder if you're up to it."

John countered, "Feelin' better and gettin' stronger every day. I think a little work will help me heal faster."

"I hear you there, friend," Cady agreed, "a little sweat felt good to me too when I was loadin' the ore wagon." Cady spoke again, to himself but out loud as if thinking. "It's lookin' like the sheriffin' is coming down to Ben and me, regardless. It would help if I didn't have to worry about the place. The boarding house is fine short term, but isn't like havin' a home. And in good weather, we're only a couple of hours away, one of us could come up and help you out now and again."

John was nodding, following the logic. "We'd probably need to borrow the mules and wagon for haulin' hay, timber, and such. Might even be fun to get my hands dirty in the mine like old times."

Cady could see that his friend had let his imagination take over. God would take it from here. "Well, let's try it and see how it goes with the women," Cady said, "and we sure do appreciate your help." Cady had to chuckle at the exchange, wondering if he and John had just been fencing or if he had really not seen through the ruse.

Two days later, the Days were headed up with the Miller's wagon loaded, trailing a couple of horses behind them. Ben, who was eager to go, rode along on his mare with intention to stay to get them situated and help John as long as necessary. Cady and Shawna moved their meager belongings into the Day's home, while Faith and Dog spent most of their time exploring. Even though temporary, it felt good to all of them. Kate and Ben elected to stay at the boarding house until their situations changed, with school starting in a month.

By the first of September the trees had colored up with yellows, reds, and browns joining the several shades of green up and down Mores creek and the surrounding mountains. While the days remained warm, there was a bite in the early morning air promising frost, to be closely followed by snow.

Leaving Ben in charge, Cady, Shawna and Faith took a horseback ride up to the claim with provisions they knew would be savored. John proudly showed off the hay crib stacked high with timothy grass from the meadow and several logs which had been dragged in, waiting to be blocked up, split, and stacked. Inside the cabin, Helen had made it her home, having sewn fresh new curtains, having cleaned and folded the others carefully away, and likewise putting their own bedding on their bed. The meadow was lush with grass that had begun to grow back, with game evident in it both at dawn and dusk. John pointed out a young buck hanging in the shade, proudly announcing his kill.

A quick lunch together reminded them all of their close bond before the men headed together into the forest with the wagon, mules, and saws. Several hours later found them returning with a wagon loaded full of tamarack, yellow pine, and red fir of various lengths and diameters. Smoke from the chimney promised a hot supper while the hot springs served as a relaxing bath.

During the evening Cady gave a report on situations in town while hearing about the adventures John and Helen were sharing here. Shawna asked straight out what their plan was for the winter at which they looked at one another before answering.

"We kind of hoped we could stay on and experience it together. It's been fun and we are getting to know each other more every day," Helen offered.

Nodding, Cady added, "workin' out for us too, nice for Faith to be around other kids and Shawna with other women, and with our new one coming in June."

The men started out early, following a nice breakfast, most of which the Millers had brought with them. Cady tried to prioritize where his help could best be utilized. The men agreed that framing up the roof structure over the stairs was a two person job more than cutting firewood. They went to work designing and installing the rafters and supports, using the loaded wagon as a scaffold to work from. By the early afternoon they were ready to overlay it with tin.

Having made such good progress, Cady made the decision to stay on to help finish it and leave the following morning. After a good night's sleep and hot breakfast, Cady and Shawna mounted the horses and headed home, the last pony following behind them. John and Helen waved goodbye and committed to make a final trip to town at the first sign of snow to stock up on provisions.

Late morning found the town as they had left it but with Faith very anxious to be reunited with her parents. She had begun jabbering and occasionally said something that made sense if you were to listen carefully, like "K-dee" or "Cha-na."

The big news in town was the engagement of Stephen and Kate. They heard it from Ben before Kate could tell them. No date had been chosen for the wedding, but smart money was betting that before Christmas they'd be married.

Cady filled Ben in on the progress made during the short visit and their decision to winter at the claim. Ben told Cady that the news of Kate's betrothal had caused a stir between he and Phil. She had indicated more than a passing interest in following in the same shoes.

Cady listened, then offered some fatherly advice, "Ben, you'll know when you find the right one and when the time is right. Trust in God, then follow your heart."

Ben nodded. "My heart says she's the one, my head says wait until you are sure. How do you know when you are sure?"

Cady smiled, "A man cannot answer that for another man. We are all different. Pray about it together, God knows who He has planned for each of His children."

That night the Millers joined the rest of their family and the other guests at the boarding house for supper, enjoying the lively talk about the coming wedding. At home later, Shawna and Cady enjoyed a long talk discussing things they'd not shared before, before drifting off to sleep.

Sunday morning, the church was filled both services, with Orville and Sarah introducing a young man who hoped to become a preacher. Under Orville's tutelage, he was allowed to preach at second service. Stephen and Kate received congratulations from the pulpit among jokes and laughter from their friends. Cady arose and gave a short report on the Days and John's rapidly returning good health. At the end of the service the question was asked about plans for enlarging the church building.

Orville answered that it appeared that it was late in the season for construction, however, an account had been opened at the bank for a building fund. Those wishing to contribute were encouraged to do so.

Right in the middle of the closing prayer, the congregation was alarmed to hear the bell on the fire wagon. As they rushed outside, they could see the Mercantile engulfed in smoke, with flames coming through the roof around the stove pipe. Volunteers fought through the morning and into the afternoon before losing the battle to save the structure, but saving the building where Smitty lived and worked.

– ELEVEN –

A sense of loss filled the town, the Merc had been central to many lives since the town was founded. Ironically, the owners had been in church when the fire began. Had they been open for business they could have put it out before the chimney fire got into the rafters. Sometimes God's plans make no sense to those who live it. Pastor Orville called for an evening service to gather, pray, and discuss how the community could help.

It was the same man who had asked earlier in the day about church construction who stood again with a suggestion, "Maybe God is telling us that His house is working out just fine the way it is. Maybe He's sayin' that the building fund might be better spent helping out our neighbors."

There were amens and nods before Orville stood to speak. "I agree with you brother, you just stole my thunder. I was going to suggest just that myself, but it sounds better coming from you." There was laughter before they came to order again and Orville continued, "if our board concurs, I vote to use what we already have and whatever God provides to help rebuild the Merc."

Amens again came from throughout the room.

Cady started it off, "We'll donate a wagon load of ore, quick as I can get it out of the mine."

Others pledged materials, labor, and funds as they were able, with Catherine offering Sally and her husband free room and board until their living quarters were rebuilt.

Monday morning, many hands began tearing down and hauling off what could not be saved. Little could be salvaged except the cause of the blaze itself, the cast iron potbellied stove. It stood like a black giant, covered in soot, but intact.

Ben, Cady, Al, and Orville left the following morning, leaving the town without a Sheriff, blacksmith, or pastor, riding up the canyon to the claim. They quickly helped John unload the remaining logs from the wagon before diving into the mine. Within six hours they had it loaded and were heading home, exhausted, but happy. The mill owner donated his usual fee back to the cause, allowing the voucher to purchase more lumber.

Wednesday morning, more volunteers gathered than there was room for them to work, so Al divided them into groups. Half worked mornings while the remainder worked afternoons, as the town's women kept them all fed and watered. By Friday, the new Mercantile was framed, sided, and roofed, with windows on order from the lumber yard. Funds kept coming in from the community; bake and rummage sales, and donations from all quarters covered the cost of materials, even leaving some left over for replacing personal property.

That left nothing, however, to restock the lost merchandise. Since most suppliers wouldn't ship before payment was received, Cady talked with Shawna and she agreed with him to donate still another wagon load of ore to the cause. Another trip to the cabin with a fresh crew of helpers found the ore waiting for the mules to pull it out and load it. John had spent the week working but lacked the mules to bring the ore to the surface.

With the mules, wagon, and many eager hands the ore was quickly loaded. Helen and John elected to make the trip down with the men, wanting to support their friends and help where they could. There was a kinship among many but an urgency among others to have a place to purchase supplies necessary for the quickly approaching winter. They arrived at the mill amid cheers, quickly unloading the ore and scattering to their various chores.

Thus far the new Merc was a shell, heated by the now notorious stove, but without a single item of merchandise in stock. The men worked inside putting up shelving and cupboards in anticipation of merchandise. As quickly as the value of the ore was tallied, the voucher was deposited and an order went out via telegraph. Much of the initial stock would come from Salt Lake City via rail and should be delivered in less than a week. Food stores would come first, while other items from suppliers further east would take more time.

The peal of the church bell Sunday morning welcomed a tired but proud community to worship. Many, if not most of those in the pews had worked long and hard in the reconstruction of the Merc during the previous week. Orville appropriately chose a theme of sharing for his sermon. At altar call three came forward to receive salvation, all three had worked on the project and had seen God's grace in action first hand. It felt like a time of renewal for all involved and a feeling of contentment pervaded the town.

October welcomed the first snow to the valley floor while the higher elevations already sported a couple of feet. John and Helen had returned home with provisions, taking the wagon and mules with them. The Merc, while still lacking some stock, was doing a whirlwind business in an effort to fill cupboards and pantries all across the surrounding area. The Millers were comfortable in the Days home, grateful for the break in the harsher routine at the claim.

Twice they had ridden up to visit for the day, checking to make sure Helen and John were doing well. Cady could see why their loved had endured through disappointment, separation, and pain. They acted like children experiencing their first love; arm in arm, sharing glances and knowing smiles as they went about their day together.

The Sheriff's job became routine and uneventful, with folks mostly keeping to themselves and inside to avoid the cold. Ben went back to work at the mill part-time while helping Cady part-time as well. By mid-month the weather had turned unseasonably cold and the streams frozen solid under a blanket of snow. Cady did a good deal of checking up on the older folks in town, making sure they weren't lacking food or fuel. He and others from the church often would spend hours splitting, stacking and carrying firewood.

Shawna had her hands full with Faith, showing, teaching, reading to her, and answering a thousand questions each day. They saw less and less of Kate during the week but made a point of spending Sundays as a family, often including Stephen, Ben, and Phil in their dinner plans. Cady could see that there was little difference whether in town or at the claim, circumstance forced folks to pay attention to detail and face life head on.

A barn dance was scheduled for Halloween, to usher in the winter that had already arrived. It gave opportunity to gather and visit for those who had been forced inside by the cold. The snow had stopped falling, leaving less than 12 inches underfoot, but the bite of the wind continued to chill to the bone to anyone forced outside.

Logging had ceased for the season, with some having brought the last loads of logs to town to sell for firewood rather than lumber. They had set up a chop mill at the edge of town where the dry logs were blocked, then hauled away in wagons for sale. Cady noted that it had only been a year since the last barn dance that resulted in the events leading to his near death, and the deaths of two men. That lingering thought brought back that familiar sense of dread with it.

John and Helen arrived in town unexpectedly on horseback, the buggy not rugged enough to brave the snow and winter roads. As Cady and Shawna opened their own house up to them, it felt rather odd, but good at the same time to see them. Shawna worried if she had made their home too much hers and might offend Helen, but Helen countered with, "you should see what I've done with yours."

As they both laughed, the tension was gone and they visited like old friends. John asked how the job was going, with Cady describing the lack of marshaling but the task of babysitting.

John nodded. "Some need more care than others for sure."

The snow at the mine was over three feet in some places, less in others. John went on to explain how the crib was working out for feeding the livestock and especially how nice it was not to have to shovel snow to go to bed at night. "Bad enough to shovel my way to the privy," he laughed. They only stayed the one night, wanting to get back to the livestock and beat any new snowfall.

At the dance, Cady made himself conspicuous, keeping watchful eyes on the crowd. Ben, however, joined in the revelry without gun or badge, but watching and listening as well. Al joined Cady and shared an idea with him that he had just perfected. A wagon was nothing new, likewise a sleigh, but Al had found a quick way to turn the wagon into a sleigh by removing the wheels, then using the existing axles and steering on which to mount runners. He was hoping that would give the wagon and the sleigh more utility year 'round.

Cady was impressed, asking if his own wagon was a good candidate for the conversion and if the weight hauled would be reduced. Al said that it could be converted quickly and easily by two men, but he believed it would haul the same load over the snow. He had hoped to use Cady's wagon as his first trial until he reminded him it was still at the cabin.

There were high spirits among those at the dance, many still feeling the comradeship from their part in rebuilding the Merc. Inside the music played while outside a bonfire kept many warm as they discussed the weather and other topics of special interest. Mayor Fitch sidled up next to Cady with his wife on his arm exchanging pleasantries before joining the crowded dance floor. Harless and Catherine changed partners with Orville and Sarah, then Al and Linda, as they made the square with the Mayor.

Cady wished that John and Helen had been able to stay on another day and join them. He finally gave a nod to Ben and took his place on the dance floor with Shawna. Ben and Phil took a breather while keeping an eye on the crowd. Unlike the last year, when the weather had been mild, few strayed long outside in the bitter wind to imbibe. That more coffee and tea was drunk than alcohol, making the likelihood of fights far less, pleased the Sheriff a great deal.

At first Cady just noticed a knot of men gathered at the barn door, then he could overhear their excited voices. He excused himself from Shawna, joining them only to find there had been an accident at the mill. Two men had been badly hurt when a conveyor collapsed while loading ore onto the waiting train. Cady quieted the music, then made a hasty announcement telling the crowd what little he knew and asking for volunteers to accompany him to the mill.

A dozen or more men joined him, leaving Ben to keep an eye on the crowd. They piled into a couple of wagons and quickly left. The night shift only worked when the train over-nighted in town, then only employing a skeleton crew. Stephen, Burt, and a young apprentice had been on duty when the accident occurred. Burt had been buried in the ore and rubble during the collapse. When Stephen had gone to help him, timbers had fallen on him also, pinning him underneath them. It was the young man who had ran run for help after failing to be able to release the men.

Someone had gone for Doc, who arrived at the same time as the rescue crew. Cady assessed the situation, first having the remaining timbers secured to prevent them from falling as well, then dispatching men to begin digging and moving the debris aside. He worked along-side Doc, assisting him as he could, to restrict bleeding and to prevent additional injury to Stephen. Burt was unconscious and nearly buried under tons of rock and wood, as the crew rushed to free him.

Cady noted that Stephen's broken leg bone showed through the skin and was bleeding badly. Smitty worked quickly to stop the blood-flow, then treated wounds to his head and left arm before returning to immobilize the leg. Finally Doc gave instruction to several men who moved him to a waiting litter, where he was warmly wrapped in blankets. Doc's attention now turned to Burt who had been partially unearthed, but expert fingers noted no pulse, his stethoscope no heart-beat. Burt had been killed in the initial collapse.

All at once the scene was flooded with others from the dance, Kate principal among them, all wanting to get a look or help if they could. Cady moved the crowd firmly out of the way, telling them what he knew as he did so. Turning to Kate, he told her that Stephen was alive but badly injured, soon to be moved to the doctor's office, promising to ask Doc if she could ride along. Several men lifted Stephen, who had lost consciousness, into a wagon where he could lie flat. Doc joined him in the wagon with Kate, while Cady took the wagon slowly across the snow as the crowd followed. Behind them Al, Harless, and others continued to excavate Burt's lifeless body.

Eager hands took Stephen inside, following Doc's instruction, lying him on the work table, before being ushered out. Both Cady and Kate stayed on, offering what help they could as they watched Smitty deftly ply his trade. Talking as much to himself as to them, Doc explained what his was doing and the order in which it was done, seeming to organize his priorities as he went. Checking the heartbeat, he nodded encouragingly, then administered something made from opium for the pain. It was plain that Doc would need additional help if he were to reset the leg without further damaging surrounding tissues and blood vessels.

Smitty spoke clearly but in a low tone to Kate, asking if she could assist in repositioning the wound. She nodded, eyes wide. Doc slowly and carefully asked a second time, describing what she would need to do, again asking if she was up to the task. Again she nodded resolutely. Doc had her put on a gown, tie back her hair, and wash her hands carefully, before bringing her close to him across the table. Cady had recruited two husky young men, who were eager to help, and returned to the room.

Doc slowly and carefully explained what was expected of them, the order of how things must go, before asking them to look directly at the wound. Within seconds one of them fainted and fell to the floor, while the other reached out and caught him. Again Cady left and returned with another volunteer, and again the doctor repeated the message. This time the new man remained standing and ready to help.

Two men held Stephen's shoulders immobile while Cady had been assigned to the booted leg. Doc opened the wound up with a scalpel, asking that Kate use her fingers to pull the tissue away from the bone. Cady strained to keep a constant even pull as the bone was eased back between the tissues and into place by the doctor. Doc had placed a tourniquet above the wound to minimize blood loss, but still it filled with blood, causing the doctor to feel, rather than see, what he was doing. After what seemed like hours, but had been only minutes, Smitty let the men release the tension to Stephen's body.

He cleansed the wound with alcohol, mopped up blood, then inspected his work before releasing the tourniquet gradually. A pleased look affirmed that all was well. While the wound was bleeding, it was only bleeding superficially and even that quickly ceased as Doc expertly sewed up the wound.

Kate looked exhausted, drenched in sweat and blood, but smiled weakly as Doc complimented each of them. "He should be fine, won't walk for a good time, may limp a little, but all in all he's a lucky man."

Doc retrieved three wooden staves from his back room and asked Kate to wrap them in cloth. He then, with help, placed them on three sides of the leg, leaving the wound accessible to future treatment, and bound them securely in place. Stephen's arm was cut and badly bruised, requiring stitches before bandaging. As Doc inspected his head, he carefully used his thumb to inspect each eye, gauging the pupil and its reaction to the lamp as he passed it by. Satisfied that the wound was superficial, Doc washed and dressed the it before sitting down with a sigh.

"You folks need some sleep, me too. I'm going to ask you to go home now and rest. I'll ask Sarah or one of the other women to sit with him through the night," said the doctor. "They can wake me if something comes up." Looking directly at Kate, he continued, "tomorrow you come back and stay with him when you are not dead on your feet."

Kate started to object, but could see the wisdom in his plan.

By the time they returned to the barn dance it was breaking up. Cady gave an update to the curious, then took Shawna and Faith home to rest, dropping Kate off along the way.

It happened that Burt was a single man about whom little was known. At the funeral, testimony revealed he was a good worker, quiet and personable, but had no known family in the area. Several mused that they wished they had gotten to know him better. He was buried amid prayers and compliments to his character, the funeral paid for by the owner of the mill. Orville made a special point to remind those present that no man knows the day or the hour when he may die, thus all should accept the free gift of salvation before it happens.

Following the rebuilding of the Merc, the town enjoyed a time of optimism and fellowship. After the tragedy, the opposite was true, a pall fell over it, only to lift with the promise of Christmas soon approaching. November brought heavy snow but an easing of the cold. Stephen was able to go home ten days after the accident but required daily care. At first Ben moved in with him during his convalescence, staying nights, while Kate stayed days.

Then, on November 15th, a wedding ceremony was held at the church with friends and family present. Stephen was still unable to walk, hardly even able to stand with a crutch, long enough to say his "I do's." Shawna and Cady had never seen Kate look so beautiful or happy. Ben was working full time at the mill now and as a deputy only when Cady asked for a break. Kate had to rely upon the former school teacher the majority of the time, because of the necessary commitment needed for Stephen.

Having heard nor seen nothing from John and Helen for over a month, Cady and Al took a day to ride up with supplies and check on them. Shawna elected to stay home with Faith. When they arrived they were glad they did, John had taken ill a week before, leaving Helen to care for him and the animals all alone. Cady doubted that the cold air and long ride were a good choice for John. He and Al hooked up the wagon with a promise to return with Doc, then headed out the next morning, trailing their horses behind them. The trip proved long and difficult in the unbroken snow, but unladen they made it in four hours. In town, Al borrowed a single horse sleigh, then made preparations to take Doc back to the cabin with him the next day. Meanwhile, Cady stayed in town to man the Sheriff's office, while Ben returned to his job.

The light sleigh with the two men made good time, arriving at the cabin well before noon. Smitty appraised John's cough and listened to his chest, pronouncing pneumonia as a diagnosis. While serious, pneumonia was not fatal to a healthy person who followed his doctor's directions. Doc asked Helen to put a pot of water on the stove, and when it began to heat, he added a few drops of strong smelling oil. Before long the room was filled with the scent and John's cough had subsided some.

Together, Doc and Al had fashioned a cot downstairs with the head raised several inches on wooden blocks. As he lay down with his head raised, his cough diminished even further. The doctor recommended he continue to use the bed long after the cough had gone to prevent its return. He also suggested that they either return to town where they could be cared for or have someone come to help Helen out with the chores. Doc emphasized that John should stay inside and out of the cold air, wearing a bandana over his face even when walking to the privy.

Helen looked worried even with the cough subsided, asking the men for prayer and God's direction. Doc and Al left the following morning, after laying a hearty supply of firewood inside for the stove and over-feeding John's two horses. They left with a promise to return by the weekend to look in on them again.

In town several of the church's leaders met, including Doc, Cady, Orville, Harless, Mayor Fitch, their wives and others, to discuss how they might help. As they listened, Doc laid out the reality of the situation from a medical standpoint. Then Orville lead them in prayer, asking God for His answer, before they began discussion.

Just as everyone began offering suggestions, the door opened and the new pastor-in-training entered, unknowing of a meeting in progress. He attempted to excuse his intrusion, but before he could, he was invited in and asked to sit. William Williams was his given name, but of course he went by 'Bill'. Bill was in his early twenties, single, and eager to begin his career as a preacher. He told them that his family lived in the east but that he had felt called west to serve. Although he was small in stature, he was an articulate young man with an engaging smile and quick wit.

As the group resumed their discussion, laying out each possible scenario with its strong points and weaknesses, Bill interrupted again.

"I'll go," he said simply. "I'd be happy to help them out and get to know them better."

It was just that simple. No debates or long drawn out plans to shuttle volunteers back forth while trying to maintain life in two locations. Shawna was the first to pick up on the reality of God's answer to their prayers, but soon everyone marveled and thanked God for His provision.

Doc and Bill left town Saturday morning in the sleigh, with Bill's clothes and personal items tied on beside a bundle of salt pork and a few food staples. Smoke from the chimney welcomed them to the cabin where Helen greeted them at the door with a smile. John was already looking and acting stronger, but seemed grateful for Bill and his generous offer to stay. Bill laughed and promised to subject his captive audience to ongoing sermons as repayment. Doc's examination found John's lungs less congested but strongly cautioned him again, not to consider himself healed just because he started feeling better. Seeing no reason to delay, Doc had a quick bite of food, prayed and left for town alone.

Sunday morning's bell called believers from the warmth of their homes out into the blowing snow before making them feel blessed to enjoy the warmth and friendship inside the church. Sarah played hymns while the faithful worshiped and late-comers were seated. Orville began his sermon on God's faithfulness by recounting the events of the meeting and how God had answered their prayers. Amid many Amens, he asked Doc to stand and bring the congregation up to date on the Days' situation.

After service, Cady helped Stephen hobble to their buggy and get seated. He and Kate then invited Cady and Shawna to join them for supper. With all the recent events, they had not seen much of each other and had little time to visit. Thomas, Phil, and Ben were invited as well. Kate moved about the kitchen as though she had been there for years, taking delight in serving their first guests since marrying.

It had been two months, more or less, since the accident at the mill, but Stephen seemed no closer to walking. He spoke of the lessening of pain and the healing of the visible wound but told his audience that Doc would not let him put weight on it yet. During supper, Kate said she had been able to return to school, enjoying her teaching position once again. Cady noticed that Ben and Phil sat quietly, holding hands and speaking to each other in whispers.

Thomas spoke finally, "little sister, you've been quiet, what's going on in your life?"

Uncharacteristically Phil blushed before looking toward Ben for reassurance, "Ben has asked me to marry him, and I've said yes."

The room erupted in laughter with everyone then speaking at once.

"About time!"

"Congratulations!"

"When?" were the remarks.

"Well," she said, "we've discussed Christmas day. We can celebrate our union and Jesus' birth together each year."

On the ride home, Shawna took Cady's hand, placing it on her stomach just as the baby moved.

"I think she's excited for them," she said.

Cady just nodded and smiled.

Christmas day, thankfully, did not come on a Sunday that year, allowing the church to concentrate on the birth of the Savior first, followed by the blessing of marriage. With housing at a premium, Thomas graciously moved out of the home he had purchased and shared with Phil, into the boarding house. Ben and Phil agreed to pay the extra expense and have him over often.

Cady and Doc made another trip to check on John and Helen, bagging a fat doe on the trip in. The fresh meat was welcomed with relish since their supply had dwindled with three to feed, and John unable to hunt. Doc and Cady brought them up to date on the recent events in town over a supper of fresh deer liver and onions.

It appeared that both Helen and John had unofficially adopted Bill, treating him like the son they had hoped to have. Bill had, in turn, found great joy in studying the Bible with them and learning about their lives. Once again Doc was pleased with John's progress, and once again warned him to stay inside, out of the cold.

Bill and Cady went out together to feed the stock early the next morning, returning with several loads of firewood. On his second trip Cady spotted a pair of fool hens high in a spruce tree. He returned with the double barrel, bringing them both down with a single shot. Bill was both amazed and impressed, having had no father figure in his life since moving out west. Cady vowed to put bring he and Ben together in the future, where they could learn from one another. Helen was overjoyed at the fowl, having tired of a deer meat and salt pork diet, wishing they could stay longer and enjoy the grouse with dumplings. Doc took a list from Helen to be filled at the Merc when they returned.

The Mayor and council affirmed Cady's position as full-time Sheriff at the beginning of the year, setting aside money for a full-time deputy. Cady had been paying Ben from his own salary, since he had gone full-time at the mill, whenever it became necessary to use him.

Mid-January found Shawna in discomfort, visiting Smitty for reassurance, which he promptly provided. He had not seen her in an official capacity since her second month, she having had no reason to bother him.

Doc beamed as he delivered the news to her. "They should be born in about a month."

Shawna nodded her confirmation, then repeated, "they?"

"Yes," said Doc, "you're having twins."

Moments later she waddled her way at maximum speed down the boardwalk to the Sheriff's office to deliver the news.

"Two," Cady repeated, looking stunned. "We're going to have two?"

"Yes, that is what Doc says, he heard two heartbeats," Shawna repeated.

They had not eaten at the boarding house for several months, keeping to themselves and out of the cold. But tonight they wanted to celebrate with their friends. Cady rode up to ask Catherine if she had room at her table, and finding she did, he invited Orville, Sarah, Al, Linda, Ben, Phil, Kate, Stephen and Doc to join them. Harless had to improvise a second table to accommodate them but was pleased to do so. Cady sat at the head, being the benefactor and organizer, with Shawna by his side. Only they and Doc knew the reason for the gathering. After blessing the food Cady stood, hesitating just a moment before announcing the good news. Faith, oblivious to the goings on, laughed and chattered as though she understood everything.

The food was fit for the occasion with everyone eating to excess, then many taking a helping of cobbler also. No one was ready when the door opened with a messenger announcing that there had been a shooting at the saloon. Cady, Ben, and Doc stood together before Cady asked Ben to stay and enjoy the party, promising to send for him if needed.

On the saloon floor lay a man unknown to Cady, a 'fancy Dan' by his dress and a gambler by the look of him. Blood was pooling behind his left shoulder and he appeared unconscious. Doc got right to work, finding a pulse then working to stop the bleeding by applying pressure to the wound. Across the room a local was being restrained by the crowd. They had also taken possession of his gun following the incident. When Doc assured him that he had the wounded man under control Cady crossed to the man.

Without waiting to be asked, the man volunteered, "he was dealing seconds, cheating me all night."

Although Cady was not a gambling man, he understood the complaint. The dealer was holding the better top card for himself, while giving the poorer 'second' card to his opponent. He had seen this done before, either by a card mechanic in a heads up game, or with an accomplice who was fed the better hand by the dealer. Cady looked at those gathered before asking for their witness.

"That true?" he asked.

While several chose to remain silent, two affirmed the story, "cleaned us both out, not until we got up from the table could we see why he was so lucky."

Cady looked directly at the assailant, "did he draw on you?"

"I didn't see his gun, but when I called him on it, he reached inside his vest." "

Cady called over his shoulder to the doctor while keeping his eyes on the man, "Doc, is he packing inside his vest?"

"Got a derringer in an inside pocket," answered the doctor.

"Thanks Doc, you need help moving him?"

"Yes, in a couple of minutes I could use about four willing men," was his reply.

"Let him go," Cady ordered to the crowd holding the man. "What's your name?" he asked speaking directly to the card player.

"Tom Irons," was the man's reply, "I work at the lumber yard."

"Well Tom," said Cady, speaking slowly and clearly, "I see no reason to hold you, but I am going to hold onto your gun for a while. You can pick it up at my office in thirty days." Turning to the two witnesses he asked, "how much didja loose?"

One declared $50 and the other $40.

Cady asked them, "are you family men?"

Their reply was affirmative.

"Can your family afford to loose that much money?"

Both men shook their heads, not speaking.

Cady then spoke to the crowd at large, "men, you've witnessed a man nearly killed, and three others fleeced of money they couldn't afford to risk. I hope you will take that into consideration the next time you sit down at a table." Cady scooped the money off the table, handing each man his due, then holding up the balance he declared, "this will go into the charity fund. Doc needs you, Tom, your two friends, and one other to move the 'sharp' to his office."

The four men lifted the gambler and carefully carried him down the boardwalk and into the doctor's office, while Cady followed. Doc elected to stay with his patient, whom Cady had handcuffed to the table.

Cady returned to the boarding house to find only Shawna, Kate and Stephen still remained. He recounted the events to them before dropping them off on his way home with Shawna and Faith. As they lay in bed together talking softly, Cady was pleased at how the native culture allowed Shawna to accept hardship and danger more easily than his own. Although he knew she worried about him, she was more able to deal with his job as Sheriff than Helen had John. He supposed that life as an Indian held little promise of a long, peaceful life, making danger less frightening to them.

On February 13th, a day before St. Valentine's Day, Shawna and Cady were blessed with Hope and Charity, just as Shawna had promised over a year before. In total, they weighed twelve pounds, one just under six, the other just over. Cady could not tell them apart so Shawna tied a ribbon on Hope's toe. Both girls showed the strong influence of their mother's heritage as had Faith, with dark hair and eyes.

While Mother Nature had provided enough equipment for feeding two, Shawna found it impossible to feed both at once. It became necessary for Cady to frequently take time during the day to go home, caring for one while the other nursed, or holding Faith while mom rested. Often Phil would also drop by and help out, as her schedule permitted. The Miller family thanked God frequently that they were not living life alone back at the cabin. By the second month, they had a routine which worked for them, but left Shawna time for little else but the children.

Every couple of weeks Al and Ben alternated taking Doc up to the property to check up on Helen, John, and Bill. John seemed to have fully recovered and was pronounced able again but was reluctant to allow Bill to leave. The three enjoyed a deep and abiding friendship, bonding in love and enjoying God's Word together daily. Bill refused several offers of a ride home saying "maybe next trip."

The Mercantile was back in full swing, catering gratefully to the needs of its benefactors. However, the weather had turned cold again, with a bitter March wind blowing constantly up the valley. Snow evaporated rather than melted, with little fresh falling, as it settled and was packed down.

Upon his release from medical care, the gambler found himself in custody, waiting for the circuit judge to come through and pronounce sentence. Often because of the delay between his visits, that sentence would be time served. With the town hunkered down waiting for the spring thaw, the Sunday worship call gave friends and neighbors an excuse to leave the warmth of their homes to meet and visit. Faith regularly showed off her sparkling white teeth to anyone who would look and eagerly pointed out her new sisters.

There had been considerable excitement and consternation when word had come about the train, which ran from Salt Lake, being blown off the tracks somewhere south of the Idaho border. Apparently heavy snows, coupled with high wind gusts, had caused the accident. While only two were killed, several more were injured and the lifeline to the northwest was cut for several days. Stock at the Merc was sufficient to see the community through the crisis, with only a few items running completely out. Families were used to borrowing or making do in times of shortage.

As the Miller clan, now three separate families, gathered one evening to share supper, Cady brought up the subject of the Sheriff's job. Although he and John had not reached a final conclusion on the matter, Cady was certain that John had no intention to returning seasonally as full time Sheriff. The most they could hope for might be he to accept a deputy position in time of need. There was a general agreement around the table. Ben stated that he had learned as much from him during his frequent visits to the mine.

"I'd like you and Phil to discuss the offer that I am going to make privately," said Cady before continuing. "I'm going need to start working the claim soon, but cannot be in two places at one time. Shawna and I have talked about it and have agreed that while the twins are small, she needs the help of family and friends. For her and I to go back alone, trading places with John and Helen, won't work."

Shawna nodded as did Kate.

He continued, "I haven't considered that Stephen and Kate might want involvement, up to this point, because of his injuries. But, we are family and everyone should have equal say. Ben, would you consider moving up and working the claim full time? As you can guess it comes with both upsides and downsides. Phil would need to take a leave from the bank, if they'd let her, and you from the mill. You'd no longer have to pay rent and Thomas could have his house back. You'd keep what you dug from the mine, God willing you could lay up quite a nest egg by fall to build your own house in town or whatever you choose."

He paused to let it all sink in, before continuing, "Ben knows, and

Phil would soon find out, that the life there together is wonderful six to eight months of the year, but difficult during the winter months."

Kate spoke up, "Stephen is still unable to work, but praise God, is walking now with only a cane. Doc is not sure if he will ever be able to return to the mill full time."

Everyone listened, then nodded.

"If Ben and Phil decide to try it this year while school is out, we might join them."

"Stephen added, "only if they want us and only if we can add some value to help pay our keep."

"Pie?" asked Shawna, purposely interrupting the conversation, allowing them all time to think.

Cady nodded, noting that she was getting good at reading people. While they ate, ideas and thoughts flew around the table. Cady made it clear that at least until the twins were weaned, they'd stay in town and he would work the Sheriff's job full time. He was becoming comfortable with the fact that God was indeed in charge. Another thought arose that maybe Stephen might serve as deputy if Ben was away. When they broke up and each went to their own homes, it was clear that John and Helen should have been included in the discussion.

The Olsen family lived out south of town, they owned a nice covered two-seat buggy that would provide enough room for the women and babies, with Stephen driving. Cady borrowed it for the day, leaving right after church, he and Ben on horseback leading the way.

Twice the men stopped and pulled dead-fall off the trail that had been taken down by heavy snow. Previous visits had been on horseback which allowed these trees to be easily skirted. Stephen and Phil had never been there before and Faith had been too small to remember. Shawna and Kate were amazed at how much had been added and changed since they'd been there last.

When John and Helen greeted them warmly, they felt like it was truly a homecoming in a deeper sense than just the location. Cady made it clear that they could not stay overnight and, with the children, would not risk traveling after dark. That made it necessary to keep the visit short.

Both John and Helen looked well, the cabin and surrounding area looked like paradise, clothed in a winter blanket. Everyone was happy to see that Bill had become a valued and necessary part of the family. The women had known the Days would not be prepared for guests and had taken precaution to bring cooked food with them. After Bill blessed the food they all ate heartily, catching up on the latest news. John bragged about the elk hanging in a tree, taking it with a single shot, his first in twenty years. Then came discussion of the business at hand, with Helen and John listening quietly before commenting.

"Sheriff here," John said, pointing to Cady, "is going to need a place to stay with his growing family, while keeping the peace. Seems to me that'd be a shame to go back and leave them on the street."

As everyone smiled at the picture, he continued, "after I got over my cough, Helen and I have enjoyed every moment up here, especially when we got company."

Bill spoke next, "me too, it has been a wonderful experience which I will always cherish. John and Helen have become like my own parents."

That brought smiles.

Ben looked at Phil before speaking up, "we have discussed it together, and with the mill, and bank. We think we'd like to give it a try before we get too old or start a family."

Everyone laughed, looking at Cady and Shawna.

Stephen spoke next for he and Kate. "We think the best course for us may be to stay in town and help Shawna out. I'd also like to see if the deputy job is something I could handle."

As the discussion deepened, it had become apparent that God was guiding them and that they seemed to be listening.

While the group said their goodbyes and piled into the buggy, they had agreed that Ben and Phil would return and join John, Helen, and Bill at the cabin, while Cady and family would stay put in the full-time Sheriff position. Stephen would begin learning the duties of a deputy while Kate continued to help Shawna with the children. Bill seemed eager to have more added to his flock and to help Ben in the mine.

On the return trip they were fortunate to see two ermine playing alongside the stream and a snowshoe rabbit in the trail ahead of them. The ground remained frozen, allowing the trip to be made with little difficulty. Ben told Cady that he planned to return with the mules, wagon, and supplies before the melt made the ground soft and the trip difficult. Cady noted to himself that the city kid had done well, to learn in less than two years what took many a lifetime.

Cady and Stephen stood before Mayor Fitch and laid out the whole plan just as the families had agreed. In his usual manner he listened, took notes, and asked few questions until they finished speaking. He nodded, then looked directly at Stephen.

"You feel up to the job?" he asked pointedly. Before continuing, and without waiting for response, "has your leg healed? Can you ride a horse?"

Stephen hesitated, "yes, Doc has given me the nod, but has told me it will be weak for some time, and I may always have a limp. 'Far as riding, I am not sure, haven't felt the need to try it yet."

"Fair enough, good answer," Fitch said, leaning forward toward him, "I trust the Sheriff's judgment and will take the matter to the town council, with my recommendation to hire you full time."

Before wearing a badge or gun, Cady began as he had with Ben, explaining the job and proper moral values which made one worthy to serve. Stephen, already a Christian, had little trouble understanding and agreeing with him. He repeated what John had told him about using force only as last resort, common sense always as the first, best option. They walked mostly, with Stephen struggling at first to keep up. Within a week his leg strength had improved noticeably, although he continued to limp.

Mayor Fitch, with due ceremony, affirmed his position as deputy by swearing him in. To this point, Cady had never seen Stephen wear a gun, or seen him shoot. He had only asked him the cursory question, "can you shoot?" As it turned out, he could shoot quite well, but was left handed and cross-drew his gun, wearing it on his right hip and reaching across himself to draw it. As they grew to know each other they became friends as well as relatives.

With April now approaching, Ben and Phil left town, the ore wagon loaded with food and personal gear, the big mare trailing behind them. Amid hugs and promised visits, they headed up to join John, Helen, and Bill at the mine. Al and Ben had installed the runners on the wagon turning it into a sleigh, then putting the wheels in the wagon to convert it back when the weather warmed. The mules pulled the sleigh easily over the snow and through soft or muddy areas. Ben hoped to get a load or two of ore to town while there was snow and the ground still frozen.

Everything came in twos, when Hope caught a cold, so did Charity, when one was fussy, it woke the other so she could fuss also. Cady felt guilty going to work, knowing he had it easier than Shawna, who was on call 24 hours a day. He thanked God for his sister, who came daily, helping to relieve the strain. Faith, now in her 'terrible twos', was beginning to miss the lavish attention she had previously enjoyed, with the twins now being the new focus of attention.

The town was beginning, like a bear from hibernation, to awaken and stir, as the sun shone more and snow receded in the valley. The mill, which had been closed much of the winter, was gearing up, doing maintenance and repairs, in anticipation of the approaching season.

In nearby Atlanta, a smaller mining community inhabited mostly by confederate sympathizers, the mines were already open and piling up ore to be delivered when the road cleared. Because of the terrain, they were cut off from the outside nearly half of the year, except by saddle horse or snowshoes.

Ben and John arrived together early Monday morning over a frozen, muddy road, interspersed with snow and ice. They dumped the load at the mill before stopping by the Merc, and Sheriff's office to visit. Cady was out but Stephen was there to welcome them. They quickly caught up next door at the café, over coffee and warm cinnamon rolls.

The women had become close friends, and Bill was gaining skill in the outdoors as well as helping in the mine. The three of them had pulled out a second load of ore before leaving with the first, making it likely they would be returning within another day or so. Ben was enjoying the ease of the sled as opposed to running the wagon in mud and the sink holes which would soon blossom as spring came. He made a mental note to congratulate Al on his ingenuity.

Cady arrived just as they were finishing up, having gone home to help Shawna with the twins for a few minutes, so they sat back down and shared another cup.

Both John and Ben were eager to get permission and advice from him concerning an idea they had come up with. They wanted to cut a hole in the floor, install a trap door, and a pull-down ladder for access to the upstairs. Cady immediately endorsed the idea, remembering that he had considered an emergency exit himself before moving to town. He also reminded them to purchase a pair of hinges that he had robbed from the old cabin when they cut in the new door. It all seemed so long ago now, though it was really just less than two years.

Taking Cady aside, Ben wanted to get his views on how to divvy up the voucher money from the ore. He said he needed direction as how to be fair, knowing the other men had worked hard. Cady thought for a moment before responding, then answered in the same way Jesus had instructed His disciples concerning the proper amount of tithe.

He also recalled a verse that said, "don't muzzle the ox who grinds the wheat." It wasn't the answer that Ben was looking for because it forced him to look inside himself and to God for answers. Borrowing horses, the two men made the rounds of the town, quickly saying hello to friends, before hitching up and heading back home.

– TWELVE –

In the East, the war raged on with the Union army holding the upper hand, but much of the West remaining detached from it. While many held strong convictions, they were not directly involved, if not for friends or family. It often inspired heated debate and less often a fist fight, as tempers flared at the saloon. It was not uncommon in the warmer months to have confederate soldiers come to town with ore and mix it up with the locals, after having a too much to drink. Cady made an effort to make his presence known when they were in town to help avoid gun play.

He had enjoyed long debates with Orville on the subject of slavery, which occupied a big part in the Bible. Neither man claimed to know the heart of God, but both agreed that a man, any man, regardless of skin color, was made in God's image and should be treated as a man and not a possession. That, they supposed, made them sympathetic to the North.

Ben and Bill made the trip with the ore this time, returning before Cady could visit long with them. They supposed that they would have to reinstall the wheels for the next trip and fight the mud as spring rains had began begun in earnest. The twins were nearing three months now and were beginning to eat soft foods, much to Shawna's joy. Kate was looking forward to the end of the school year for a break in her routine. Neither Harless and Catherine, Al and Linda, nor Orville and Sarah had been highly visible during the severe winter months. Social lives in the town were often limited to church functions or weddings and funerals, until spring thaw.

By June, logging and mining were in full operation, with mud and snow still hampering travel in some locations. The mill was busy, keeping the train running two days a week hauling ore and timber to the lower elevations. Ben, Bill, and John were averaging about a trip every other week with ore, occasionally bringing the women to town for an overnight visit when they came. Stephen walked with confidence now, though limping badly after he had been on his feet a few hours. Cady had come to trust his judgment the same as he had Ben, not worrying when he needed to take time away from the office.

Faith was putting words together now in both Shoshoni and English, sometimes in the same sentence, causing everyone to laugh. One Sunday after church, Cady overheard Kate and Phil conspiring together to trade places. She and Stephen would spell Ben and Phil off for a week to enjoy a change of scenery.

Back in town, Ben rejoined his uncle as his deputy while Phil spent a great deal of time with Shawna and the children. Ben confided that he had worked out a financial agreement with John and Bill, who labored with him in the mine, and also that he and Phil had saved quite a nest egg. Phil confided to Shawna that she and Ben were eager to begin a family and hoped they might have a baby soon. Although the week went rapidly, it was an enjoyable change for both families.

John, Helen, and Bill had made the trip to town Saturday to stock up on provisions, reacquaint with friends, and hear pastor Orville's message. When they all met on Sunday at church service, Kate and Stephen looked refreshed as did Ben and Phil. The second service was followed by a pot luck that made the reunion perfect for everyone.

Orville's sermon was on the subject of 'surrender', of allowing one-self to be truly governed by God. The Pastor noted that bending to God's Lordship is one of the most difficult lessons a Christian has to learn, and then relearn daily. Cady was amazed at how the sermon seemed to be pointing at him personally and mentioned it after the service. Only then did he find out that many had felt the same, that they were also being convicted by their attitude of stubborn independence.

After a short conversation with Shawna, Cady approached John with the idea that he might take responsibility for the town, over seeing Stephen for a week or two while they returned with Ben and Phil to the mine.

After last year he knew that he must be in town for the 4th of July celebration, but was ready for a break. All were in agreement when they left town together on Monday morning for what would be the first time the twins had seen their home. Cady had almost forgotten how spacious the cabin felt compared with the John's home in town. He was also pleased with the improvements which had been made in his absence. John had proved to be quite a craftsman, giving attention to detail and design. Ben pointed out the escape ladder that afforded access and exit to the bedrooms upstairs. Two deer were in the meadow with their fawns when the group arrived, causing a squeal of delight from Faith.

They spent the first day unpacking, relaxing and remembering before enjoying a hot supper together, followed by a soak in the warm springs. The twins and Faith loved the warm water. John and Helen had left the house in good order needing nothing fixed, cleaned or repaired, so Cady and Ben went right to work in the mine.

When they stopped for lunch they had made good progress, both men enjoying the hard labor. And so it went day after day, weather warm, food good, relationships growing and deepening. At the end of the first week the wagon was loaded, with a second load nearly ready to haul to the surface. Both women elected to remain at the cabin while the men went to town and returned the same day. That early evening ride rewarded the men with two grouse for supper the following day.

Relaxing, Cady could feel the years falling away from him as the reality of the responsibility of his job became clear to him. That knowledge made him respect John all the more for having shouldered the burden alone for five years. Returning from having deposited a second load of ore, it was decided they stay a second week. In town John and Stephen had things well in hand while the women were enjoying the social life that town provided.

Ben and Cady took a break from the mine to enjoy a change of pace at midweek, choosing rather to haul some dead timber in for firewood. With July just around the corner, all but the highest peaks were bare of snow. Cady decided to work the trail with the fresno one more time before returning it to its owner in town. With regrets, they left Ben and Phil behind, taking the wagon filled with ore to town, the fresno tied on top. Faith, as the older child, was privileged to ride in her father's lap, while Shawna wrestled with the twins all the way to town.

Before unloading the ore, Cady took Shawna and the children home, all of them badly needing a nap. Then he dropped off the fresno, thanking them for its use. Finally, he left the ore at the mill, deposited his voucher, unhitched the mules from the wagon, then went to the jail. He found both men enjoying a game of cards as the afternoon sun threatened to put them to sleep.

"Forgot how easy the job was," joked John. "A guy should feel guilty to take money for doin' it."

"Yup," agreed the deputy," "unless you're healin' from a gunshot that is."

They all laughed.

Cady turned to them, "which of you lazy bums are gonna help poor Ben out up at the claim?"

"John quipped, "Stephen and I here were about to draw high card to see who has to go to work."

"You better check with the wives first, see who is stayin' and who is goin'," was Cady's answer.

The three families met for dinner at the café where the subject was discussed and decided. Bill had elected to stay in town for a time, working with Orville to improve his preaching skills, while John and Helen were anxious to return to the claim. But it was expected that they'd return soon with Ben and Phil for the 4th Fourth of July celebration. Although Idaho was nearly 30 years from statehood, it still enjoyed celebrating the event as a territory of the United States.

"How'd it go?" Cady asked Stephen next day at the jail.

"Went fine, 'cept for some southern boys who came dressed in gray, lookin' for trouble." He continued, "Sheriff saw them comin' in, figured they'd be lookin' for a fight. Had me come in quiet by the back door 'o the saloon with the double barrel and just stand there. Was four of them, drinkin' and getting loud, pushin' the locals around a little. When the Sheriff came in the front door they got even louder, showin' off like. I thought for a while they might draw down on him."

Cady nodded, feeling anger and anticipation, while waiting for the story to unfold.

"That's when he says, calm as you like, "Deputy, these boys are gonna lay their sidearms on the bar, would you pick them up for me?" Up to now they didn't know I's there. Quick as they saw me with the double behind them, they got real quiet and accommodat'n."

"No trouble?" asked Cady.

"Nope, we walked them down the street, locked 'em up a couple of days, and let 'em go. Kept their iron though. I 'spect the Sheriff will give them back next time they come through, if they mind their business," said the deputy.

Cady was in awe of John and his ability to maintain the peace in the face of conflict. He secretly wondered how he might have handled the situation. From reports, it appeared that the south was losing the war, Cady surmised that the Confederate soldiers locally were taking their frustration out on whomever they viewed as their foes. He promised to discuss the situation with both John and the Mayor, guessing the problem was not resolved.

"How's the mine doin'?" came the question, throwing Cady off guard.

"Fine," Cady answered, "looks like the vein is holdin' up for the time being."

"We enjoyed it up there, I think the exercise was good for my bad leg too," Stephen volunteered.

"I hear ya there," answered the Sheriff, "I find the hard work more satisfyin' than sittin' here waitin' for something bad to happen. It's nicer here for Shawna though, with the babies and all."

Independence Day celebrations were scheduled for Thursday of the week, with a barbecue during the day down on Main Street sponsored by the business community, and fireworks at night. A pit had been dug with the anticipation of roasting a whole beef and two hogs in it. It was Tuesday and the fire was already burning, heating the ground and building up a bed of coals in which the meat would be buried overnight.

Visitors had been pouring into town for several days, filling up all accommodations and putting a strain on available food and drink supplies. Mayor Fitch and Cady had met with the city council to discuss the possibility of checking firearms, but found their plan too little and too late. It should have been done as they entered town rather than trying to disarm them after they were already spread out. Cady hoped to conscript both John and Ben, when they arrived, to help him keep an eye on things.

As it turned out, John and Helen reoccupied their own home with Cady and family while Ben and Phil joined Thomas at his house for the ceremonies. While the women visited and fretted, the memories of last year still fresh in their minds, the men laid plans to work two shifts, John and Stephen during the day with Cady and Ben during the night. On Wednesday, Cady was forced to start filling the jail as high spirits and hard liquor took its toll on the revelers, causing multiple fights. Disarmed, they were released with stern warnings the next morning to rejoin the festivities. However, many returned to the saloon where they started all over.

Daytime activities on Thursday included games and contests, speeches and acknowledgments, horse races and pulling contests, weight lifting and for the loggers, pole climbing and ax throwing. As the day wore on, some contests became heated and needed the Sheriff's intervention to prevent escalation in to fights or worse. As the meat was pulled from the ground, volunteers cut and served it with side dishes and soft drinks to the waiting public.

John and Stephen became the necessary crowd control when the bar crowd spilled into the street, many not wanting to wait their turns in line for the food. Both Cady and Ben came early for their shift, wanting to enjoy the food with their families before taking over the responsibility of the office.

However, they arrived just in time to help John and Stephen out with a pair of colored families who were being ridiculed by several men in gray. It turned out that they were the same four Confederates whom John had jailed previously. The men were told to leave town and not return or they would be re-jailed for a longer term.

While no one was naive enough to believe that this would be the last they would hear of the four, they lacked cause to proceed further, until laws had been broken. Mayor Fitch, John, and Cady spoke privately with the two families involved, promising to keep an eye out, while at the same time warning them to also be vigilant. Both lived south of town not far from the Olsen family who had loaned their sled to Cady earlier in the winter. The Mayor deputized two locals to keep an eye out for trouble, reporting directly to the Sheriff, but not carrying weapons.

As darkness fell, the crowds became less apparent, finding places off the street to celebrate. John and Stephen left to be with their families while promising to stand ready should they be needed, leaving only Cady and Ben to keep order. They broke up two arguments before they became fights, sending the participants home with warnings.

By 11 o'clock, most families were home in bed, and most rowdies back at the saloon and off the streets, making it easier to keep track of them. Cady had just stuck his head in the saloon, satisfying himself that things were under control, when he heard an explosion and saw fire south of town. He mounted the gelding, stopping briefly at the jail to apprise Ben of the situation, then left at full gallop. Taking the main road which ran north and south down the valley he was nearly to the turnoff when he was passed by four horses with riders going north. With only the moonlight, he could not recognize faces but noted their dress was gray military uniforms.

When he arrived, two small homes were wrapped in flames and several bodies lay in front of them, illuminated by the fire. A man, badly burned but alive, and one child had survived while the rest had become victims of the fire. The Olsens arrived just after him in their surrey, viewing the destruction, then rushing to the survivors to offer help. Cady could see that no part of either house could be saved, noting anyone still inside was already dead. He directed the Olsen family to take the victims to Doc, then lit out after the riders, stopping only long enough to grab Ben and a double barrel as he passed through town.

They rode hard, traveling northward at full speed, faster than a prudent rider would in the dark, but eager to make up for the lead the four had on them. Anger welled up in Cady, anger that he had not felt in years, more akin to rage. Even in the moonlight, the hoof prints in the mud of the four horses were easy to follow, fresh enough to still be filling with water. They couldn't ride and converse, so the two men just rode without discussion, unknowing of what they would do when they might overtake finally overtook the four.

As his anger quelled, thoughts filled Cady's mind; thoughts not of just himself, but also of his family, his future, his belief in God, of men already killed and those waiting ahead to kill or be killed. No answers, only questions flooded his consciousness. His mind was filled with feelings to the point of overload, but feelings were of no value to him. Decisions based upon feelings would give him false direction, he knew that. And so he prayed... for clarity, for guidance and direction, for help in overcoming his own selfish rage. Slowly, a peace came over him, he reigned in his horse and stopped.

With a questioning look, Ben followed suit asking, "something wrong, Uncle Cady?"

"No Ben, things are fine," his uncle answered, "we just need to take a deep breath and think this thing out." Ben nodded as Cady continued, "when we catch them, we'll likely either kill them or they us. Is that the way you see it?"

"I 'spect so," came Ben's answer.

"And then, are you ready to die?" Cady continued, "or ready to take a life knowing you have condemned him to certain hell?"

Ben seemed unsure of what the correct answer should be.

Cady spoke again, "truth is, if we play it smart, we can likely surprise them and take them without getting hurt. It seems to me that after what they did, they deserve it."

Ben found his tongue, "I agree."

"But," Cady said now making his point, "if we try to capture them and take them back to trial, things are likely to get dicey. We could get hurt or killed ourselves."

Again, Ben nodded his agreement.

"So, it comes down to faith, doesn't it, it always does," said Cady slowly. "Do we have faith to trust God to judge these men or will we make our own judgment and take our chances?"

As Cady was speaking, he was also listening, listening to himself speak God's words back to him.

Ben sat quietly, absorbing the message, then he spoke. "Seems like we done pretty good so far trustin' Him, guess we should keep on."

This time it was Cady who nodded. "Let's get after 'em then." he said as he spurred the gelding to a gallop.

Forty minutes later they rounded a turn in the road, only to find a horse lying beside the road with his rider pinned under him. Nearby, another horse, with it's rider still in the saddle, who seemed uncertain whether to flee or dismount and help. Cady noted both wore Confederate gray and both horses were lathered up from exertion.

"Your friend alive?" Cady asked.

The rider answered, "Think so, but he's busted up some, horse fell on him."

"Got a rope?" Cady asked again.

"Ya sure," the man answered pointing to the lasso tied just below the horn."

"Looks like the horse just gave out or broke his neck when he fell, lets get a rope on him," Cady said aloud to no one in particular. "Ben, when we lift up the horse's neck, pull the rider clear."

Ben nodded.

The rider tossed the loop to Ben, who had dismounted. Ben pulled it down over the horse's neck, nearly to its chest, before signaling the rider to dally the horn and ease the horse back. Cady remained mounted and ready to help where needed but said nothing more. Only a minute went by before Ben pulled the unconscious rider clear and announced the welcome news, "he's breathin'."

Cady swung a long leg over the saddle and dismounted away from the stranger. As he did so he pulled his .45 and said, "son, I need you to drop your pistol in the mud and dismount slowly, your friend needs your help."

The young soldier hesitated only a moment, then replied, "yes sir!" Cady could see he was just a boy, younger than Ben, still just a child.

Cady retrieved the gun, then spoke, "seems like your friends didn't have the loyalty that most military men do. It's good to see you's raised right."

"He's my brother," came the choked reply, "we joined together, don't have any other family."

By this time the man on the ground had his eyes open and was groaning in pain. It appeared that one leg was badly broken and some damage to his ribs as well. His brother was holding his head and talking softly to him, tears running down both cheeks.

"Ben," Cady said softly, "'pears were gonna need Doc and a wagon to get this boy back to town safe. Would you mind going to get him?" It was a gentle request rather than order. "I'll stay with the boys."

Ben first looked uncertain about leaving Cady alone but then realized he was not alone, he never had been.

"Should I bring help?" Ben asked, referring to a posse or Sheriff John.

"No, just bring the Doc and a fresh horse or two if you can. I'll be just fine." As Ben left, Cady extended his hand to the young man, "name's Cady, Cady Miller. I'm the Sheriff."

The boy took his hand, "Theodore Black, most folks call me Ted. This is my brother, Thomas."

"Tell me Ted, what happened back south of town," Cady asked quietly.

Ted looked stricken, then offered, "Griff and Duke wanted to have some more sport with the darkies after we was run outta town. Tom and I rode along with them. Griff's our sergeant, we followed him here from Georgia to get gold for the cause."

Cady nodded his understanding.

"Griff and Duke followed them home, then kicked in the door and began yellin' at 'em. Their neighbor musta heard and came to help, 'cause he and his family showed up right away. We stayed on the horses, didn't see what started it, but all of a sudden there was some shootin'. Then Griff took a coal oil lamp and started both houses on fire. By the time we left, the screamin' had quit and we followed them to here." His tears had resumed as he mentally relived the nightmare.

Tom had awoke while he was telling it and began to cry also. Tom seemed even younger than Ted to Cady, just a boy in his teens. He was not even wearing a gun. Cady unsaddled the dead horse, using it to support Tom's head and the blanket to cover his shivering body.

"I 'magine it'll take a couple of hours for Doc to get here," Cady began, "meantime, you got any water or food with you? Tom needs water."

Ted went to his horse, coming back with a military canteen and some hard tack, which he gave to his brother before covering him with his own coat. Tom began sobbing again.

"You hurtin' boy?" Cady asked.

Rather than answering, Tom asked, "are we gonna hang?"

Cady took a moment to compose himself before he answered the young man, "I don't expect you will, son. It's up to the judge to say though, what your part in it was, and up to God to sentence you. Do you boys know God?"

Cady learned after much discussion that both boys were from the Bible belt, both believing Baptists, both church goers before the war had taken their Ma and Pa. Cady encouraged them both to pray and ask for forgiveness while he left to find the makings for a fire.

The fire was burning down by the time Ben and Doc arrived with the surrey, two horses trailing behind it. Doc had brought not only medicine but also food, water and blankets. As Smitty bent to the task with Ted helping him, Ben and Cady discussed their plan for further pursuit of the remaining two men.

Cady told Ben the story as told by Ted, making both men believe that the two would come hard. They also thanked God that they had not come in with guns blazing and killed the two boys. As Doc headed back, Ted was holding Tom's head in his lap in the back of the surrey, unconscious from pain killer. Cady's gelding and Ted's horse followed behind the surrey on ropes.

Cady had learned that they were only a few miles from Atlanta and that there was no law enforcement there. He also was told that many of the miners were like Ted and Tom, conscripts from the Confederate army who had come to dig for gold to aid in financing the war. It looked as he and Ben might be facing overwhelming odds who had a dislike for northerners. As fear and doubt tried to elbow its way into his consciousness, Cady used his memory of Scripture to recount the numerous times that God had caused Israel to overcome impossible odds.

They were riding slowly now, unable to catch the fugitives before they reached sanctuary, so they talked and shared their feelings. They reached an agreement to shoot only if necessary to save their lives, then only to disarm and not kill their quarry. They also agreed to put their badges in their shirt pockets, they had no reason to show them, having no authority in this town.

The town was little more than an encampment, with the saloon and general store the only wooden structures. The rest were temporary shelters, mostly tents, numbering forty or more. Men walked about, heads down, on their way to or from somewhere, uncaring of the strangers arrival. From within the saloon harsh voices could be heard amid curses and laughter.

Cady led the way and seated himself at an empty table, with his back to the wall facing the crude bar, Ben joined him sitting to the side. Only a couple of men had noted their entrance before turning back to their drinks. The bartender made a vain attempt to wipe the table off with a dirty rag before sitting down a bottle and two glasses.

"Six bits," he declared before collecting his due and leaving.

Cady poured both glasses half full but made no attempt to drink, while watching the activity at the bar. Ben counted seven men, five at the bar and two at another table, four of the seven wore gray uniforms. Covertly Cady and Ben poured their drinks in the spittoon beside the table and refilled them several times, leaving the impression that their bottle was on the wane.

Finally, the barkeep noticed the bottle was near empty and returned with a second. As Cady thanked and paid him, he leaned close and said a single word, "Duke?" in the form of a question. The man jerked his thumb in the direction of the other table and left without a word.

Certain that the two at the table were Griff and Duke, Cady was encouraged to see that they were isolated from their compatriots along the bar. He slipped the double barrel from its case on his back, cocking both hammers before sliding it across to Ben without ceremony. Motioning Ben to stay put but alert, Cady got to his feet, grabbed the bottle by its neck and stumbled drunkenly across the floor toward the men. As he got near both looked up, but before they could object he sat and poured them a glass.

"One o' ya Griff?" he said, slurring the words. Then without waiting for an answer continued, "fella named Ted sent me to ya." By the look in their eyes Cady could tell which was Griff before he spoke.

Griff looked at him hard, appraisingly, then said, "what fer?"

Cady continued, filling the glasses again, "said his brother didn't make it and he needs help."

Duke jumped in, "kid's dead, what can we do for 'em?"

Cady shrugged his shoulders, "can't say, I only told him I'd tell ya. Ask him yerself, he's outside with the dead 'un."

Cady stood shakily, grabbed the bottle and turned as though returning to his table. Both men stood also, walking toward the door, while Cady sidled along behind them. As they exited, Cady motioned into the darkness, "over there to the right, by them horses," as he pulled his .45 after they passed.

Behind him, Ben had left also, facing into the bar, covering their backs. Just as Griff started to turn his head, Cady shoved the .45 into his back, "on your knees, hands over your heads, either of you move, Griff takes one in the back."

Both men stood speechless, raising their hands slowly. Cady relieved them of their weapons before shoving them roughly forward toward the horses tied at the rail, saying, "make a sound and I'll drop you where you stand." Carefully, Cady handcuffed first one, then the other, their hands in front of them to allow them to get onto the waiting horses.

As Ben joined them, Cady cut a small leather thong from the rigging using it to tie the cuffs to the saddle horn, then tying the reins together dropped, them over the horn. Mounted, the four melted into the darkness with Ben on one side, Cady on the other.

Neither of the prisoners said a word on the three hour trip back to Idaho City. It was only after they dismounted at the jail that Griff boasted that he had taken ten 'niggers' with him. Duke was more contrite as they were locked away to wait for trial.

Just as the sun rose over the little valley, both Cady and Ben wearily got to bed, leaving the town's business in the capable hands of John and Stephen. Before Cady drifted off to sleep he thanked God for His faithfulness but wondered how many more 4ths of July Independence Days he could endure.

He slept nearly eighteen hours without waking, before dressing and heading into town to see what was happening. Ben, being younger, was already there having coffee and swapping stories with John and

Stephen. Ben had made Cady, in his version of the story, 'larger than life', retelling of how they slipped the prisoners out without a shot fired. John gave Cady an approving nod which said more than any words could have. Next door Doc gave them the sad news that both of the burn victims had died of their injuries and the good news that Tom was recovering, with Ted remaining at his side.

"I don't 'spect there's need to jail the two boys," said Cady to John, in the form of a question.

John answered, "I don't see them going anywhere soon, I imagine they'll be here to give their story when the judge comes. "'Sides," he added, "can't see puttin' them in with the rough necks. That's how they come to be in trouble in the first place."

Everyone concurred with John's estimation.

Ben turned to John asking, "murder's a hanging offense, have you had any hangings since you been Sheriff?"

John answered after thinking for a moment, "No, not here in town. I saw a couple of rustlers hung down Silver City way, years ago. Messy affair, I never want to witness one again."

Ben pressed, "so are you against hangin'?"

"No, sometimes it needs done," John answered, "ain't no other way sometimes. What I'm sayin' is that some folks like the spectacle of it, come just to see, bringin' their kids 'n picnic baskets. I hold that life deserves more respect than that, no matter whose life it is."

– THIRTEEN –

Moving forward a year... it is one year later, July 4th, 1865.

Once again the town has filled with visitors looking for a good time. Once again Cady has responsibility for the safety of the town's people. The three Miller children have been shooed inside by their mother as warm raindrops, as big as twenty dollar gold pieces, fall from the sky. Heavy, dark clouds cover the summer sky from horizon to horizon, with bolts of lightning revealing the darkened landscape every few seconds. Claps of thunder frighten the young ones and warn the older of nature's pending fury.

Up on Grimes Pass, the heavy rains had been falling steadily for over an hour and were now moving down toward the valley floor. In the higher reaches, the powder dry summer soil had turned to a slurry of mud. Gold Fork Creek, which followed the terrain down from the pass toward the town, had begun to run high and muddy.

It was nearly 4 o'clock and the planned outdoor festivities had been canceled as rain continued to fall. The fury of the thunderstorm bore down on them with full force, with the increasing wind forcing even the heartiest inside. The Sheriff excused himself from his duties, telling his deputy that he was slipping home to catch an early supper with his family. He would return to relieve him a short time later.

As Cady donned a heavy oilskin slicker, he pulled his hat down against the wind, before throwing his leg over the gelding. Kicking the horse in the flanks with the heel of his boots, they turn toward home, the falling rain and thunder cocooning them in its embrace.

Cady rode first past the Merc and the boarding house, neither showing signs of life except the oil lamps burning in the windows, then on toward the school which was now empty in the season. As they came to Gold Fork Creek, Cady saw that the water had risen to the bottom of the bridge below him, full of mud and debris.

With the speed of an avalanche and without warning, a wall of muddy water, boulders and trees whirled down the canyon, thirty feet high, sweeping Cady and the horse off the bridge, before engulfing them within it. His mind turned inward... remembering the events of the last three years, of his first vision of Shawna standing by her horse in the meadow, the hours they spent together building, first a home and then a life together. Of the birth of their children and their mutual embrace of Jesus.

He remembered those whom God had brought into his life, those upon whom he must now depend to help Shawna raise his children. Most of all, he felt fulfilled and complete, at peace within himself as the torrent took down the school building and everything in its path with a thunderous roar, continuing toward the flat of the valley floor.

The horse was found later, dead and broken among the boulders, and debris was strewn over a half mile. Cady's hat and slicker were found buried under silt and mud, but his body was never found.

Epilogue

In later years, Shawna was appointed by the territorial governor as Chief of the Bureau of Indian affairs for the northwest. She never remarried but served God and His children faithfully. Ben became a U.S. Marshal, a father, and grandfather before his death in 1908. Kate and Stephen worked the claim in season, while opening an orphans home with their own money in town. Thomas married a lovely Scottish woman widowed by the Civil War, they moved back east when the gold rush ended. John and Helen moved back into town, John resuming duties as Sheriff until his death, with Al as his deputy.

The church burned to the ground and was rebuilt on the same site by the community, remaining there still to this day. Orville and Sarah never had children, but worked with Stephen and Kate at the orphanage after their retirement. Bill took over the responsibility for leadership of the church.

Ted and Tom were acquitted of charges, becoming evangelists later in life, who traveled preaching the equality of man under God's law. Heirs to their faithfulness marched years later in Montgomery, Alabama beside and with men and women of color still seeking equality.

Ironically, Idaho became a state on July 3rd, 1890, celebrating statehood 25 years after Cady had died. Following the gold rush, Boise

(Les Bois) became the capital city of the new state, being closer to the Oregon trail and main rail line that tied the northwest together. Faith married a Baptist minister, lived in Boise and taught nursing, while raising three children of their own. Their great-grandson was a senator who's name lives on, given to Idaho's highest peak, Mt. Borah. Neither Hope nor Charity married, both becoming nuns in the Catholic Church where they served in the Order of the Sacred Heart, working in the hospital founded by it, until their deaths after the turn of the century.

– THE END –

– DANisms –

- The real value is not in the length of the commitment, but in the depth of it. (apply this to anything in your life)

- Those who wait until the right time to get started often may find that the train has left the station while they are still packing their bags. (apply this to your witness)

- It is more desirable to do a small kindness quietly than to do nothing with great fanfare.

- Small things become big things when viewed through the eyes of small people. (nit-pickers beware)

- The humble view the extraordinary as ordinary.
  (bio of a committed servant)

- Those unwilling to act have many plans for action, but always for tomorrow.

- The critical eye and sharp tongue are the tools of fools, while the busy hand and committed heart can accomplish much. (dedicated to the few who do much, which the many know nothing of)

- While they say "talk is cheap" it may cost us a great deal in the end. (don't gossip)

- In spiritual warfare we cannot lose unless WE choose to do the fighting. (stand strong in His might, not your own)

- A man's lips like a dog's tail, it only wags when he is not working. (we all know someone)

- There are NO disposable people, not the old, the infirm, the young, disabled, or the unborn... they are all God's creation.

- What guides your heart, guides your hands, what your hands produce is a testimony to the fruit of the Spirit within you.

- Even if you pick only the worthy one, there are too many challenges facing us each day, too many battles to fight, too many wrongs to right. Let God guide you to the place where your efforts will be blessed and multiplied, as were the fishes and loaves.

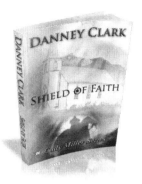

SHIELD OF FAITH

"One more thing, Red, then if you want I'll shoot you, okay? Thing is, if you should beat me, I go to Heaven to be with the Lord, but if I beat you, where do you suppose you'll go for all eternity? Have you thought about how long forever in Hell might be?"

Red cursed again. "You don't worry about me miner, you worry about your little family here after I shoot you!"

SHIELD OF HONOR

Amid the explosions and aerial displays that marked our nation's Independence Day, he heard a yell followed by a louder and sharper report that was closely followed by a second and third. Cady, in his blue uniform with Kevlar vest and duty belt, was lifted off his feet by the impact and fell fifteen feet from the pier into the East River.

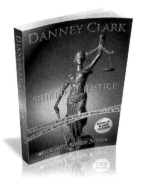

SHIELD OF JUSTICE

Unknown to others, Cady Miller was a dangerous man, having the physical and technical abilities to inflict mortal injury. His lean stature and rapidly advancing age belied his physical prowess. His pale blue eyes now retained their 20/20 vision by the use of contacts lenses, but more importantly he used that vision to see things others often missed. Skills honed through years of training and discipline allowed him to maintain an edge others frequently lost as the years caught up with them.

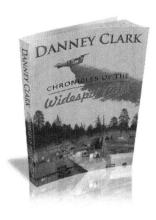

– ALSO AVAILABLE –

Searching for...
LIGHT in the Darkness

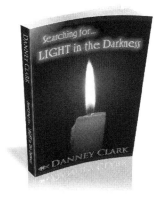

Cremains / Dementia / The Birth of a Book
The Conversation / The Means to Murder
The Trigger
The End Game: An American Prophecy

Often we forget how great our God really is, by letting the fallen world overwhelm us and take away our joy. We should recognize that God created the world in the image of Himself, perfect and without sin. Man then, through his disobedience, opened the door to the sin about which these pages tell. Pay special attention to Cremains and recognize that the GOD who is great enough to create mankind is also great enough to forgive mankind and return him once again to perfection.

These and other offerings available at the Author's website:
www.danneyclark.com / www.danscribepublications.com

About the Author

Danney Clark is first a practicing Christian, then a husband of nearly 50 years, a father of two daughters, and grandfather of two granddaughters. He is also an Idaho native who values and enjoys the outdoors in all of its varied forms that are so apparent in Idaho.

When he finds a challenge, he is passionate about pursuing it with diligence before moving onward to the next. Questionably an accomplished cook, he devotes much of his time to serving the homeless community and his church home.

His passion for many years has been writing and most recently, God-inspired Christian fiction, or "adventure with a spiritual message" as he calls it. He sees life as an adventure to be enjoyed, appreciated, and shared. Recent retirement has encouraged him to do so.